Passionate Deceit

"Come here now and take the blasted pins from your hair," Scarblade said in a deep-timbred voice. "I'm in a mood for loving this night."

Tori blinked. Did he mean . . . could he mean . . . Her mind raced, frantically searching for some diversion to occupy him while she tried to think of an escape. He truly believed she was Dolly, and what he expected of her brought a hot flush to her cheeks.

His dark, heavy browed eyes explored her with thinly veiled passion. Tori struggled to gain control of her shaking knees. Then in one step he was against her, holding her fast to his lean, hard body, his lips, hot and wine-scented, pressing against hers. She struggled to free herself, but he held her closer, enveloping her within the strong fold of his arms.

And slowly, unbidden, from deep within her came an answering response . . .

Vixen in Velvet

Fern Michaels

BALLANTINE BOOKS • **NEW YORK**

Library of Congress Catalog Card Number: 76-10609

ISBN 0-345-29611-7

Manufactured in the United States of America

First Edition: September 1976
Seventh Printing: December 1981

Vixen
in
Velvet

Chapter One

A myriad of golds and oranges was fast fading into the gray that precedes nightfall. With the setting sun, the warm summer air was taking on the chill of early autumn. Dusk was growing deeper as the ornate coach drew to a halt long enough for the liveried footman to jump down from his seat next to the driver and light the pewter-sconced lanterns alongside the doors.

Lord Nelson Rawlings, distracted from his thoughts, sat uneasily in the plush interior and gazed into the pool of yellow light the lanterns spilled onto the hard, rutted road.

When the coach started again, Lord Rawlings tried in vain to settle himself comfortably in his jouncing seat.

"These roads are a horror," he complained to his three companions. "If we aren't killed before we get home it won't be any fault of the driver. I daresay he has yet to miss one rut in this—" He stumbled over the curses which caught in his throat in deference to his wife and daughter and completed his statement in a garbled voice, "—road!"

"Yes, Nelson, you must speak to the driver, this trip is unbearable! Every bone in my body aches," Lady Rawlings said in a soft, high, childlike voice.

"We have but two hours to ride and we'll be home, my dear," the lord assured his wife in soothing tones. "We must be brave and put up with these inconvenient conditions. After all, we did enjoy the summer at our country home. Now it's time to realize the hardships of travel."

"You're right, Nelson," Lady Lydia Rawlings concurred, her small delicate face lighting up at the

1

thought that soon they would be home in their London
quarters.

Once more, Lord Rawlings leaned back on the heavily padded seat and closed his eyes. His stomach was
punishing him cruelly for the greasy lunch he had
bolted down. Way-station food! he complained silently,
as the dull ache was fast becoming more insistent,
cramping his innards into tight fists. He fumbled in his
vest coat for his mints and withdrew a plain, shell box
which held the small, white cubes.

"Stomach troubling you, dear?" Lady Lydia asked
with concern.

"Nothing to worry about," Lord Rawlings grumbled
as he deftly hid the box within the palm of his hand.
He didn't want Lady Lydia to notice that his gold pill-
box had been replaced by one so inferior. Lord
Rawlings emitted a sigh, and replaced the case in his
vest coat. It seemed to him he had spent the entire
summer concealing small items of value within the
folds of his coat and driving to the money lenders and
pawnbrokers to exact the pittance of cash the items
would bring. Under no circumstances did Lord
Rawlings want his treasured wife to know the hard
straits which the family now faced.

What was he to do? Since he had lost favor with the
Crown and his rental lands had been seized, he had
been sinking deeper and deeper into debt. Rawlings
knew that once he was again in London the creditors
would be after him with a vengeance. There was
nowhere to turn. He had exhausted every possibility
before leaving the city.

He shook his head and opened his eyes and let them
come to rest on the beautiful face of his daughter Victoria, who was seated across from him. His heart
smiled as he gazed on her. A bonnet covered her
golden hair but for a few wisps which escaped at her
high forehead. Green eyes flecked with gold enhanced
her pink and white complexion. Heavy, dark lashes
fringed those strikingly colored eyes and concealed
them from his view.

There was no other way, he debated with himself; he
would have to sacrifice his daughter to Lord Fowler-

Greene. As Rawlings thought of that portly gentleman who was older than himself, his stomach issued a sharp stab. He had wrestled with the problem throughout the summer. Victoria was twenty-two years old, much beyond the age when most girls married. Yet, he argued, this was the eighteenth century—modern times! It was foolish to consider as spirited a girl as Victoria an old maid, a spinster past her prime.

Still, he was getting on in years himself, he would be fifty-nine next birthday, and he wanted to see Victoria settled nicely. In case something should happen to him, he needn't worry what would become of Lady Lydia. Victoria would see to her mother's comforts and Victoria's husband would see to Lady Lydia's bills. And what person was more able than the wealthy Lord Fowler-Greene?

Although the general consensus held that Fowler-Greene was an overaged fop, Lord Rawlings had long ago decided that the guise of dandy covered a keen intelligence and a dedication to duty that very few were ever able to discern.

The lofty Lord Fowler-Greene had long had his eye on Victoria, and upon hearing of Lord Rawlings' difficulties, had more or less offered to help the latter out of his enigmatical problems, provided of course, that Lord Fowler-Greene would win a place in the Rawlings family, preferably as a son-in-law. All Lord Nelson had to do was convince his daughter that Lord Fowler-Greene would make a most suitable husband.

After the first encounter with Victoria concerning Lord Fowler-Greene, in which she unleashed an incredible verbal attack on him, the girl had not said another word on the subject. But Lord Rawlings was not one to be fooled into letting down his defenses. If he knew anything of anyone, it was his own daughter, and he knew the worst was yet to come on the subject of this marriage.

She was a wild one, he would give her that. Lady Lydia had long ago thrown up her hands in despair at their daughter's brazenness and unruly tongue. Nelson, too, had oft chosen to look the other way, but he also knew that if his circumstances were to come to her notice, she loved him enough to do anything for him, even marry a man she could hold no affection for. But he did not want it that way. He would have Victoria's cooperation because she thought it best for herself, because he would convince her she needed a strong man. He would rather have her wild and screaming, kicking at the idea, than have her quiet and complacent, silently suffering.

He took another look at his beloved daughter as she rested her head against the back of the seat. Her expression was sweet in repose, like an angel. Lord Rawlings shuddered again as he thought of how her remarkable eyes could freeze someone in his tracks one moment and, then, flash and change to so beguiling an expression that a person wished to stay in her presence indefinitely.

"Are you taking a chill, dear?" Lady Lydia asked solicitously. Shaken from his reverie, Lord Rawlings answered, "No!" more abruptly than he intended. More than likely his conscience was guilty over the slight matter of selling his daughter into bondage. Still, there was no other way, and he must provide for Lydia. Sweet Lydia. His gaze rested on his wife's face as he ached to reach out and touch her. The same golden hair as her daughter's, paler now, peeked out from under her bonnet. Chapeau, he corrected himself. Lydia always referred to her hats as chapeau. His eyes raked over her slim body as he thought she'd not gained an ounce since their wedding.

Lady Lydia, too, had married for convenience, yet Lord Rawlings believed that she had come to love him. Not as much, surely, as he loved her, but enough to make him secure, enough to care about him and worry about his welfare. Dear, sweet Lydia. Her loyalty was much to be admired, even in the face of her only child marrying a man who was so much her senior. She had stated simply to Victoria, "If your father wishes it, darling, then it must be so." He imagined that when she and Victoria were alone, Lydia had spoken to Victoria of her own arranged marriage and tried to show the girl how well things worked out after all.

"Granger," Victoria called softly to her cousin, the

fourth member of their party, who was seated next to her father. "Are you asleep?"

"No, Tori. Damned if I can sleep with this carriage jostling about." Granger cast an eye on his uncle, Lord Rawlings, and apologized. "Sorry, sir."

Lord Rawlings muttered something under his breath and turned his head toward the window. Granger gave his cousin a bold wink. Tori, as she was known to her family, laughed lightly as she glanced toward her father. Granger was always blaspheming, much to Lord Rawlings' annoyance, and Granger was constantly apologizing for it.

"Granger, please tell us of the highwaymen. The stories you tell are always so exciting, and we could all do with a bit of amusement. How do you know so much about highwaymen?" As an afterthought Tori added, "Gentleman that you are."

Granger Lapid glanced at his uncle warily. Why did Tori insist on upsetting the applecart by reminding Lord Rawlings of his knowledge of the nefarious characters that plagued the roads of England? The little minx, he thought, she likes nothing better than the bit of excitement that occurs whenever my presence is made known to Uncle Nelson.

Tori cast her green eyes on her cousin and did not fail to note his discomfiture. A smile played over her full lips and she lowered her heavy lashes to conceal her amusement. Poor Granger, she thought, so cowed by Father. Perhaps if he did not have to rely upon Father for his keep he would demonstrate more backbone. As she watched him it seemed as though she could see through his thin, wiry body directly to the spine which she was sure was absent from his anatomy. Granger nervously ruffled his light-brown hair, and a pinched expression played about his thin features.

"Go ahead, amuse the child," growled Rawlings. "If she hasn't the sense to see you've no knowledge of anything, much less the deeds and secrets of those scoundrels who plague our roads, then she hasn't the sense to be affected by your tall tales."

Granger looked questioningly at Tori, and she could see the hurt her father's statement had caused him. She was sorry she was the instigator. Tori was well aware that Granger indeed knew criminals and highwaymen. But she could never defend him to Lord Rawlings; to do so would be to admit that Granger visited those dark cellars and disreputable inns those felonious scoundrels frequented. Granger, not having the heart for a rogue's way of life, nevertheless sought his thrills by association with thieves and through those acquaintances, however remote, gained for himself some measure of importance.

"My dear Tori," Granger said in a nasal tone which he knew irritated her, "everyone knows about the highwaymen. They are a passel of thieving rogues. There is one in particular, Scarblade. They say he has a black heart, and," he added ominously, "he does not care whether he robs women or men. He shows no favoritism."

"How absolutely delightful. I should dearly love to be robbed by Scarblade." Her eyes lit up and took on a sparkle that set Granger's nerves on edge. He knew his cousin well. She would go out of her way to be robbed if it were possible.

"Tori, you are impossible," Granger said sourly. "I, for one, don't want to be robbed. First of all, I have not even a farthing to my name." For an example he turned out the satin lining from his trousers' pockets for her to see. "What do you think Scarblade would do when I tell him I have nothing to give?"

"Why he would probably slit your throat. I do so hope it doesn't happen today," she said, fingering the fine yellow muslin of her skirt. "Blood does spurt so." Granger paled perceptibly as he looked at the laughing eyes of his cousin. "Please don't worry, Granger; if it happens I will throw myself at the mercy of this Scarblade and plead for your life. I'll tell him I'll do anything to save you. Besides, if I absolutely must, I can defend myself." She added, pouting her full, pretty mouth, "It's not been so long since you taught me to throw a knife. I am quite an accurate marksman, if you remember."

Granger blanched and nervously glanced at his uncle. He had been accused so frequently of teaching

Tori unladylike behavior that he almost forgot it was Tori, not he, who led the way in social transgressions.

"It will make no difference, my dear cousin, this man wants only money and jewels. He doesn't care what he does to get them. A man's blood on his hands would not concern him. But I will tell you this: If we can get through the next few miles without being accosted, then we'll make it home safely. This section of the road is Scarblade's lair."

Lord Rawlings groaned aloud and Granger began to tell him that what he had spoken was the truth when he realized his uncle's disinterest. Granger knew when he was being ignored and allowed the matter to pass. What he did not know was that Lord Rawlings was thinking that if they should be robbed, his last shilling would be taken and he would be even more beset by financial worries.

Tori noted her father's attitude and prodded Granger further. "Do you really think this is his lair? And that we'll be robbed and our throats cut?" she asked softly, in an effort not to disturb Lord Rawlings.

Lady Lydia gasped, "Cut your hair? I won't hear of it! Did you hear the child, Nelson? She wants to cut her hair! My dear," she said, not waiting for a reply from her husband, "only madwomen and criminals have their hair cut. I won't have it! Do you hear? I never heard of such a thing! Foolish girl, what will you think of next? I knew it was a mistake to let you play in the kitchens when you were a child. I forbid it, Tori! Now let the matter rest. I want to hear no more of it!"

Resigned, Tori nodded her head. She knew from past experience it did no good to explain that her dear mother had misunderstood. Lady Lydia's hearing had been getting worse of late. Tori and her father pretended there was nothing the matter, for vanity's sake. But now, Tori wondered, what *would* she look like with her hair cut?

"What does Scarblade look like, Granger?"

"He's handsome, all right, at least that's what the ladies say. A scar on his left cheek in the shape of an S that flames brightly with the heat of passion. S for seduction," Granger smirked. "I've heard in town that one or two wealthy ladies have actually made arrangements for him to rob them a second time. A slip of the tongue, a casual mention, next they know they've found themselves in his clutches once again."

"Imagine that," Tori mused, "making arrangements to be robbed. Tell me more."

"He's said to have coal-black eyes. He rides a magnificent chestnut stallion that makes him ten feet tall. That's all I can tell you, Tori." Warily, Granger eyed the dusty windows and prayed silently that Scarblade was somewhere else this day.

"Oh," Tori breathed, enraptured by the tale, "I would like to meet this man."

"Victoria!' Lord Rawlings shouted, shocked at the words coming from his daughter, though why he was stunned was beyond him. She had been doing much as she pleased since she had learned to walk. It would be just like the girl to make an appointment to be robbed by this uncouth fellow. "I want no further talk of this nonsense!"

Tori always remained calm under her father's furious gaze and sudden shouts. She knew his bluff, she had cut her teeth on his outrages. Inwardly, Tori believed he had a kind heart, even to where Granger was concerned. Besides, she mused, the poor old darling really was frightened by Granger's story. She stifled a smile as she noticed Lord Rawlings fumble in his waistcoat for his purse.

Suddenly a shout from the top of the coach and the quickening of speed made the occupants fall over in helter-skelter positions.

"What is it? What's happened?" Lady Lydia quivered.

"I think we're about to be robbed," Tori laughed, as the pounding of hooves could be heard coming from behind the coach and thundering closer.

Chapter Two

As the yellow light from the side lanterns swayed back and forth, Tori could see the decidedly green cast to her cousin's pale face. She couldn't help but prod the barb again.

"Don't look so sick," she hissed. "Haven't I already promised you I would do everything possible to save your throat?"

Granger shot her back a venomous look and sneered through clenched teeth. "Hold your tongue, Tori. You shall be lucky if your own life is spared."

Lord Rawlings said in a whisper, "Hold! The pair of you! For if the robber spares your life, I promise you I shan't!"

Lady Lydia, whimpering to herself in fright, came around long enough to side with her husband. "Tori, now is not the time for your ill jokes! Hush!"

Peering out the window, Tori could see that the coach had finally stopped in a thickly wooded glade. She heard scuffling atop the coach as the footmen were forced from their seats. A wave of fear washed over her, and in her ears a roaring sound echoed, making it hard for her to hear exactly what was happening outside.

Abruptly, the coach door opened and an authoritative voice boomed over the roar in her head, commanding the passengers to come forth.

Tori grasped her mother's hand, and with the help of one of the highwaymen they stepped down. Lord Rawlings and Granger were close behind.

Three men in rough clothing stood in a semicircle, while a giant of a man sat astride a huge chestnut. All wore soiled cloths, with eyeholes, tied around their heads, covering half their faces.

Tori tried to see the rider of the stallion in the

9

deepening light, knowing she had the advantage because the coach lanterns were to her back and the thieves were bathed in yellow light.

"Your money and your jewels!" the rider demanded imperiously.

"Why should I give you my jewels?" Tori asked. "Who are you that you hide behind a mask and dare not show your face? I refuse to part with the emerald ring that I carry in my pocket!" she said brashly.

"Oh, no!" Granger muttered. Standing as close to Tori as he was, he could feel the quivering of her body. The vixen, Granger thought angrily, she's enjoying every moment of this. The little fool will see us killed!

"I think you will be more than glad to hand over your valuables," the man astride the chestnut replied in a dangerous tone.

"You sound very sure of yourself. Masked bandit, I have no intention of handing anything over to you, much less my ring! And you dare not molest a lady!"

Lord Rawling stepped forward and grasped his daughter's arm, pulling her back from the point to which she had advanced during her last speech. "Forgive her, sir," he addressed the horseman, " 'tis but my addlepated daughter. She's not the sense she was born with. An embarrassment to my wife and myself." He tapped his head near his temple and nodded despairingly. "We're just returning from the country where she was staying. The doctor said she would be better, but now I'm afraid all this excitement has only brought her back to her former, invalid state."

"Father!"

"Calm yourself, child, else you'll find yourself back at the house in the country," he hissed through clenched teeth as he grasped Tori's arm cruelly. Lady Lydia, unable to control herself any longer, began a fit of weeping, and Lord Rawlings left her to herself, feeling it would serve to convince the robbers of the sad state of their daughter.

Tori, resigned to being quiet for the moment, took to studying the three men who surrounded her and her family. They wore incongruous hats; brushed beavers and silk toppers, quite incompatible with their shoddy, rusty black suits, and no doubt supplied by their past victims. One of the three smiled at her lewdly, showing broken, rotted teeth. Tori felt disappointed. Granger had always said the highwaymen were handsome, but these were no more than street beggars. Feeling repulsed by the robber's lecherous smile, Tori retreated backward a step. Granger came close behind her and whispered, "What do you think you're doing? You don't even have an emerald ring! You'll kill us all yet, Tori!"

"Silence!" the lead horseman thundered. "I will repeat myself once more only: Your money and your jewels."

"Pay no heed to my daughter," Lord Rawlings protested in a commanding tone. "She is but a child and I can assure you, she owns no such ring. None of us has any monies or jewels. My wife wears only her wedding band, surely you would not deprive her of that small trinket?"

"If what you say is true, no. But such cannot be the case. You are persons of some quality and I see by the coach that you bear a seal of Parliament. Up to now I have been patient, but it is wearing thin. I am known to give only one warning, then the result you will bear alone. Now, hand to my men your money and jewels!"

"Nelson, why does he keep calling us fools?" Lady Lydia whimpered.

"Hush, dear. All will be well," Lord Rawlings comforted.

"And if we do not, will you slit our throats, Masked Bandit?" Tori demanded. "Will you draw and quarter us? Will you drag my mother and myself off to your lair and make slaves of us? Take me!" she cried dramatically, "for I will never part with my precious ring. It was given to me by my betrothed."

"Tori, for God's sake, keep still!" Granger hissed.

"Come here!" the rider demanded.

Brazenly, Tori walked to within a foot of the huge stallion and looked up into the face of the highwayman.

"Is it true? Would you become my slave rather than part with your betrothal ring?"

Tori nodded, suddenly at a loss for words. She had
never seen such black eyes. He was a handsome brute,
even with his face half covered. When he spoke to her,
he punctuated his statement with a smile and Tori saw
that his teeth were white and strong and, more, they all
seemed accounted for, no gaping holes in this smile.
He sat on the horse with an ease that made him and
the magnificent beast seem as one. A lover of horse-
flesh, Tori found herself distractedly trying to keep her
hand from feeling the hot, quivering animal.

"Beware of your answer," the horseman shouted.
"One word from you and your family could be dead in
seconds. Think carefully!"

His shouts had startled the chestnut, and the bandit
felt the beast begin to rear up in fear. Tori, too, saw
the horse move and she reached her hand out to touch
its muzzle. Her gesture had the required effect, the stallion calmed. Its rider found himself awed by the girl's
knowledge of horses and admired the stance she took
in the face of danger.

"No!" Tori exclaimed softly. Suddenly, she started
to tremble, shaking in her shoes. She had gone too far.
She could read murder in the black eyes. "Let my
family go. They mean you no harm. We have no
money with us. My cousin is destitute. We are returning from our summer home and our luggage and personal belongings have gone before us in a flatwagon. I
beg of you, let my family go!"

"You plead prettily for your family. Is this true what
you say? Don't lie to me, for I can seek you out within
an hour's time and have you all murdered in your
beds."

"It is the truth," Tori said meekly.

"I will spare them if you give me the ring."

"I can't do that. It's from my betrothed."

"You must love this man very much to be willing to
die for his ring."

"With all my heart," Tori said quietly.

Suddenly, without a moment's warning, a long arm
reached down and grasped Tori under the shoulders.
Feeling herself being lifted from the ground, she
struggled, but the man's grip was firm.

He lifted her in one swoop onto the saddle before him. So quick was his action, Tori found herself caught between excitement and fear. Turning her head to face him, she determined to brave out her predicament. From somewhere she could hear her father making noises demanding her release, but his words became indistinct. Looking into dark, brooding eyes, Tori gazed at the deep curling scar that ran across the highwayman's cheekbone. It stood out sharply in the dim evening light. The girl fought an almost uncontrollable urge to reach up and caress the snakelike indentation. As the man's jaw tightened the scar moved to form a letter S. Tori's thoughts choked her as she remembered Granger's smirk and his words, "S for seduction!"

Forcing her gaze away from the fascinating line, Tori found herself locked in a stare with the highwayman. In his night-dark orbs there was an excitement, a passion! Her heaving breaths knotted in her throat.

The fast-fading light of late evening threw Tori in shadow. Scarblade peered beneath the brim of her bonnet but could not see her face. He could only discern a loveliness there and a voluptuousness of figure as a ray of light from the lanterns on the carriage slashed across her rising bosom. He noted her scent, the feel of her weight against his thighs, and the slim fragility of her ribs encased within the silkiness of her gown.

Tori sensed his appraisal of her and her senses reeled as she became aware of his masculine scent mixed with the pungent smell of horse sweat. Feeling the rippling muscles beneath her, she noted a stirring tautness in his loins. Her breath came in choking rasps. She felt his fingers pressing into her ribs, drawing her imperceptibly closer. Then, just as she sensed he would kiss her, she became frightened of her own soaring emotions. Drawing away from him, she cut the air between them with a sharp retort. "Don't tell me you're that facetious sort of highwayman who warrants laughter in the ladies' bedchambers. That most low and ridiculous form of scoundrel known as a 'kissing bandit'!"

The highwayman froze, struck by her words, angered that she had sensed his intentions. "I give you your choice: You will hand over the ring or I will take it from you."

Tori could feel his breath upon her cheek and was aware of the oddly disconcerted emotions he stirred in her by his nearness. Slowly, Tori searched the pocket of her gown, her fingers grasped the small ring and withdrew it. She felt the wild beating of his heart as she leaned against her accoster. Her own fluttered madly within her breast and she felt herself being gently lowered to the ground. Half falling, she quickly regained her balance and stood tall.

"If you must have it, then it is yours." She tossed the ring into the air and watched as it was deftly snatched by Scarblade.

"That's enough, child; quickly now, come here to us," Lord Rawlings sputtered.

"Yes, please, dear," Lady Lydia entreated, a tinge of hysteria edging her voice.

"You hear your parents," Granger hissed, "now come here to us!"

Heedless of the frantic words of her family, Tori was only aware of the eyes of the highwayman upon her and their thinly veiled desire.

"I think, sir," she said haughtily, "we shall meet again one day. I am allowing you to safeguard the ring for me—one never knows in these times what dangerous men are lurking about on the highways. I trust you will guard it well!"

The bandit's jet eyes bore through her, and to her terror she discerned the scar on his cheek had deepened in color.

Chapter Three

Hidden in a woody glade, the bandit Scarblade quieted his nervous chestnut and watched the Rawlings' ornate coach rumble by. He took no pleasure in these robberies and found it hard to believe that he, Marcus Chancelor, would land himself in this unlikely position.

Like the pages of a calendar flipping backwards, his memory brought him to a point in time less than a year ago, and there before him were the reasons behind his banditry.

Evening fell silently on his sprawling, two-storied white clapboard home, wrapping the Carolina countryside in tender arms. He paced the spacious half-beamed room impatiently, stopping now and again to peer out the mullioned windows into the darkness, anticipating the sight of the horse-drawn cart. Marcus's long, easy strides were unhindered by the provincial furnishings that graced the room.

Carver, an inky black manservant, entered the informal sitting room with a questioning look in his watery eyes. " 'Scuse me, suh, but yo' father ain't home yet?"

Marcus turned abruptly to face the elderly Carver. "No, dammit, and if you come in here once more asking for him, I swear I'll skin your hide!"

Carver watched his young master, a sullen expression drawing the corners of his wide mouth downward.

"Yassuh."

"Sorry, Carver," Marcus apologized. "If it weren't for the damn redskins, I wouldn't be so jumpy. Samuel's not as young as he thinks he is, and he might take on more than he can handle. You know how the Indians in the North Carolina area are plaguing the colonists with frequent raids and war parties."

"Ah knows, suh. Them redskins jus' luvs ta torment us. They sho' do!" Carver mumbled to himself.

In two easy strides Marcus reached the desk in the corner of the room. He toyed nervously with the familiar rolls of blueprints, his ears pricked for the sound of approaching horses. He picked up the heavy parchments and opened them as he had on many occasions, studying the white lines etched in the thin coating of blue wax. These were the plans for the house that was in progress on the other side of the rise, closer to the river. The house his mother had dreamed of and which his father, Samuel, had promised to build for her. Now it was to be a shrine to her memory, she being dead these twenty-four years. Samuel was determined to see the house built just as she had dreamed, before he was called to rest beside her for all eternity.

Carefully, Marcus rolled the parchment and replaced it on the desk. Sorrowfully, he doubted his father would ever realize his ambition. Materials were expensive when one had to purchase them on the black market, and the constant threat of Indians made progress slow. Twice now they had burned the strong cedar beams to the ground, and Samuel, refusing to admit defeat, had sighed wearily, cursed soundly, and had begun over again.

Marcus punched the fist of one hand into the palm of the other, the soft buckskin of his shirt tightening across the bunching muscles of his back. "Blast and damn!" he swore just before he heard the anticipated sound of hooves on the path to the cabin. He raced to the window, his moccasins soundless on the rough wooden floor.

Carver hurried to the door as fast as his big, thick calloused feet would carry him. "Ah heard them. Ah knows ah did. Now don't yo go a-teasin' an ole man, massa Marc, ah tell yo they is heah."

Marcus paid no attention to the wiry black man and pushed ahead of him, putting Carver at a distinct disadvantage as he tried to stretch his knobby old frame to see out in the darkness over Marcus's tall bulk.

Samuel Chancelor and Myles Lampton slowly

climbed out of the flat black wagon, the ancient boards of the vehicle squeaking in protest at each man's portliness. Marcus stepped out of the lighted house to greet his father and the old man's lifelong friend. One look at Marcus's worried face and Samuel hurried to explain their absence to his son. In a voice which matched his son's deep timbre, Samuel told Marcus of an emergency meeting of the Chancelor's Valley Association.

Marcus, not satisfied with his father's excuse, berated the old gentleman. "But why did you and Myles leave so suddenly? Surely there was time enough to send me word in the lower acres. I would have gone with you."

"Now, son. Don't go fretting again. There'll be time for that later. Right now I want you to hear what Myles and I have to say."

Marcus settled back in the small provincial chair—his size and bulk incompatible with the furniture's delicacy. He studied Myles Lampton, measuring his face for a clue as to what they were referring to, knowing the man's countenance was more open and readable than Samuel's. Seeing no sign there, Marcus instead turned his concentration to Samuel.

"We were at a meeting of tradesmen and farmers," Samuel began, "and some of those rapscallions we're forced to deal with. Those bandits have boosted their prices again and they know we're at their mercy." Samuel was referring to the black-market traders who were the mainstay of Chancelor's Valley.

"Naturally we once again were forced to agree to their prices."

Myles broke into the conversation. "Yes, Marc, they only offered us half of what our tobacco is worth and demanded five times the worth for what they've smuggled."

"Marcus can imagine what went on, Myles," Samuel said impatiently. "Get to the point. Can't you see he is near jumping out of his skin to know?"

"All right. Here it is, Marcus: The Chancelor's Valley Association has decided to send you to England to plead our case directly to the King."

"I won't go!" Marcus stormed, his voice booming. "I'm needed here with you! What can I do that our *'honorable statesmen'* have not done?" he demanded sarcastically.

"You've every right to feel that way," Samuel soothed. "We all believe we're being sold down the river by our House of Lords, and our colonial governors. That's why someone from Chancelor's Valley must go and plead our case. Someone who is educated, well spoken, and authoritative. You were educated in England, hence you're the logical choice."

Marcus looked at his father and knew that Sam would never suggest the plan to him if he weren't convinced it was the best for all concerned. The unselfishness of his father struck him once again. It would be as difficult for Samuel to send his son across the ocean as it would be for Marcus to leave. Samuel had not displayed the best of health lately, and Marcus felt the old man had not much time left. Well, he wanted that time, he demanded it. He wouldn't leave Samuel alone here with Carver, with himself months and an ocean away.

"There are others as suited for the 'honor' as I," Marcus insisted.

"It's all arranged," Samuel broke in, his face an older replica of his son's, displaying the same authority. He did not fail to see the faint, barely discernible scar on Marcus's cheek turn a deep crimson. In anger the scar twisted like a slithering snake, wrested into the shape of an S by the tightening of his jaw. While he was still a student, a trip to Paris and a dalliance with the young and beautiful wife of a dragoon had precipitated a duel with rapiers which had left Marcus's left cheek inscribed.

Samuel had never been able to induce Marcus to speak of it, but he knew from witnesses that Marc had allowed himself to be cut rather than kill the French army officer, whose sense of honor demanded he fight to the death.

Samuel looked at Marcus with clinical interest; the scar did not detract from his handsome features. On the contrary, it made him a dashing rogue, a man to be reckoned with.

"You'll travel to Boston," said Samuel, "and there you'll meet Jason Elias. He is captain of his own ship and a trusted friend. He has guaranteed you passage and, above all, any assistance he can give you." Samuel's face wore the closed look Marcus knew so well. The look stated that, in Samuel's mind, the decision had been reached and there would be no need for further argument. Marcus felt a swollen, hard lump in his chest and knew his arguments would be fruitless.

"Think about it, son, that's all I ask. Think about it!"

"Marcus, your father's right. Think about it," Myles added, his round, heavy face flushed from brandy. "Chancelor's Valley seems to be lacking in eligible young ladies suited to your taste. In England you'll have the flower of womanhood to choose from—that would be to your liking, I think. A gentle mixture of business and pleasure, eh, Marc?"

Myles Lampton was taken aback by the scowl on Marcus's face, and he glanced at Samuel, who was evidently amused by his son's reaction.

"You'll get nowhere with that statement, Myles. Marcus's view of women is disdainful, to say the least. What is it you call them? Grasping, greedy, and willing to ride the back of any man to attain their ends?"

The white heat of anger rose to Marcus's features. "I have yet to find evidence to the contrary. Women are a breed unto themselves. Grasping and greedy, true, but that is a trait common to men as well as women. What I find so abominable is the conspiracy to be found between them and others of their sex. From birth they are raised and schooled in the talents to snare a man into marriage and use him to supply all those things which they feel are their due. And all the while they wink and smile at one another, bragging of what they suppose is their ingenuous charm in twisting a man, a mere mortal, around their little fingers. It would not occur to a woman to be sincere and forthright, not when flattery and trickery will profit her."

Samuel sighed heavily, the image of grandchildren at his knee fading into oblivion. "I think, Myles, that Marcus has been too long in male society."

"But Sam, what of that bit of scandal concerning Marcus and the attractive wife of the wealthy shipbuilder that filtered down to the valley last winter?"

"All true, Myles," Samuel answered, enjoying Marcus's discomfort. "Marcus may deride women for their faults, but that does not hinder him from enjoying their charms. I've almost given up hope for grandchildren. It seems as though I'm destined to die a lonely old man with an embittered, bachelor son for my only company."

"Don't make me laugh, Sam," Marcus smiled, calling his father by his Christian name as he had been wont to do since he was a boy. "I can only promise you this; if I should ever find a woman who contradicts all I've said about her sex and who offers a great personal sacrifice for the betterment of another, I would snatch her up and carry her to the valley immediately."

Myles looked sympathetically at his friend Samuel. "It would seem, Samuel, that your visions of grandchildren are indeed futile."

"Marcus has yet to learn, Myles, that life has its way of turning the oddest corners. Marcus has not yet met the young woman who will make him eat his words. I can only hope that when he does it will not be too late. Who knows, you may be correct, Myles. Marcus just may meet the young woman to suit him in England," Samuel said pointedly in his son's direction, settling once and for all the question of Marcus's pleading their case with the King.

Not caring to hear any more, Marcus rose from the chair and walked out into the clear, crisp night.

Moments later, Myles Lampton joined him, puffing on a long-stemmed pipe, exhaling fragrant clouds of smoke. "Marc, Sam would never ask this of you if he didn't think the situation warranted your going. Here we are, well over a hundred families striving to make a living off this new land. The Indians have raided and plundered our granaries and burned our fields, and still we remain. And why? Because the people here in Chancelor's Valley have the courage to stand up for their rights. We are a community peopled with political refugees. Men who have spoken out against the corruption of our governors. So, in retribution, we are virtual prisoners. The King has placed an embargo on our products, a blockade on our port. He's forbidden any trade with us from our neighbors. Marc," Myles said vehemently, "we are being starved out of existence. I know it pains you to leave Samuel . . . if I'm any judge, he's on the decline. But when he asked you to think about it, I believe he was telling you to give a thought to how he would feel if Chancelor's Valley, a community named for Sam himself, were to be driven out of existence. That would kill him more quickly than any ailment on the face of this earth. Sam himself suggested you as the man for the job. The others would have come to the same conclusion sooner or later, but the fact is, Sam wants you to do this, indeed, *needs* you to do this . . . for him."

The sun burned its way through the thin morning fog so typical of England at the start of summer.

Marcus left the dining hall of the House of Lords with the sound of those revered gentlemen's jeers in his ears. He had failed, miserably. He could feel his soul retreat into a small, dark corner of his heart. What was he to do? How could he return to North Carolina and tell his father that the King refused his audience? For two weeks he had hounded the King's secretary to no avail. Then, thinking himself to have a better chance if someone from the House of Lords would plead his cause, he had tried persistently for an audience with one of these gentlemen. Here, too, he had failed. Finally, in desperation, he tricked and bribed his way into an early luncheon, and there, with his heart on his sleeve, Marcus told the lords of the plight of his people. Their answer was to have him thrown out on his ear.

A hackney driver called to him, begging a fare. Marcus waved him on, preferring to walk back to his lodgings. His heart was heavy, his pride wounded. He wanted to smash out at something, someone. He heard the sound of his name being called, and he turned to see a footman running down the wide, cobblestoned street after him, waving a piece of paper in his hand. Marcus stopped and waited for the footman to catch up with him.

"Mr. Chancelor! Mr. Chancelor," the footman cried breathlessly, "wait, please, sir!" Marcus stood in his tracks until the footman reached him and handed him the piece of paper. " 'Tis from Lord Fowler-Greene, sir, he expects a reply."

With trembling hands, Marcus opened the paper. There, in a broad, scratchy hand, was an invitation to come to the Lord's home and discuss his problem further. "I promise you nothing," the note stated, "but perhaps we can come to some kind of agreement beneficial to both of us."

"Tell Lord Fowler-Greene I shall gladly come to his home at the appointed hour."

Still trembling with anticipation, Marcus bounded into the road to hail down the first hackney that came his way. This hope was too good to keep to himself. He had to get back to his rooms and share the news with Josh.

Josh will be as hopeful as I, Marcus thought exultantly. He could almost see the great blond giant dancing with glee and he could imagine him reaching for the brandy and proclaiming a toast.

Josh was Marcus's closest friend. Although the man was reaching his fiftieth year, they had much in common. A love of the outdoors, hunting, fishing, and a good long talk by a fire on a cold night.

Samuel had helped Josh out of a serious difficulty when both were just young men. After that, Josh had devoted himself first to Samuel, then later to Marcus. When Marcus had arrived in Boston to take Captain Elias's ship to England Josh had been there to meet him. The burly man would have it no other way than to accompany Marcus and be of any assistance he could.

Marcus knew this cost Josh dearly. The man's health was not what it should be, and the warm climate of North Carolina would have been more conducive to his recovery.

Marcus and Josh rode in the hired trap to Lord

Fowler-Greene's home. The ride seemed interminably long, and both men clenched their fists tightly in expectation. "This could be the opportunity we've waited for, Josh," Marcus said stiffly. "Pray God, the man has a heart and decides to help us."

"Aye! Marcus, me lad, but how can he refuse when the need is so great?"

The trap pulled into a long, tree-lined drive and stopped before a tall brick structure. "The lord does well for himself, Marcus," Josh said in a husky whisper.

A manservant in formal livery pulled open the door, and Marcus and Josh announced themselves. The servant admitted them, curling his lips with disapproval at Josh's rough appearance. "My Lord is expecting you, Mr. Chancelor. I will announce you."

Shortly, the manservant came back into the foyer and asked them to follow him into the library.

Lord Fowler-Greene, a man at least a decade past his prime, stood in the center of a room lined with deep bookshelves and lighted with several chandeliers. Josh was plainly impressed with his opulent surroundings, and his eyes darted from one corner to the other, drinking in the elegant furnishings.

Lord Fowler-Greene offered the men some port. Marcus watched his labored movements, noting the lord's obesity hindered him as he trod across the Persian rug to pull the bell cord to summon his butler. "I understand you have a serious problem in your colony—North Carolina, is it?"

"Yes, sir," Marcus answered, looking grim. "I had hoped you could intervene with the King on our behalf."

"Precisely," the lord expostulated, "although intervening with the King was not exactly what I had in mind."

"I don't understand, sir," Marcus said, a puzzled look on his handsome face.

In a lighter tone the lord said, " 'Tis a shame the King refuses to be a willing patron to your needs, but perhaps you would find it amenable to allow the King to be your . . . shall we say . . . not-so-willing ally?"

Still puzzled, Marcus remained quiet in order to allow the lord to explain this statement. " 'Tis a known fact, Mr. Chancelor, that our roads are traveled by people of wealth as they gad about from one place to the other. I hear tales of some of our country's most beautiful ladies wearing the most ostentatious of jewels as they traverse from here to there. Would it not be a shame if these ladies, the wives of the very lords who had you . . .er, removed from the House of Lords this day, were to be relieved of the cumbersome jewels," quickly adding, "to be returned to them, of course, for a trifling finder's fee. In this way it could almost be said that the lords are contributing to relieve the plight of your colony."

Josh, immediately grasping Lord Fowler-Greene's words, said pointedly to Marcus, "Look sharp now, Marcus, me lad, the Lord is making some good sense!"

"Of course, Mr. Chancelor, the risks would be entirely yours. Perhaps I could find my way to notify you of a great shipment of this year's taxes which are being collected now, at this very moment, from the whole of England. Of course, you understand this is only half a year's taxes. I'm afraid you missed the last shipment."

Fowler-Greene's plan intrigued Marcus. Adventure and danger had always appealed to him, but to have this suggested by a member of the House of Lords! And what of the law? Marcus held a deep and abiding respect for rule and regulation. Could he intentionally defy the face of justice? The image of hunger-sunken faces of the people of Chancelor's Valley swam before him. Starvation induced by the purposeful misrepresentation of the same edicts he was having doubts about violating.

"I think, Lord Fowler-Greene, your meaning is clear to me. But I am obliged to ask you why? Why should you turn against those of your own class, your friends, and propose they should be subjected to robbery?"

Lord Fowler-Greene grasped the back of a high

Duxbury chair fiercely; the knuckles of his bejeweled hands shone white. Looking at Marcus with a gaze so concentrated it seemed to bore through the younger man, he said in a voiced edged with anger, "Because of a vision I have. A vision of the colonies peopled with a society that works and strives for an ideal—founded on trust and certain inherent freedoms . . ." Lord Fowler-Greene stopped in midsentence, glowering at the amused look on Marcus's face.

"It would appear, Lord Fowler-Greene, that you have made the acquaintance of Mr. Benjamin Franklin when he was envoy to England last summer."

"Yes, how astute of you." The lord visibly relaxed. "And I find I agree with him. England owes something to the colonies, and much as I try, I don't seem to be able to convince the House of Lords or the Crown of this fact. During this past decade or so, business and trade have prospered here in England because of the colonies. The results upon our own society have been small as yet, but I don't think them negligible. New-found trade and wealth for the Crown without the rewards due to those who have made it possible rankles me and now I see my chance finally to offer tangible aid."

Marcus looked squarely at the man before him, mentally questioning the general impression the lord created, that of a bigoted old fool.

"I can see by your expression, Mr. Chancelor, that you are amazed that, contrary to all rumors, I have some faculty of mind. In spite of my love for luxury and certain other . . . er, idiosyncrasies, I do have the glory of England at heart. But I know that England's glory can only be enhanced by the success of the colonies, and hence, it is America's betterment which I seek."

The butler entered the room bearing a silver tray with a decanter of port and three long-stemmed glasses.

"Shall we drink to your success, Mr. Chancelor? Perhaps you would be wise to assume a pseudonym for your ... er, ventures. Say, something with a bit more style, which will appeal to the lower orders. You might consider the title of Scarblade. It has a certain flair, don't you think?"

Chapter Four

"My God, Tori. What got into you? We could have been killed! Your father's right, you need to be horsewhipped!" Granger went on and on, seeming to enjoy the luxury of railing at her. It wasn't often he could best Tori in argument, but since they had driven away from the highwayman she seemed not to be listening to anyone. Her indifference pricked him and leaning closer, willing to engage her in argument, he said again, "You should be whipped!"

"Clip? What kind of clip?" chirped Lady Lydia's puzzled voice. "Clip? Victoria, I won't hear another word about cutting your hair! Nelson, speak to the girl! Do something!" Lady Lydia cried in her soprano voice as her fingers plucked at her reticule nervously. Worry pinched her delicate, pretty features. "You must attend to her marriage, Nelson, she needs a strong hand. On the morrow you'll attend to the matter, for I'll not have another night's sleep otherwise!" This last Lady Lydia said in a lowered voice meant for her husband's ears alone.

Lord Rawlings patted her small hand comfortingly. "The matter will be attended to, my dear. Rest, Lydia, soon we will be home." He cast a wary eye in the direction of his daughter, who was engrossed in a heated conversation with Granger on the merits of Scarblade. Once again, he let his hand travel to his waistcoat pocket to feel the slim purse. He heaved a weary sigh of relief now that the decision to wed his daughter was made.

"Granger, I swear I would have protected your life, truly, I would. You must learn to manage your allowance more carefully. Always keep a few farthings in your pocket. This way you won't tempt a highwayman to slice your gullet. Dear Granger, what am I to do

with you? I shan't always be around to protect you."
Tori teased unmercifully, smiling with pleasure at the
perspiration which bathed his face.

"Wha ... what? Victoria," Granger sputtered, "I
envy the man that marries you."

"You do? Why?"

"Because if he has just one small part of a working
brain, he will whip you three times a day and four on
the Sabbath. You, dear cousin, are headed for one
mighty dreadful time."

"Granger, in this day and age, there is not a man
alive who would beat his wife," Tori said loftily.

"Cousin, when the man that marries you gets to
know you, he will regret his bargain immediately. He
will return you to your parents posthaste, and demand
to be rid of you!"

"Granger, dearheart, the man who marries me shall
love me for all time. I shall make his life exciting and
full of meaning. I shall bear him rosy-cheeked
children." As an afterthought, she added, "When I am
ready, that is."

"I can see it before my eyes," Granger snorted.
"You'll have a ring through his nose in a day's time."

"You see, Granger, when you put your devious mind
to work, you truly understand," Tori said happily.

Granger ignored Tori's words and looked deeply into her sparkling green eyes. Seeing Granger's intent,
she lowered her thick, dark lashes.

Too late, Tori, Granger thought. I know you too
well. Something happened back there and you're
frightened. That's why all this inane babble. It's to
draw my attention from the fear in your eyes. You're
not half as brave as you would have everyone think,
dear cousin. But there was something else glittering in
those catlike orbs. And I don't think I miss my guess
when I think it was something akin to ... lust?

Tori heard Granger's snicker and she shot him a
staggering look. "Ah, I think we are home!" she announced, her discomfiture disguised by her forced
gaiety.

"Yes, my dear, we're home," Lord Rawlings said,
happy as Tori to have neared the familiar surround-

ings. He glanced lovingly at his daughter. Soon, all his worries would be over. She really was too trying for a man reaching sixty. As he thought this last, he brightened. *Why, if she's too much for me, and I am only fifty-nine, she surely will be too much, much too much, for that old badger Fowler-Greene. I give him a year with her before he's burned out.* His smile broadened. *My dear Tori will make a handsome widow, a handsome, rich widow.* He beamed as he speculated on this saving thought.

"Granger," Tori whispered, "come to my sitting room later. There is something I wish to discuss with you."

"What is it, Tori? I'm sorely tired this evening."

"We will discuss it later. Now don't forget!"

"How could I forget? You will nag me unmercifully if I don't do your bidding. But I warn you, Tori, I shall not help you in any more of your dastardly schemes."

"Well, if you prefer to live the life of a pauper, so be it. I happen to be in a position to help you line your pockets—somewhat, that is."

Granger's eyes took on a curious gleam, as they always did at the mention of money. Tori, looking at him in the dim light of the coach, knew he would do her bidding.

"Come, Mother, I'll help you. I know that you must be as weary as I this night. All that terrible excitement! What is this country coming to?" she said, her voice raised so Lady Lydia would hear. "Imagine being accosted this night!" She shook her head for her mother's benefit.

"Your father is going to arrange a marriage for you, Tori, so that should put your mind at rest. Soon you will be someone else's prob . . . worry," she corrected.

"What do you mean, Mother?" Tori asked fearfully, a knot of panic clutching her stomach.

"Your marriage is to be arranged for only a fortnight from now. Is that not happy news?"

"Mother, I'm not ready for marriage," Tori wailed. "I thought we had this all out at our summer home. I can't believe you agree with Father in wanting to pack me off to Lord Fowler-Greene. I'm not ready!"

"My dear, there is nothing to it! Soon as you've become accustomed to the ways of the marriage bed, believe me, you shall be most happy. Your dear father assures me that you'll be happy. It's what you need, dear girl. If you're happy, then your father and I will be happy. We'll have a great feast. If I'm well enough tomorrow, I'll undertake to arrange all of the details. We must have a suitable gown for you . . ."

"But, Mother . . ."

"Hush, child, let me think. I know that you're overcome. Don't try to thank me now, or your father; we're only too glad to attend to the details."

"But, Mother . . ."

"Not one more word! I'm sorely tired," Lady Lydia sighed as she walked on shaky legs up the marble steps to her bedchamber.

"Ahhk!" Tori squawked indignantly to herself. "I'll not marry unless I'm in love, and I certainly shall not marry some fat old man with hoards of money. It would be just my misfortune that he'll snore and snort all night and in the morning he'll belch and scratch. All I need is enough money to line Granger's pockets. If I have to, I'll join Scarblade's men and secure my money the way highwaymen do!"

"Tori, I wish to discuss a matter of some importance with you after the evening meal," Lord Rawlings commanded as he saw a familiar belligerent expression cross Tori's face.

"Very well, Father. I shall oblige you as a good daughter should," Tori said, suddenly meek.

Lord Rawlings did not miss the submissive tone. Suddenly his own stomach knotted in panic. He could feel in his bones that she was up to some form of trickery. Never in all of her twenty-two years had she agreed to anything, no matter how small, without some form of obstinacy. This time, though, he'd tie her and lock her in her bedchamber if she didn't agree. With this resolved and the happy thought that his daughter could not best him this time, he followed his wife.

Tori cast a loving eye in Granger's direction. He paled. Tori never looked lovingly at anyone, only at her reflection in a mirror. She winked roguishly as she mounted the steps. "Don't forget, Granger. Later, in my sitting room," Tori whispered. A thrill of apprehension shot through him.

Chapter Five

Tori flung herself on the high bed and stared up at the sculptured ceiling. She had to come up with some kind of plan to thwart her father! She would not marry that odious Lord Sidney Fowler-Greene, monies or no. Father would just have to come up with another way to see himself through the difficulties she knew he was having. He hadn't been as sly as he had thought when he would creep out of their summer home with some article of value beneath his frock coat. He had underestimated her perceptive eye. He can lower himself to the station of a scullion, as far as I care! Let him beg or, better, steal or, still better, crawl on his belly to curry favor with the Crown. He could not barter his own flesh and blood. She knew it was a lost argument. She also knew her father well. If necessary he would lock her in her chamber till the marriage vows were said. Granger was her only hope. He would have to help her. Granger would do anything for a price, as long as it didn't involve putting his head in a noose. Soon her father would have to oust him. There would be no money to keep him—to say nothing of his handsome allowance. She giggled at the thought of Granger at the mercy of the elements, not to mention the highwaymen. He would not last two days on his own. What could she offer to entice him to help her. Quickly, she climbed from the bed and opened her jewel box. She looked in dismay at the paltry baubles that rested in the velvet depths. The lot wasn't worth ten sovereigns. Oh, why hadn't she pleaded with her father like the other girls did to acquire jewels. She pounced on her reticule and counted out the small hoard of money. Perhaps Granger would be satisfied with the meager sum. She would have to beg, plead, cry, and if all else failed, threaten. She knew a few secrets about Granger that he would not want bandied about, especially to Lord Rawlings.

Dinner was a dismal affair. Everything was cold, the meat, the eggs, the bread. Tori had no appetite and Lady Lydia soon retired, pleading a headache. Lord Rawlings escorted Tori into the library.

A fire had been laid in the hearth to ward off the chill of the rooms unused throughout the summer. Lord Rawlings pointed to a high-backed leather chair by the low fire and requested Tori to seat herself.

"There is a matter we must discuss. Please, my dear, listen to me with an open mind. As you well know, I have lost favor with the Crown. What you do not know is that without the rentals from those properties which have been removed from my title, we are in grave financial straits. I have barely enough to see us through the next several months. After that," he said, piteously eying Tori for reaction, "it will be debtors' prison for me. Now I know," he said, raising a hand to forestall an objection Tori might be inclined to make, "that you do not want that to happen. Therefore, my dear, I had to arrange the marriage for you with Lord Fowler-Greene. You must put these romantic notions out of your mind. 'Tis a cruel world we live in and you are of an age when marriage is imperative. Why, in a few years we won't have an opportunity to marry you off. You don't want to see your dear mother languish and die for mourning me, locked away in Newgate, do you?"

At Tori's meek denial, he continued. "The purse that Lord Fowler-Greene has offered for your hand will take care of all my debts and leave your mother comfortable till I regain favor with the Crown, if ever." He added sorrowfully, "You will agree, won't you, Tori?"

"But, Father, couldn't we sell Mother's jewels? Perhaps I could take a post as a governess somewhere?"

"My dear, much as it pains me to say this, I fear I must. However, not a word of this to your mother. The jewels have been gone these many months. What remains in their place is trinkets made to look like the real ones. All that remains is the wedding necklace I gave your dear mother. I had not the heart to sell it!"

"The ruby and diamond necklace that is to come to me on Mother's death? Is that what you mean, Father?"

"Yes," he nodded wearily. "Your mother prizes it highly. That is why she keeps it beside her bed at all times."

"What you mean, Father, is that you could not get your hands on it," Tori said spiritedly. "Otherwise, you would have sold it also. Is that not a fact?" she asked brazenly.

Lord Rawlings flinched at his daughter's hard tone, or was it at the truth of the statement?

"Will you agree to the arrangement? Will you, Tori?"

Tori nodded affirmatively. She would agree to anything at that moment. She needed time to think and to plan. The whole night was before her.

"I want you to give me your word that there will be no trickery, Tori, else I will lock you in your bedchamber. Your word, Victoria," he said imperiously, "your word as a Christian."

"Father, let me remind you that I am not a child and do not wish to be treated as such. No, I will not give you my word. You will have to accept me as I am. You will arrange the marriage. I won't stop you. Let us leave it at that. Now if you will excuse me, I wish to bid Mother goodnight."

The little whelp, she's up to something, Lord Rawlings thought. I'll have the footman watch out for her. It is too late in the day for her to mix things. He poured himself a glass of port and sat back contemplating his soon-to-be-found wealth and the marriage of his daughter. All his worries would be over. Soon he would have grandchildren to bounce on his knee. Thinking of the age of Lord Sidney Fowler-Greene, he amended, "Well, children aren't all there is to a marriage. Besides, if they were to be as troublesome as Tori, it might be best not to have any."

Tori mounted the steps slowly, her heart beating quickly. She entered Lady Lydia's room and quietly walked over to the huge bed where her mother lay in a half-doze.

"Mother, may I have another peek at your wedding necklace?"

"Mmm. Yes," the childlike voice answered sleepily.

Tori bent and picked up the small leather bag that held the diamond and ruby necklace. She held it near the flickering flame of the bedside light, removed the gems, and held them so their luster sparkled and gleamed.

"Mother, is it not your plan to present me this necklace at some future date?"

"Hmmm."

"Then, perhaps you'll not mind too much if I take possession of it now, to do with as I please. Can you hear me, Mother? I'm going to take the necklace. It's all right, is it not? Somehow I feel it fitting that I should have the necklace since my own marriage is to be arranged."

"Yes, yes," came the sleepy reply.

"Oh, thank you," Tori exclaimed as she placed a resounding kiss on Lady Lydia's pale cheek. "You've saved my life!"

"That's nice, dear." Lady Lydia snuggled down further into the warm bed and turned her face deeper into the pillow.

Tori crept out of the room, feeling guilty for tricking her unsuspecting mother.

Back in her own suite of rooms, Tori sat on a small settee by the idle fireplace. The double glassed doors leading onto the balcony were open, allowing the gentle breezes of late September to waft into her room, bringing with them the fresh scent of fallen leaves rotting in the damp.

She placed the sparkling necklace on the delicate end table before her, putting her too few jewels beside it. With this as an added incentive, Granger was sure to help her. She never for a moment considered his refusal. Granger would do anything for money. So near poverty was he, Tori had no doubt of this. Poor Granger, ensconced in his mother's sister's household, dependent on Lord Rawlings' goodwill and generosity.

When Granger was fifteen, he had lost both mother and father in a shipwreck off the coast of Spain. Sir Lapid, Granger's father, had been a successful privateer and shipbuilder, dabbling in imports and exports. Pirates and heavy embargoes had put his livelihood in jeopardy, and Sir Lapid risked all he had on a venture in North Africa. Granger had stayed in England to complete his schooling and await his parents' return. Lady Sylvia, Granger's mother, had begged her husband to allow her to accompany him on his newest ship. After much cajoling and pouting, Sir Lapid had finally agreed. Then an ill-fated storm off the coast of Gibraltar had robbed Granger of both mother and father and, not the least, his inheritance. All Sir Lapid owned was tied up in the venture, and when the estate was settled and the debts paid, Granger was left with a small yearly allowance, barely enough to keep body and soul together.

Since that time, Lord Rawlings had taken the responsibility of his wife's nephew. If the truth were to be told, Lord Rawlings was fond of Granger. If only the boy were not so irresponsible and shiftless, Lord Rawlings had told himself and his wife countless times, he would not find Granger so irritating. And what did the boy think to gain by regaling his innocent cousin Tori with tales of misadventure? Lord Rawlings blamed most of Tori's high-spirited ways on poor Granger.

Tori had just replaced the ruby necklace in its leather pouch and her own jewels in her pocket when a tentative rapping sounded on her door.

"Come in, Granger," she called cheerfully.

Warily, Granger entered, his eyes raking the room for some hidden message.

"Pray, cousin, sit here by me." Tori patted the cushion. "I'll not bite you. Come, come, don't be shy." She measured his mood. "We've been cousins and known each other too long to stand on ceremony. Pray, sit, Granger."

Still wary, Granger sat on the edge of the settee as if poised for flight. "Come on, cousin, let's get this over with. I told you before that I'm sorely tired."

"Dearest Granger, if that is to be the case, then I must tell you my little predicament immediately. I find myself in a very precarious predicament. I'm sure you know of my father's plans for me to wed Lord Fowler-Greene." Granger nodded. "Are you also aware that after his debts are paid there will be precious little left for my father and my mother?"

Granger looked puzzled, not liking the course of the conversation.

"That, Granger, means you'll have to find other lodgings and look elsewhere for an allowance. My parents will close this house and take up residence at the summer house. There, they'll live modestly and quietly. And Granger, there'll be no room for you," Tori stated ominously.

"But . . . but . . ."

"I'm truly sorry, but that is the way of it. I sorely wish there was some way I could help you."

"Oh, but there is, dear cousin." Granger smiled meaningfully, his emphasis on the "dear." "When you have wed Lord Fowler-Greene you will invite me to stay with you."

"Granger!" Tori said, shocked, "I cannot do it! Why, Lord Fowler-Greene will want me all to himself. After all, he is buying a wife, not all her poor relatives. Think, cousin, how will it look? Surely you jest!"

Granger examined the sincerity of Tori's expression. "You're right, Tori, I was jesting." The glumness of Granger's face almost gave Tori up to her secret laughter. Poor boy, so worried was he for his future he could not see past his nose to her tricks.

"But, Tori, what am I to do? Turn into a beggar?"

"Better yet, why don't you join Scarblade's men? They could use a member who has some breeding. I feel so sorry for you, Granger."

"Don't waste your sympathies on me, Tori; I still have my wits to live by. But you, poor cousin, you'll have naught but a pretty face and a fashionable figure with which to secure your future. And once Lord Fowler-Greene learns of your temper and lack of breeding in the wifely arts, you can be sure you'll be kept at home, away from polite society, where your spirit will not embarrass him."

"Embarrass him? What are you speaking of, Granger? How could I embarrass Lord Fowler-Greene? He should be ecstatic that I should consent to this marriage!"

Granger smiled wickedly; his recriminations against Tori always carried weight. He knew which road led to her sorest parts, the one that led directly to her pride. "But of course if you're a good girl and only speak with the ladies and never smile in a gentleman's direction, Lord Fowler-Greene will have naught to complain of. So you see, Tori, once again you are mistress of your own destiny."

"Granger," Tori exclaimed hotly, "if you do not drop this, this . . . I demand you speak the King's English! What do you mean I'll be kept at home? You know I cannot live a life of solitude. Speak now, Granger, explain yourself!"

Granger sat for a moment arranging the lace at his sleeves, pretending Tori's excited statements were unheard. At last, unable to withstand the sheer willfulness of her stare and the pitiful picture she made sitting there with her future at stake, actually fearful of his next words, Granger's core of cruelty rejoiced in satisfaction. How often Tori had placed him in just this situation, how many times she threatened to do something which would see Granger cast out on his ear, left to fend for himself. But then, she was his cousin and he loved her only slightly less than he loved himself. No matter how great was his enjoyment of this verbal sparring in which Tori ranked among the most witty, he must now make his move to put an end to her anxiety over his statement.

"Odds fish, cousin, what I am about to tell you is the honest truth, I swear on my sainted mother's watery grave." Tori sighed audibly and settled back in her seat. "Of course, this is only taproom talk, but you know as well as I that there is no smoke without fire."

"Yes, Granger, now get on with what you have to tell me. I fear I cannot abide your philosophizing this night."

Granger sneered slightly in annoyance at Tori's disinterest in his sage impressions. "All right then, if you would have me come straight to the point, here it is. Lord Fowler-Greene has been a bachelor these many years, his first wife succumbing to a fever almost thirty years ago. Lady Fowler-Greene was a woman of quality and title. A bit long in the tooth when she married, true, but nevertheless, her wit and charm won for your betrothed the titles and manor which he now holds. One cannot say it was a love match, but the good lord fawned and doted on her. Who would not, seeing the great advantages one could gain by association with her?"

"To the point, Granger, to the point!" Tori said impatiently.

"It is this, Tori. Lord Fowler-Greene has been heard to say time and time over that never would he bed a woman who could not match his wife for manners and culture. The poor gentleman has never been known to avail himself of the wenches who would fall at his feet for the recompense he could well afford. Rumor has it that he has been celibate these many years since the demise of his dear wife."

"Hrmmmph! And why would anyone, be she wench or lady, seek to *faire l'amour* with that obese, sweating, scratching . . ."

"Tut, tut, Tori! Have you forgotten, you speak of your intended?"

"Oooh, Granger!" Tori raged, "I believe you are actually enjoying my predicament!"

"No, Tori. I know better than that! Our fortunes have been too closely linked these past years. I know that whatever is best for you is also best for me."

"On that you can depend. Were it not for me, Father would never have increased your allowance to much above that of a schoolboy's. I have not yet decided on a plan to gracefully withdraw from this engagement, but when I do, Granger, I will depend on you to assist me."

"Your imperious tone irritates me, cousin. Do not be too sure of me. For once it might bring me pleasure to see you brought down."

Tori swallowed her rage. At all costs she would deny Granger the satisfaction of seeing her cowed. She gathered her poise and smiled sweetly. "As I said, you will assist me. Think, Granger, soon it will be cold and wintry. I can see you trouncing down the road, cold, hungry, destitute, begging for a crust of bread. Just when you think you cannot go one step farther, the highwaymen will be upon you. Oh, Granger, what they will do to your poor person. I can see it as if it has happened already. I will cry openly over your poor frozen body. The tears will freeze upon my cheeks. I shall pray for you, dear cousin," Tori mocked sadly. "Alas, it appears only the women in this family have any kind of stamina. Poor, poor Granger."

Granger trembled at her softly spoken words. He, himself, could picture the scene she had painted.

Tori reached out a slim white hand and offered him three gold sovereigns and her meager jewels. "You jest, cousin. This paltry sum would not keep me but a month."

" 'Tis all I have!" she protested.

Granger looked Tori in the eye. "Lazy I may be, but a fool, never! Let us see the rest of the booty."

Grudgingly, Tori withdrew the small leather pouch from her pocket and threw it on his lap. She watched the greedy leer spread over Granger's face.

"That is more like it! You snitched this, didn't you?" he said suddenly. "You never owned anything like this in your life. Where did you get it? Never mind, I have no wish to know. This way, when I turn it into cash I'll not see your poor mother's face before me." Deftly Granger tossed the brillant necklace into the air and caught it.

Suddenly Tori snatched the necklace and stuffed it into her pocket. "Not so fast, cousin, you only get this," she said, patting her pocket, "when you agree to help me in whatever course I decide to take. A promise, Granger, your word as a gentleman!"

"Develop your scheme, Tori; you can rely on me for my assistance," he said, eying the pocket.

Later that evening, a weary Tori climbed into bed and pushed aside all thought of her predicament concerning Lord Fowler-Greene. Instead she clung to the memory of strong arms pressing her closer and black eyes caressing her.

Morning brought no solution to Tori's problem. Tori rose hollow-eyed and exhausted, feeling as though she had never slept. Dressing hurriedly in a pale-green morning gown which matched her eyes, she trudged tiredly down the stairs. She breakfasted in silence, picking at her food and glancing out the high, wide windows.

"Tori, you're not listening to me!" Lady Lydia's high, clear voice complained.

"Yes I am, Mother. I heard you. I fear I had a bad night. You are going to have a dinner party tomorrow evening, and, yes, it is quite all right with me."

"Your betrothed will be here, Tori," Lady Lydia chattered brightly. "The footman, just this past hour, has left with the invitation from your father. I am sure Lord Fowler-Greene will accept with haste. Do you not agree?"

"Yes, Mother," Tori said wanly.

Lady Lydia looked at her daughter with something akin to fear. The child looked ill. 'Tis the thought of the coming marriage. Lady Lydia brightened as she remembered how nervous she had been at a similar time in her life. That's all it is, she consoled herself. The child is just nervous. Immediately the lady felt better; after all, the child was bound to marry *someday*, and it might as well be now when she would still look lovely in a wedding gown. There are too many brides I've seen who were too long in the tooth. They never should have had formal weddings. Posh and tother to all that business about doing it for their mothers. The dear ladies should be grateful enough to see their daughters marry, let alone quibble over the grandeur of large ceremonies.

Her attention came back to Tori, who was picking at her food. "I hope, dear, that you will wear the green silk, it brings out the color of your eyes. We do so want to leave a good impression with Lord Fowler-Greene, don't we?"

"Yes, Mother." Tori pushed a thick slice of ham from side to side on her plate as her stomach heaved. She thought of her eager bridegroom and her years of association with him. Tori had had occasion to meet Lord Sidney Fowler-Greene numerous times since her childhood. She moaned inwardly as she remembered his fat, white, eternally damp hand which never lost an opportunity to tweak her chin or pat her cheek. His distasteful teasing, instructing her to hurry and grow up so he could make her his bride. Thank God, he had restrained himself when she had become a young lady. Only then was she saved from being pulled onto his lap and pressed against his enormous belly to suffer his foul breath on her face.

The years had not improved the lord. If anything, they had been most unkind. Where his face had once been round and plump, it now had fallen into folds of flesh that quivered at his every word. His nose resembled a lump of bread dough molded into a swollen ball and pressed into the middle of his face. His mouth was overgenerous, overmoist; a hint of what in his youth must have been sensual still remained, but now it was disfigured by years of imbibing and discolored by too frequent use of Indian snuff. The thought of coming into intimate contact with that mouth caused Tori to gag. Abruptly, she stood up and asked to be excused. Without waiting for an answer, she clamped a white hand over her mouth and ran from the room.

Startled by her daughter's abrupt action, Lady Lydia looked askance at the fleeing figure. "Nelson," she cried, "where are you? I must speak with you!" Her cry went unanswered. Lady Lydia's thoughts began to run together. She must be mistaken. It was probably due to her restless night's sleep. She dreamed that Tori had asked for the marriage necklace. Tori, who had no use for jewels!

Chapter Six

"If I need you, Annie, I'll ring for you!" Tori snapped. "I'm perfectly capable of dressing myself this evening. My head is pounding and I wish to be alone!" The little maid scuttered away. She had never seen her mistress in such a bad humor. She should be happy, what with her wedding so close.

Tori dressed in a state of dejection. Bovine, pompous old man, she fumed inwardly. I don't love him and I could never learn to love him. I don't want to marry him. I don't want to marry anyone! Silent tears splashed her cheeks and then a glimmer of an idea came to her. Granger says my good lord will only wed and bed a lady of quality, a woman of taste and manners. Why, it's a point of honor with him! Ooh, wouldn't I like to see society laugh in his face. Perhaps if I'm miserable and rude to him this evening he will change his mind and think I'm not good enough for him. "Would that it were so easy, Tori girl." She knew her father would never demand this marriage of her if it were not for the money involved. No, any overt action on her part to discourage Lord Fowler-Greene would not be taken well by Lord Rawlings, not well at all. Any attempt made in those directions would have to be subtle, very subtle indeed for Lord Rawlings not to catch on. Tori brightened. Perhaps, she thought, if Lord Fowler-Greene were to become, let us say, disenchanted with me, and he himself were to break the engagement, it might be just possible his embarrassment would incline him to pay Lord Rawlings the purse at any rate.

"If only it were so," Tori wished aloud as she looked at her reflection in her small mirror. "I have it!" she exclaimed. Hurriedly, she applied bright vermillion to her cheeks and lips and smiled at her reflection. "That should set Lord Fowler-Greene on his ear." Defiantly, she tossed her head and set a few stray curls to dancing. She sniffed and gathered up the hem of her skirt and left the room.

Lord Nelson eyed the color on his daughter's face and squirmed in his chair. If he were to make an issue of the matter, he knew full well that Tori would run off to her bedchamber and refuse to return. He could picture himself dragging her as she kicked and fought all the way down the stairs to meet her intended.

Lady Lydia looked at her beautiful daughter and smiled. I wonder if she has the fever? she mused. It was probably the excitement of meeting Lord Fowler-Greene again.

"I'm so glad you've chosen that particular gown to wear this special evening, dear," Lady Lydia said, nodding her approval at a peach-colored silk tied with soft blue ribbons. "I've always said it gives your skin the color of spun honey." Actually Lady Lydia was perturbed over the fact that Tori had not worn the green silk as she had promised, but Lady Lydia used good judgment in refraining from making a point of it. She, too, could imagine Tori using the mere comment as an excuse to argue and be absent from this important dinner.

Suddenly, there was a sound of carriage wheels and the bustle of footmen heading for the front door. "Ah, it appears our guest and Lady Helen have arrived." Lord Nelson cast a stern eye in his daughter's direction, and rose to greet his guests.

Tori fought the urge to stick out her tongue at her father's retreating back. She would do it later, she promised herself. As she reclined languidly on the small sofa next to her mother, she worked her face into a semblance of a smile. Granger would have described it as a grimace.

At the first sound of footsteps at the doorway, Tori jumped to her feet in deference to the ages of the entering guests. Lady Helen, Lord Fowler-Greene's widowed sister, preceded her brother into the room. She was a gaunt, tight-lipped woman, the direct opposite in appearance of her brother.

"Darling!" Lady Helen gushed, coming forth to embrace Tori as she scrutinized the girl's high color. Her narrow, black eyes flicked in disapproval while syrupy phrases dripped from her pinched lips. "How wonderful it will be to have you in the family, Victoria dear. I've long been lonely for a companion and Sidney must see to it that you spend considerable time with me at my home in Sussex. The country air is so invigorating."

Tori smiled politely and groaned inwardly. Why had she never thought of it? Of course Lady Helen would expect her sister-in-law to sit with her and embroider and read the French classics. As if Lord Sidney would not be enough to bear, now this too!

Lord Fowler-Greene approached, limping slightly from a recent attack of the gout. "Victoria, beloved!" he exclaimed, reaching for her hand. "You are more beautiful than ever." He kissed Tori's unwilling hand, then turned it and bestowed another kiss on the inside of her wrist, leaving a trail of saliva. His plump, hot hands clamped her shoulders and Tori could feel her flesh crawl as he pecked her on each cheek.

"Dear Victoria," Lord Sidney said unctuously, "I'm so happy to be here in the capacity of your betrothed. In fact I am deliriously happy at the thought of our coming marriage. I see that you are, too," he said, noticing the high color in Tori's cheeks. "And you, dear friend," Lord Fowler-Greene said, extending his hand in Lord Rawlings' direction, "we have been good friends and now we shall be more, much more."

Lord Rawlings smiled and allowed Lord Fowler-Greene to pound him on the back. He felt a little displaced, a bit more than chagrined that soon, very soon, the slathering Lord Fowler-Greene would be his son-in-law. And if he didn't miss his guess, the pompous ass would take to calling him "Father." A taste of bile rose in Lord Rawlings' throat and the bitterness made his lip curl.

"How good to see you smile, my good man," Lord Fowler-Greene boomed. "I know if it were myself about to lose my beautiful daughter, I would find little to smile about."

Then, turning to Lady Lydia, he said in a quite serious tone, "My good lady, I want to assure you that I will dote on your daughter day and night."

Lady Lydia smiled sweetly and then suddenly brightened perceptibly. "A moat!" she cried, thinking she had at last understood. "Lord Sidney, I did not know your house had a moat! Tori, is it not enchanting? A moat! Fancy that!" Lady Lydia tittered at the romantic thought. "Then you two shall be safe and secure against the elements, not to mention outlaws. Delightful!"

Granger, just entering the room, heard Lady Lydia's last remark. He choked slightly and had to be pounded on the back by Lord Nelson.

Dinner was announced and Lord Fowler-Greene led Tori by the arm, surreptitiously pinching her smooth skin. Outraged, Tori hissed quietly, "Do not be so familiar, sir. We are not married . . . yet!"

"Hrmmmph. Yes, yes. Quite. There are some ladies who like that sort of attention," Lord Fowler-Greene whispered. "I can see you are not one of them and I am grateful. I, myself, believe a lady should never accept advances from men; however, since I am your intended, I'm sure you'll forgive my little, shall we say, *faux pas.*" Seeing the vicious look on Tori's face, he added hastily, "I shall save my fondlings for the bedchamber," then smiled lewdly.

Tori pretended not to hear this last statement, so angry with herself was she for missing her chance to give Lord Fowler-Greene food for thought. I should have pretended to like it! she scolded herself. If what Granger says about the old fool is true, I just missed my chance, but I promise I'll not miss another. I'll have the old fool thinking I can hardly wait to jump into bed with him. Perhaps my eagerness will put him off me. Ugh! I must do something! His breath smells like a bucket of slops. As she entered the dining room, she stepped over to her seat and awaited the entrance of the others.

Granger entered, Lady Helen on his arm. Tori misinterpreted his pained look as one of sympathy for himself. Actually, Granger's sympathies were totally with Tori.

Dinner was dismal. Granger appeared to be the only one enjoying the roast mutton. He, in fact, had his dish refilled twice. Lady Lydia kept glancing at Tori from beneath lowered lids, a frown on her still pretty face.

Lady Helen was engaged in expounding the merits of a new remedy for the dropsy which she had been using on her cook. Tori appeared to be interested for courtesy's sake, but the whole while her head was pounding unmercifully.

Lord Fowler-Greene was speaking to Lord Rawlings and his voice began to get louder and louder. Even Lady Helen, used as she was to her brother's volume, stopped speaking to listen.

"No, Nelson. You don't see it the way I do and I don't expect you ever will," Lord Fowler-Greene was saying in his great voice.

"I don't expect I ever could see it your way!" Lord Rawlings raised his voice a note above that of Lord Fowler-Greene. "I don't do things under the cover as is your way. I thought the man should be given at least the consideration of a hearing and said so!"

Lord Fowler-Greene used the old statesman's tactic and lowered his voice. Immediately, all attention was on him, waiting expectantly for his next words. "You see, old friend," with a special emphasis on "friend," "you must think of the whole situation logically. You must view it in its entirety. If you would help this Marcus Chancelor, you must not incense those who would be inclined to oppose him. This you have already done by your blatant support of the man."

"Blatant?" Lord Rawlings shouted. "What am I, a crude pigkeeper, or a Member of Parliament? Sidney, you weren't there when this all happened. Now you must hear the tale from my side." Lord Fowler-Greene settled himself back in his chair and rested his eyes on Lord Rawlings, flattering his friend with his total attention.

Lord Rawlings started, in a much softer tone of voice. "We were at lunch, the other members and myself. From somewhere entered a tall, good-looking young fellow. He was well dressed, very much the gentleman. Then he began to speak. Imagine everyone's shock when this apparent gentleman addressed us in that impossible slur that is spoken in the colonies. Then, what does he do, but after he has our shocked attention, he falls back into the purest-class English, like ours, Sidney, you know? One would think he was born and bred right here in London in sight of Whitehall. But I am drifting from the point. He addressed us and said his name was Marcus Chancelor, from Chancelor's Valley in the Carolinas. He told us of the hardships his people have had to suffer because of our blockade and those renegade Indians. All they have left is a bit of seed with which to plant the next harvest. It seems that Chancelor's Valley is inhabited by those who have spoken out against the government. Chancelor made it clear that they weren't speaking out against the King. Indeed, the people are steadfast royalists. Instead they were speaking out against the corrupt governors there in the colonies who line their pockets by the sweat of the workingman's brow. Since they are to be considered outcasts, the only possible means they have of supporting themselves is to deal in the black market which in the long run is a side enterprise of the very governors who condemn them. This Marcus Chancelor was not asking for any assistance other than to have the King lift the blockade which was suggested by these governors."

"I've heard all that, Nelson," Lord Fowler-Greene commiserated. "What I'd like to know is just exactly how you found yourself in your embarrassing predicament."

"Found myself? Placed is more likely!" Lord Rawlings protested. "I took up the young man's case with several of my colleagues. They seemed very interested. Then all of a sudden, temper seemed to change against me; indeed, the ill wind was blowing so strongly it was all I could do to remain standing on the floor of the House. I've strong suspicions that the governors this Chancelor was speaking of have friends who better their own interests by assuring those of the governors. Next I knew, I was named an offensive subject to the King, and my holdings had been stripped from me."

"Now were you wise, you could have helped Marcus Chancelor, for a price of course, for if his community could afford the outrageous prices foisted on them by the black market, surely they would have been relieved to pay you a trifling sum, just in gratitude, you understand. So, instead of working behind the scenes, you made an issue of it, found yourself opposed, and stuck with it anyway. Now you find yourself with nothing and also no way to help this Chancelor fellow whose cause you've championed." Lord Fowler-Greene noted the interested and dismayed expressions as he glanced around the table. "Odds fish! Is this the first you all are hearing of my good friend's problems?"

Chapter Seven

It was less than a week before the wedding. Lady Lydia sat chatting with Mrs. Carey as the seamstress fitted the dress. The long white satin of Tori's wedding gown sparkled and shone in the few rays of the sun that filtered through the huge leaded windows of her bedchamber.

"As I feared, Lady Rawlings, the child gets thinner each time I come, and then I have to restitch the seams. I fear she'll waste away to nothing. As one of experience, having fitted more brides than I can remember, either Miss Rawlings is overcome with excitement or she is unhappy with the match," Mrs. Carey sputtered, her mouth full of pins.

Lady Lydia, herself, had the same thoughts. But she knew for certain which way Tori's emotions lay. When Lady Lydia had tried speaking to her husband of the matter, he had said it was just one of Tori's tricks. Still, she didn't like the look in the girl's eyes. Lady Lydia had never seen defeat in Tori; this was unlike her. A mother doesn't know how to help her child at times like these, Lady Lydia complained to herself. What is a mother to do? If there was only something she could say to make the ordeal easier for her child. The lady sighed deeply as she leaned forward to feel the smooth satin fabric which hung on Tori's too sparse frame.

Tori roused herself from a half-dream and glanced at her mother and the seamstress. Noticing the gleaming satin as though for the first time, a look of loathing came across her face. It was noticed by the two women. Dutifully, Tori stood complacently as the seamstress turned her this way and that, pinning here, altering there. Where the gown had once clung to her curved figure it now hung limp. Lady Lydia frowned at the appearance of her daughter. Mrs. Carey sighed audibly. The seams must be taken in again, she would be up all night sewing. And for what? They would have to carry the girl to the ceremony on a litter or she missed her guess. And then who would see the lovely gown that she had stitched for over a fortnight? "A waste," Mrs. Carey muttered to herself. "A pure waste!"

All the while she measured and pinned, Tori stood, bemoaning the fates which had brought her to this crisis in her life. Tori willed her mind to dwell on happier moments. Her first ball, the morning rides through the countryside with the wind whipping her golden hair back from her eyes. The freedom she had felt and enjoyed. Sitting in the kitchen with Cook and the maids and mimicking their melodious cockney accent to their screams of laughter and approval at her adroitness. Granger and the sometimes vile tricks she played on him, only to take her turn and become the object of his practical jokes. Girlhood seemed to be rushing away from her, leaving behind only memories of those carefree days.

Lady Lydia became so disconcerted by Tori's silence, she could bear it no longer and made a feeble excuse to escape the maudlin atmosphere of the bedchamber. When she had left, Mrs. Carey too was feeling the heavy pall of silence and she strove to divert the girl's attention.

"You look so familiar to me, Miss Rawlings. I believe I've mentioned it before. At the time I could not remember who you resemble. But I have thought and thought and at last, late last night while I was stitching the hem of this gown, I finally remembered. There's a girl at the Owl's Eye Inn. Oh, I don't suppose you know of the place; believe me, were it not for a marvelous little shop nearby, I myself would never venture into that notorious district."

Seeing the disinterested expression Tori offered her, Mrs. Carey curbed her verbal wanderings. "As I was saying, Miss Rawlings, I've thought and thought these past days and finally it came to me. The serving wench at the Owl's Eye Inn is the dead image of you, Miss Rawlings. Don't take offense where none is intended, but I dare say she could pass for you in a bright light."

Tori squirmed as Mrs. Carey adjusted a pleat and again stood quietly listening with half an ear.

"She's the same hair as yourself, or it would be if it were done up proper. But I don't imagine the eyes are the likes of yours. I declare I've never seen eyes the likes of yours in all my born days!"

"Who is she?" Tori asked politely.

Mrs. Carey, so startled by Tori's sudden interest, gagged on one of her pins. "Why, I just told you, she's a serving wench at the inn. I don't know anything about her."

"And she works at which inn?" Tori asked, a brightness returning to her eyes.

"Why, like I told you, Miss Rawlings, the Owl's Eye Inn, in Chelsea. And a beautiful girl she is. 'Tis a shame she's not quality folk like yourself."

Tori began to fidget. "Miss Carey, have you seen my cousin Granger?"

"Yes, miss. He was downstairs when I arrived, if I'm not mistaken. Hold still, miss. I'm almost finished. There, that does it, little lady. The gown will be finished in time for the wedding. Though dreading it I am that I'll have to lose sleep again to alter the gown."

Tori wiggled from the gown and hastily dressed herself. She almost stumbled, and Mrs. Carey had to come to her aid. God! She'd no idea she was so weak. She must have something to eat. She must regain her strength! There was no time to lose.

"Mrs. Carey, when you return downstairs, tell the cook to send me a heaping plateful of food. Any kind, it doesn't matter. And please have someone send my cousin Granger to me, immediately!"

"Yes, miss," Mrs. Carey managed to utter, so startled was she by the abrupt change in the girl. Still, the old woman remembered her own wedding to her Charlie. Hadn't she acted much the same way, excited one minute and composed the next? Yes, Mrs. Carey thought to herself, everything would work out. Especially now, since she wouldn't have to take in the seams on the bridal gown again. If Miss Rawlings continued to show this renewed spirit, surely she would put on the needed five pounds she required to fill out the gown.

Chapter Eight

"Aaaow, miss! That glad I am to see ye yer old self again." The maid, Annie, smiled as she watched Tori tear the leg from a succulent squab.

"Mmm . . ." Tori mumbled as she chewed excitedly. Laying the fowl aside, she ripped at a chunk of cheese and washed it down with a huge mug of milk. "I forgot how good food could taste," she said as she picked up the squab again. "You may leave now, Annie. You can return the tray to the kitchen in the morning. I won't need you the rest of the night. I'm due for a good long night's rest."

"That you are, miss. 'Ave a good night. That 'appy am I to see ye more like yer old self. I'm sure yer intended will be overjoyed t' 'ear about yer improved health."

"Mmm . . . yes," Tori said, her eyes bright. "I'm sure he will. Most happy. The lecherous old fool," she added under her breath.

As Annie was leaving, Granger appeared outside the open door.

"Granger! Come in, come in." As the door closed behind Annie, Tori cried excitedly, "I cannot believe my good fortune. I simply cannot believe it!"

"Tell me now. Has Lord Fowler-Greene met with an unfortunate accident?"

"Oh, hush!" Tori scolded, suddenly remembering her annoyance with Granger. "Where have you been? I've been waiting the better part of an hour for you to come to me. Didn't you receive my message?"

"Ah, Tori. I see by the return of your sweet nature that your health has returned. When I saw the maid carrying your tray, I thought there was an army quartered here. I see you have regained your appetite. To what do we all owe this remarkable recovery?"

53

Tori chose to ignore his sarcasm. "Granger, I cannot believe my good fortune. The gods are smiling in my favor. Listen to what I have to tell you. You will become as excited as I." Quickly, Tori recited the tale Mrs. Carey had told her of the serving girl at the Owl's Eye Inn. "Is it not fate, Granger? Aren't you happy for me?"

"Oh, I'm happy," Granger said, squirming in his chair. "Now that I know there are two of you in this world I fear I shall have to take up your father's offer of wedding Lady Helen."

"Dear Granger, he didn't! Did he—to a sixty-year-old sheep dog!" Tori laughed mirthfully. "Is it to be a double wedding? How much is your purse? What are you worth on the marriage market? Surely not as much as me. Let me look at you," Tori giggled as she eyed Granger's virile, young body. "I fear," she said sadly, "Lady Helen wouldn't know what to do with you. Pray, Granger, do you not agree?" She laughed aloud at her cousin's obvious discomfort.

"Many's the seed you've sown," Tori continued teasing. "Perhaps it is time to settle down and grow old. 'Tis a shame? Lady Helen is *well* past the childbearing age. There will be no lusty sons for you, dear Granger."

"Hah! And that old cuckold that you are to wed. What makes you think he'll even be able to bed you?"

"I have no intention of marrying and bedding that rooster. I have a plan, Granger. And if you have half the brains you were born with you will leave with me. For a man as versatile as yourself, there must be many ways of making a suitable living, or if that fails, marrying a wealthy woman."

Granger nodded morosely. He could not picture himself lying next to a shaggy sheep dog. Sheep dogs were fine creatures, in fact he actually liked them, but not in his bed! Now if Lady Helen was ripe and succulent like a fresh picked peach, he would have snatched at Lord Rawlings' offer. Still, one could not have everything. But on the other hand, what did he have? Just the promise of a ruby necklace if he helped Tori in whatever scheme she could devise.

"Let's get on with it, Tori. What exactly do you have in mind?"

"It is this, Granger. As soon as everyone is asleep, we will go to the Owl's Eye Inn and see this girl who looks so much like me. I shall offer her the chance to change places with me."

All of a sudden, Granger burst out into a roaring laugh. "Tori, do you realize what type of scoundrels custom the Owl's Eye Inn? No, I think not. In all likelihood, this wench is a slattern, a doxy. Can you just imagine that pompous ass's face when he discovers he has bedded a tavern wench? And after all these many years of boasts. Why he'll not be able to show his face in London!"

"That is what makes this so ideal, Granger. Lord Fowler-Greene will not want any publicity concerning the trick played on him. He wouldn't dare to openly accuse my father of participating in this sham, and in all likelihood he will be more than glad to forget the purse he will have paid for the honor of my hand. Don't you see, Granger, it's perfect. The most father has to lose is an old friend. Mind, I said an old friend, not a good one."

"Speaking of your father, Tori, what do you think this will do to him? He does have his code of honor, you know."

Tori snapped her fingers. "Why, dear cousin, it shall be as honorable for me to save myself from this impossible marriage as it was for Father to stretch out his hand and accept the purse. There is a word for what he has attempted to do, you know. It is called slavery. And me! His own child! I'd rather die first than marry someone named Sidney!"

"You just may at that! When Lord Fowler-Greene discovers the ruse, what then? We have already agreed he would want no publicity, true. But surely you don't think he will ignore the whole thing. No, I fear not, cousin." Granger rubbed his hand gently across his lace-cravated neck. "And that long neck of yours is so beautiful, Tori. It will be a shame to see it broken. Our Sidney does have his ways and means, you know. And think of the sympathy that will accrue to him when London hears of the fatal accident suffered by his young wife. Surely the King will see fit to bestow another land grant on the grieving widower."

Tori blanched slightly at Granger's softly spoken words. "It is no more than he deserves. I have no compassion for him."

"You have it wrong, cousin. It is you who will merit the pity. I hear you brought a healthy purse. That lecherous old fool, as you call him, willingly offered to double the purse, and your father accepted. That is how eager he is to bed you."

Tori's eyes glittered, showing more yellow than green, as they always did when she was incensed. "The man I bed will be something to behold, Granger, I promise you. No dirty old man for me! I'm young and healthy. I want a man who can set my pulses racing, not some fat, unwashed old fool who thinks the measure of a lady is her indignation at a hint of physical contact. I'll have the full experience of love or I shall never marry!"

Chapter Nine

Granger rapped softly on Tori's door a little past ten in the evening. The door swung open and his cousin stood there, excitement evident on her lovely face. "Come. Hurry. Aren't you ready yet? My neck isn't as long and pretty as yours, and I wouldn't look well at the end of a rope. For surely that is what will happen if Uncle Nelson finds I've helped you."

Tori shot him a vicious look and picked up a purple velvet cloak lined in white ermine to wrap around her slim body. "Have you arranged for the trap?"

"All is ready, and I must add that you owe me ten guineas with which I had to bribe the stableboy."

"Ten? You'll get two and not a farthing more. Don't try and make your fortune from me, you fox."

As Granger watched her arrange the cloak he said, "I see you dress for the occasion. Don't you think you'll be conspicuous? It is not Whitehall to which we go, you know," he hissed sarcastically.

"I may be robbed this evening, and I so want to be well dressed," Tori whispered. "It pays to always look one's best. Granger, you are so *gauche*. Really, I must wash my hands of you. All these years and I have tried, but Mother was right, you cannot make a brass urn from a lead one."

"Hand over the necklace, Tori," Granger scoffed. "I want it now. It is not that I don't trust you, but just in the event we are robbed I don't want you to offer it to some nefarious highwayman just for a thrill. Now hand it over."

Tori gave him the gleaming jewels. "You're so greedy, Granger! It sickens me," she said, wrinkling her nose and baring her white teeth.

Granger accepted the gems, his eyes as bright as the jewels. Deftly he slid them into his right boot. That they caused him pain was no matter. He would limp to hell if he had to. "And if we are accosted, and if you open that foolhardy mouth of yours, I'll shove my boot in it. Mark my words, Tori, I've had enough of your tricks. I want your word or we stay home."

Tori sniffed. "Very well, Granger. If you do not trust me, I give my word to you."

"Oh, it is not you I don't trust, it is that mouth of yours. It seems at times as though it has a mind of its own." He looked at her suspiciously. "You're probably some kind of witch."

"Shut up, Granger," Tori ordered. She, too, had often wondered if there were something wrong with her. But, she thought objectively, witches are ugly, so that took care of that little matter.

Granger and Tori sat in the Owl's Eye Inn. There was no sign of the girl whom she resembled.

As they sat there sipping a raw wine, Tori noted her surroundings. The interior of the inn was coarse and dirty. The rough, wooden benches on which they sat had sharp splinters projecting from the edges. The tallow candles, which were the only source of light, threw their yellow rays on the sawdust floor, and a rank smell of filth and spoiled food rose to pinch her nostrils.

"Tori, for God's sake, stop looking around as though you're quite impressed with the place. As it is, when the innkeeper noticed your dress he tripled the bill. I've only enough money to cover another glass of port at these prices."

"Be still, Granger. I've not had your advantages. I've been kept away from the seamier side of life. I'm enjoying myself. Here, look at those men on the other side of the room. Have you ever seen such wicked-looking characters?"

"Yes, I have. Those two men who rode with Scar-blade had much the same look about them."

"What look is that, Granger?"

"Hungry! Now if you don't stop staring at them, I'll find myself in the position of defending your honor."

"They wouldn't dare!"

"Oh, wouldn't they! Look here, Tori. The only

women that frequent a place like this are known doxies or the sluttish mistresses of the men you affectionately call highwaymen. Now turn around, Tori, for I don't feel like getting my throat slit on your account."

"Granger, what is this preoccupation with your throat? I worry about you, dear cousin. Perhaps a physician in Harley Street could put your mind at rest. I strongly suggest it."

As Tori teased Granger and watched for his reaction, she noticed his eyes lift and an expression of disbelief cross his face. She turned to note the object of his fascination and she, too, was aghast. There, under the flickering light of the sconce, stood a tall, slim blond girl with skin the color of spun honey and a prettiness of feature which Tori had, till now, thought her own.

"She does resemble me," Tori whispered in awe.

"Resemble you! Why, she even has that stubborn set of chin! I'd say she could be a relative if I didn't know better. She looks a bit older than yourself, wouldn't you say? Now what are you doing?" Granger said crossly.

"Shhh! Do you think I want to give it all away? 'Tis better she doesn't see me till the last moment. If seeing me affects her the same as seeing her affected me, she'll run frightened. And as far as being a relative, it may be quite possible. Father did not live the life of a celibate until he married Mother, of that I'm sure!"

"Tori, have you no delicacy?" Granger admonished in mock horror. "So now what do we do? If you're not going to reveal yourself to the girl, we have made a wasted trip."

"Oh, I'll reveal myself to her, but not here in front of all these witnesses. Do you think I want to be black-mailed for the rest of my life? And if I don't miss my guess, these shady characters in here don't miss their chance to turn a dishonest penny."

Granger scratched his head. "You surprise me, cousin. I would have thought you never had a serious thought in your head. But when are we going to approach her?"

"We'll wait till she leaves and then follow her. Now

what you can do for me is go up to the tap table and
inquire of the innkeeper about the girl. Find out as
much as you can about her. It will help, I'm sure of
it."

"Don't you think it will seem strange that I'm in the
company of a lovely young lady and here I am inquir-
ing of another?"

"Granger, I'm sure you are quite used to being considered strange. Go on now!"

It wasn't until he had crossed halfway to the tap
table that he realized the pointed jibe behind Tori's
words. He turned abruptly and looked at his cousin,
who was sitting at the table sipping the crude wine with
a look of innocence about her.

Granger returned with the information Tori wanted
to hear. The girl lived alone and had no known family.
The proprietor called her Dolly Flowers and Granger
admitted as delicately as he could that the inn keeper
would "speak" to Dolly if the gentleman so chose.

"Oh, Granger, how wonderful!"

"Eh! Wonderful, you call it? What, that the girl is a
slut and for a price she'd bed any man willing to pay?
Maybe I wasn't clear, Tori: the man would have sold
me the night with Dolly!"

"Granger, don't be so stuffy with me. I'm not an
ignorant schoolgirl you know. I've read about places
like this and girls like that. Don't look so horrified!"

"Don't misunderstand, cousin. The fact that Dolly is
an honest businesswoman—well, a businesswoman at
any rate, does not offend me. Heaven knows, it would
be a lonely life for a bachelor like myself were it not
for the likes of her. What shocks me is that you think
it wonderful that a pretty girl like that engages in the
'oldest profession.' "

"Don't be stupid, Granger. If she were a girl of vir-
tue how could we expect her to join in our plans? After
all, it is crucial that she actually bed Lord Fowler-
Greene, else we would not have an advantage over
him. What would be the use? The only club we carry is
his fear of it being exposed that he has gone against his
word of these many years to bed only a lady of quality.

And as far as Dolly blackmailing us, she would not do it, not when she has much more to gain by beleaguering dear Sidney."

"Ah, that is where you plan fails, dear cousin. Lord Fowler-Greene is a man of many moods. If she ever threatened to open her mouth, he would have her throat slit."

"There is your preoccupation with throats again! Don't be silly, Granger. Lord Fowler-Greene would never do that. Dolly will be protected simply because we know of the scheme. Lord Fowler-Greene would never take the risk of harming Dolly when he does not know for sure how many of us were involved in it. So you see, it is all bundled nicely. Lord Fowler-Greene gets the surprise of his life, my father gets the purse, you have the necklace and I—I, dear Granger—have my freedom."

"Not yet you don't. We still have to convince Dolly. Now drink up."

Tori stood with her back to the side of the inn. The malodorous refuse and slops which were dumped there caused Tori to wrinkle her nose. Granger paced back and forth beneath the single lamp that lighted their dank surroundings, checking his silver pocket watch.

"What's keeping that girl?" he muttered, limping slightly because of the necklace still in his boot. "I don't much care for waiting around here. God only knows who we'll meet!"

A few moments later a side door opened and closed softly. Dolly emerged, humming to herself. Granger approached the girl, startling her so that she almost lost her footing as she picked her way through the offal. Tori emerged from the shadows and fell in behind Granger. They walked single file down the street and crossed over to a dark alley. Suddenly, the girl stopped short.

"Aaaow, ye na be followin' me, are ye? Listen, Oi've na a ha'penny ta me naime, so get on wi' ye. Wha' are ye wantin' wi' me, anyway? Surely na a turn in th' 'ay, eh sir?" she said, eying the dark form of Tori.

"Ask her, Granger," Tori hissed. "I can't wait a moment longer!"

Granger cleared his throat. "Miss Flowers, I am Granger Lapid, and this," he said, pointing toward Tori, "is Miss Rawlings. We have a proposition to place before you," he said courteously. "I wonder if we might have a moment of your time?"

" 'Ere now," Dolly said sternly, "Oi don' loike these queer threesomes. Oi'm a good girl, Oi am. Oi don' care fer some o' th' games ye gentry loike ta play!"

"No, no," Granger protested, "you misunderstand. It's not that way at all."

"Ooh, in tha' case, sir," Dolly brightened, "la, guvnor, ye can 'ave all me toime. Oi'm na averse ta th' charms o' a gentleman the loikes o' yersel'. Ye can 'ave all me toime." Taking a close look at Granger, she added to Tori, " 'E's quite pretty, 'e is. Wouldn' ye say, miss?"

"I agree," Tori smirked. "He is pretty."

A look of consternation crossed Dolly's face. " 'Ere now, 'ow did ye know me naime?"

Granger sputtered and confessed, "The innkeeper told me."

"Oh, Oi see. Well, whazzit ye wan' o' me?"

Granger struck a match and Tori removed the hood of her ermine cloak. Dolly gasped. "It's me double! Saints preserve us," she muttered, crossing herself.

"Miss Flowers, I want you to change places with me," Tori blurted. "I want you to go through a marriage in my place."

"Yer na serious. Na ye are! Oi can see by yer face, ye are!"

"I am most serious, Miss Flowers. And I assure you I'm not crazy if that's what you're thinking. If you do this for me, you'll be richer than you ever dreamed. Please do this for me," Tori begged, tears stinging her eyes.

"An' jes' who izzit Oi'll be marryin'?" Dolly asked.

"What difference does that make?" Tori answered hotly, afraid of revealing too much of the plan. "Will you do it?"

"Jes' a minute, miss . . . Rawlings, izzit? If Oi marry

this ... person in yer name, it's na a legal marriage. It's sor' o' proxy. So where's all this money cum from?"

"Well, let's just say," Granger interjected, "marriage to you would be a bit of an embarrassment to the old boy. He'll pay you well to keep your mouth shut!"

"Ah, yeh, bu' 'old on 'ere. There's too many toimes Oi've 'eard o' people gettin' their necks broke 'cuz they've threatened ta tell some secret. Tha' blackmail, ye know."

"He'd be afraid to do anything to you, he'd worry that we'd know what he'd done. Besides, he's not that sort of man, is he, Tori?"

"Oh, no, indeed not, he's a kindly old gentleman," she lied.

"Well, if 'e's so koindly, whyn' ye marry 'im yersel'?"

"I would," Tori said pathetically, "but my heart belongs to another. Anyway," Tori added so hotly that Dolly was taken aback, "what my reasons are, are none of your business. I'm offering you a chance to make your fortune, are you going to accept or not?"

"As Oi said afore, who izzit Oi'd be marryin'? Wha's wrong wi' th' man? Does 'e 'ave only one leg? Wha' are 'is failin's? Oi've a righ' ta know! Oi'm a young girl, Oi am!"

Suddenly Tori smiled. "I see. You need have no fear, Miss Flowers. While your bridegroom is up in his years he is most active in this province. Of course, I cannot speak from experience, but knowing his pinching fingers as I do, I am almost sure he'll warm your bed on your wedding night."

"An' wha' o' yersel'? When Oi taikes yer place wha' becomes o' ye?"

"Why, of course, Dolly, I shall take your place."

"Oooh, Oi'd loike ta see tha', Oi would," Dolly laughed.

"An' would ye now? 'Ere luv, lemme tell ya a thin' er two. When yer dealin' wi' th' loikes o' Tori Rawlings yer dealin' wi' th' experts!"

"Aaaaaow! Did ye 'ear 'er now?" Dolly poked

Granger in the ribs. "Who'd 'ave though' she could speak th' cockney?"

"Oi learned it from th' kitchen maid," Tori said imperiously.

Granger and Dolly laughed heartily. "Well, it's been noice knowin' ye an' 'earin' o' yer plan, but Oi'm afraid Oi can' include mesel'." Seeing no reaction on Tori's face, she hastened to add, "At leas' fer th' toime bein', tha' is. Oi'll 'ave ta sleep on it."

"There's no time!" Tori wailed, "the wedding is the day after tomorrow. You must give me your decision!"

"Oi'll give yer me decision tomorrow, bu' Miss Rawlings, Oi migh' arrive at a quicker decision if Oi 'ad a noice warm cloak the loikes o' yers. Jus' so's Oi could get a good nigh's sleep."

Tori snatched the ties and wiggled out of the cloak. "Take it, it's yours. A prewedding gift from me to you."

"Aaaaow!" Dolly exclaimed, rubbing the soft fur of the lining. "Cum by in th' mornin'. Oi'll give me moind then. Oi lodge at th' Rooster's Crown," Dolly said as she tucked the cloak tightly about her shoulders and turned on her heels.

Chapter Ten

Tori and Granger rode within the plush interior of the trap. She was silent, casting furtive glances toward Granger. Finally, unable to stand his silence any longer, she all but shouted, "Well, what do you think? Will she do it?"

Granger nodded gloomily. "I don't see how you hope to get away with it even if she does agree. And you gave her your cloak. She might just as well take off with it, and then where will you be?"

"But I asked you if you thought she would agree—what is it, Granger, will she or won't she?"

"Who knows what a woman thinks and does? Look at you," he said, jabbing a finger in her direction. "If anyone ever told me I would be a party to something like this, I'd give that person a wide berth. You had better start to think how you're going to arrange all this, that is, if she chooses to go along with it." Granger squirmed in his seat.

As they approached the house, Tori turned to Granger. "Best tell the driver to slow the horses. We don't want to awaken anyone. How would you explain the late hour and that you have me in your company?"

"I would tell them the truth," Granger said uneasily as he peered at the darkened house. "I'll just tell them it was all your idea. Who do you think they would believe, especially with your past history of trickery?" he added sourly.

Once in her chamber, Tori ripped the clothes from her body and threw herself on the high bed. The girl had to agree, she just had to! There was no other way out! Tori pounded her fist into the plump pillow and almost wept. Time was so short.

Tori knew she would never sleep this night. Rising

from the bed, she moved over to the washstand and bathed her face in the icy water. Donning a fresh nightgown, she paced the floor, then hurried to the windows and peered out through the leaded panes. Soon it would be dawn of the day before her wedding. How could her parents do this to her? She was their only child! To sell her like a calf at auction and have no remorse was beyond all her understanding.

Quietly, she slipped out of her door and headed for Granger's room. She expected him to be sleeping soundly.

"You know, Tori, you sound like a bull elephant," he said nastily when she tipped over a vase in the darkness. "I expected you hours ago, what kept you?"

"Oh, Granger," Tori said as she threw herself into his arms, "you couldn't sleep, either. Truly, you're the best cousin I ever had!"

"Be truthful, Tori, I'm the only cousin you have," he answered dryly, but his answering embrace comforted her and reassured her that he was with her through the thick or thin of it.

"Are you ready, Granger? You have to go back and get Dolly's answer. I don't think I can bear another moment of the suspense. Granger, you must promise her anything, anything. Just see to it that she agrees!"

"Yes, Your Majesty." Just as Tori was about to speak again Granger hushed her with a motion of his arm. "And yes, I'll not forget what you explained to me. If she agrees, she is to come here tomorrow dressed in a hood and veil. She is to say that she carries a parcel from Lord Fowler-Greene and she must deliver it to you personally. When she is in your chamber, the switch will be made. Correct?"

Tori rushed over to him and helped him into his cape. He picked up a long glowing taper to light his way down the stairs.

"Granger, I implore you, ride carefully. Don't fall off the horse. Look out for bandits and, above all, don't eat anything! You know that when you eat and your nerves are jangling you cannot move for hours. And I do not have the mettle to wait for hours. Go now," she added brightly.

"I have a better idea, Tori," Granger said hotly. "Why don't you go yourself? This way you'll save yourself all this worry."

"And deprive you of another glimpse of the ravishing Dolly? Granger, you above all should know that I've not a mean bone in my body."

Granger snorted in disgust. "You wouldn't give any woman the benefit of a compliment, save our friend Dolly Flowers. Now I wonder why that could be. Perhaps it is because of the resemblance you bear to each other?"

Granger left the room without a backward glance. He brightened considerably at the thought of the beautiful Dolly, and surely if he made good time he would make her lodgings before the full light of day. He brightened still more when he recalled how Dolly remarked on his handsomeness. He rode faster.

Leaving his horse at a nearby livery stable to protect the poor nag from thieves, he made his way the few short blocks to Dolly's lodgings on swift feet. There was no way to tell which room off the long dark hall was Dolly's. Carefully and quietly, Granger opened first one door and then another. Some of the rooms were empty and others were occupied by sleeping forms snoring loudly in protest against the penetrating dampness.

After the fifth try he saw the white ermine cloak in the first faint rays of dawn that managed to creep through the filth-caked windows. He walked quietly over to the narrow cot and eyed it as though taking measurements. Dolly slept with her face pressed into the lining of the cloak. Her closed lids displayed her long lashes. A lock of flaxen hair, so like Tori's, curved sweetly on her cheek. In sleep her face bore a mask of innocence that time and a hard life would never steal. Clearing his throat nervously, Granger shook Dolly's shoulder and demanded in a hoarse whisper, "Have you decided?"

Dolly opened sleepy eyes and smiled up at Granger. "Oh, it's ye. Oi wuz 'avin' mesel' a luvly dream." Through slitted eyes she peered up at him. "Did Oi tell ye las' nigh' tha' Oi think y'ere pretty?" As if to emphasize her words, she wiggled seductively on the narrow cot. Then she stretched luxuriously. "O' course, luv, Oi made me decision las' nigh'."

She smiled again as she rubbed the fur. The cloak slid away from one shoulder revealing a creamy expanse of flesh that looked softer than the ermine. Granger drew in his breath and Dolly smiled.

"Cum 'ere, luv, an' si' by me. Tell me more o' thi' plan."

Granger, never one to dally in the presence of a lady, quickly sat on the edge of the cot and watched as the cloak slid even farther while the wiggling Dolly tried to make room for him.

Dolly made a half-move to restore the cloak, but Granger put out his hand to stop her. When next Dolly touched the cloak it was to remove it entirely.

"Oi do thank ye, Granger," Dolly said with enthusiasm as she watched Granger fasten his waistcoat. He looked puzzled. "Why dearie, this day is th' end o' me carefree youth," she exclaimed. "Tomorrow Oi'll be a married laidy!"

"I must say, Dolly, that when Lord Fowler-Greene discovers what a gem you are, he'll be cock o' the walk!"

"Providin' 'e can still walk, tha' is." Dolly laughed uproariously.

Chapter Eleven

Dolly shed her clothes, careful of her elaborate hairdo. Granger had explained that it was imperative she visit Tori's hairdresser and have her flaxen hair styled to match his cousin's. Feeling the chill of the room, she hurried and wrapped the ermine cloak around her nude body. Delighting in the feel of the silky fur against her skin, she padded her way across the room to peer into the cracked looking glass. As she studied her image a knock sounded on the door.

"Why, it mus' be th' Blade," she thought. " 'E's th' only gent Oi've ever 'ad who takes th' trouble ta knock." For a second she hesitated. What would he say when he saw her? Dolly stepped to the center of the room and assumed a graceful position, allowing the cloak to slip seductively.

"Cum in, Scarblade," she called. Scarblade's tall frame entered the room; his coal-black eyes flickered around the bare, dim surroundings. "Ow, Scarblade," Dolly said petulantly, "ye know it maikes me 'air stand on end when ye do tha'!"

"Do what?" he barked, his eyes taking her in for the first time.

"Ye, when ye rake yer eyes aroun' loike tha'. As if ye expected th' King's men ta jump out o' th' shadows an' grab ye."

"One can never tell, Dolly."

"Aye, but ta think Oi'd 'ide an enemy o' yers 'ere and let ye walk inta a trap. It's very little ye think o' me!"

"Ah, Dolly, don't carry on so. And tell me, what have you done to yourself?" His generous mouth broke into a wide grin. "Are you planning to attend a masked ball?" His dark eyes narrowed to slits and the light danced off them like quicksilver.

69

"Aye, ye say tha', milord," Dolly said haughtily. "An' do Oi offend ye?"

"Where did you get that cloak?" Scarblade said, ignoring her question.

"It's none o' yer business, Oi'm sure."

"I'm making it my business! Now answer me. Where did you get it?" He took two long strides and had her by the arm.

"Ah! Take yer 'ands off me, Scarblade. Ye don' own me, ye know. 'Tiz true we 'ad many a good roll on tha' cot o' moine, but Oi'm a laidy from this day on. Stop pawin' me loike this!"

"Don't you like it?" Scarblade asked roughly, as he pulled her closer to him. Dolly could feel his heart pounding within his massive chest and she discerned a tightening of his body as he held her against him. "I can remember days, Dolly, love, when your passion equaled mine." His lips were in her hair and Dolly regained herself enough to remember her new coiffure. She pulled away from him and the effort left her breathless.

"Well, dearie, those days is gone and Oi don' loike it any longer!"

"I can see you've become a grand lady since last I've seen you. What are you up to, Dolly? Who did you steal that cloak from?"

"Oi didn' steal it! It wuz given ta me. By a gent, Oi migh' add!" she said sweetly as she caressed the velvet. "An why are ye so concerned abou' wha' Oi wear? Ye never were before! Oi'm weary o' ye, Scarblade. They say yer th' busiest 'ighwayman in all England, an' yet 'ave ye ever given me more'n a few shillin's ta pay me ren' or get me shoes fixed? Naw, never!" Her voice rose to a decibel below a screech. "An' who're ye savin' all tha' gold fer, tell me tha', Scarblade? Jus' tell me! Ye fer sartin don' spend it on yersel'!" she said, eying his plain, black frock coat and cotton hose. Her eyes darted over his tightly fitting dove-gray trousers and she fought back the memory of his strong, muscular legs as they had forced hers apart.

"Dolly," he said smoothly, fighting to control his

laughter, "one word of advice. If you want others to think you a lady you must keep your composure."

Dolly shrugged elaborately, and the cloak slipped again to reveal a creamy shoulder and the sloping curve of her white breast. Scarblade drew in his breath, his desire mounting. With a smile, Dolly drew the cloak more snugly about her.

"If it's gifts you want, Dolly, you'd better stay with the er ... gentleman acquaintance you've made, for you'll not receive gifts from me," he said quietly as the twinges of desire bloomed to an ache. "You never asked for anything before this. I thought our passion was a mutual thing. Come on now, Dolly, take the pins out of your hair and come to me."

"Ye'll no' be gettin' any luv from me this nigh', Scarblade," Dolly said as she peered at her reflection in the cracked glass. Even as she said it she could feel the hunger for him growing within her.

"I'll give you a few shillings to have your hair done in the morning if that's what's wrong," he said quietly, coaxingly.

Quickly Dolly glanced over her shoulder, puzzled by the softness in his tone. But then she thought of sitting a whole morning having her hair dressed and felt revolted by the memory. Besides, she thought craftily, this is me chance ta make me a fortune. Oi'll not lose it fer a roll on th' cot, no matter 'ow sweet!

"No, thanks," she said regally, noting the effect on Scarblade when he closed his eyes to slits and glared at her. "Now, if ye don' moind, Oi wish . . . Oi wish ta . . . be alone." Her voice shook slightly with indecision. "Oi've other fish ta fry, Scarblade, an' ye'll no' stop me!"

He laughed, a deep booming sound, starting from within his broad chest. "So, Dolly, it seems you're more a lady than I gave you credit for. You share the same qualities as the more high-born of your sex, namely greed." He stepped over to the narrow cot and sat down, casually placing an elbow on his knee.

Dolly watched him, steeling herself for his wrath. Instead, she was rewarded for her silence with still another insolent laugh. "Come here, Dolly. You know you want to," he said quietly, outstretching his muscular arms to her. For an instant Dolly was undecided, remembering how warm and safe his arms could make her feel.

"An' wha'll ye give me? Eh?" she asked huskily, desire for him deepening her voice.

"Anything you wish. What shall it be?" he asked, measuring her through narrowed eyes that burned through her.

"A gold guinea!"

"A gold guinea it shall be." He reached into the purse hung from his belt, retrieved a golden coin, and hurled it toward her.

Dolly skittered across the floor in an effort to capture the coin, disbelief stamped on her face. " 'Tiz abou' toime ye've cum across wi' sumpin fer me, it is. A girl 'as ta watch 'ersel' an' make 'er own way in this world, she does."

Picking up the gold coin and dropping it into the pocket of her cloak, Dolly stood and looked at the man who lounged upon her cot. She gasped when the full force of his gaze came to rest on her. His mouth was drawn into a tight line, and she saw the scar on his cheek color with anger. His dark, heavy brows netted together and the black eyes beneath them burned into her, shaming her.

Dolly affected a pleasant smile. "Oi wuz jus' teasin' ye. Oi never wanted yer money. Oi jus' wanted ta see wha' ye'd do. . . ."

Scarblade turned his head and rose from the bed, gathered up the frock coat that he had so carelessly tossed upon the solitary chair, and walked out.

Tori, clad only in her petticoat, paced her room on the morning of her wedding day. She kept an open watch on the delicate ormolu clock and drew no comfort from the slowly moving hands. Granger knocked on her door and whispered, "Is she here yet?"

Tori leaned against the oak doorframe. "No, Granger, do you think she's changed her mind? What if something happened to her? Perhaps you should start out to look for her."

"Be sensible, Tori. Where on earth could I tell your father I was going, dressed in all this finery? Don't dither so, she'll be here. I promise you."

"But Granger, I have but an hour left!" Tori said, panic making her voice shrill.

"Don't forget she has to walk from her lodgings," Granger reminded her. Then he whispered, "Wait a minute, here comes your maid and there's someone behind her."

"Pray that it is her," Tori cried.

"There is a servant here for you, Miss Victoria. She's sent from Lord Fowler-Greene. Seems that he's sent you a present and she is instructed to place it in your hands herself. I'll wait and show her out," Annie added curiously.

"That won't be necessary. You'd better see if Mother can use some help. Granger will see her out. Hurry now!" Tori pleaded. Annie left the room reluctantly, glancing over her shoulder at the wrapped parcel the servant clutched in her hands.

Quickly, Tori closed the door and threw the heavy bolt. "What the devil took you so long to get here?" she demanded of Dolly. "I'm so glad you could come!" she added sarcastically.

"Me pleasure, miss," Dolly cooed, ignoring the caustic tone of Tori's voice. Dolly looked around the handsome room and marveled at the costly hangings.

"Hurry, Dolly! Hurry! There's not much time. Take off all your clothes. I hope you had a bath this morning!"

Dolly bristled at this questioning of her personal hygiene.

"Soon you'll be rich," Tori said as she feverishly ripped off her petticoats and handed them to Dolly. "Everything has to be right from the skin out."

"Oi can see, a real laidy," Dolly smiled as she fingered the rich, embroidered lace on the petticoats.

"Never mind the lace. You'll have time enough to look at it. Just put them on, hurry! My mother will be here soon and there are several things I must tell you. Quickly now!"

Fifteen minutes later Dolly was resplendent in Tori's

wedding gown. "Now the veil, Dolly." Tori placed the heavy seeded-pearl crown on Dolly's head and threw the net over her face. Then she finished dressing in Dolly's worn gown and fastened a soiled apron around her waist. "Ugh! How can you go about in these rags?"

"Well, miss, when ye've got no' a crown ta yer name ta buy soap or a crumb o' food ta fill yer belly, th' state o' yer clothes is th' las' thin' ta worry about!" Dolly shot at Tori.

Tori said, "You must keep your mouth shut from now till tomorrow morning. Whatever you do, don't lift the veil in my parents' presence. If you can manage to smile and act sweet and agreeable to Lord Fowler-Greene till he gets you to the bedchamber, then you can let your other er . . . accomplishments take over. If you just play coy with the lord you should do fine. I think it only fair to warn you, though, he loves to pinch."

"Oh 'e does, does 'e? Well Oi'll soon cure 'im o' tha'!" Dolly giggled.

Tori joined in the laughter. "Listen to me now, Dolly, I shall take your place at your lodgings till Granger comes for me. When the lord finds out he's been duped, you're on your own. You will have to out-think and outsmart him. Do you think you can carry it off?"

Dolly nodded. "It's no' me brain Oi'll be usin', miss. But yes, Oi think Oi can carry it off. Coo, imagine, Oi'll be a real laidy. Me old mum should only see me in this getup. Oi'm no' a virgin, ye know," she said, ey-ing the white gown and frowning.

Tori smiled. "Somehow I didn't think you were."

"Do ye think th' old boy'll notice?" Dolly asked anx-iously.

"It's up to you to see that he doesn't," Tori snapped.

"Luv, however in th' world do ye think Oi can man-age tha'?"

"I'm the wrong one to ask for advice."

"Oi can see tha'," Dolly scoffed.

"I must go now, Dolly." Impulsively Tori hugged the white-clad Dolly and whispered, "The best of luck to you, Dolly. And thank you from the bottom of my

heart." With a jaunty salute Tori left the room, headed
for the back stairway, and fled down to the kitchen
regions. Once out in the open road, she paused a moment and looked back at her home. She felt a small tug
at her heart and blinked back the tears. "I had to do
it," she said to herself as she trudged into town to
Dolly's lodgings. She would have to get herself settled
and wait for Granger.

Lady Lydia opened the door to tell Tori that the
judge was waiting. "I am so happy that you're ready.
You look lovely, my dear," she said happily. "Your father will be so pleased. I think he thought this day
would never come. And your intended!" She rolled her
saucer-shaped, bright blue eyes. "He's beside himself! I
don't think he yet believes his good fortune in winning
you."

Dolly bobbed her head, saying nothing.

Both women left the room and started down the
steep stairwell.

Lord Rawlings looked lovingly at Dolly. So it was
true. She was actually going to go through with the
wedding. He could hardly contain himself at his good
fortune. He patted his waistcoat and felt the key to the
strong box. Still, something niggled at him. The wedding
wasn't over with yet. Once the "I do's" were said then
he could breathe easy.

"Victoria, you have been a good and faithful daughter. I love you dearly, as does your mother. I want to
say that I know you will be very happy." When he received no response to this declaration his stomach
turned over. I knew it, he muttered to himself; she
won't go through with it. At the time she is supposed
to say "I do", she'll say "I won't!" He clasped Dolly's
hands in his own and whispered fiercely, "All I can say
to you, Victoria, is that you'd better say 'I do.' Do you
understand? If you bollix this up, I'll have you
whipped, which isn't such a terrible thing. I should
have had it done before. You are much too strong-
willed. This wedding is to go off as planned. Do you
understand, Victoria?"

A slow smile spread over Dolly's lips. The whole family was crackers. She had every intention of getting married. In fact, wild horses couldn't drag her from here. Catching a glimpse of her intended, she blanched slightly. So wha', she chided herself. 'E migh' be a dear old duck. 'E's probably starvin' fer affection. If there's one thin' Dolly's an expert at, tha's it. Oi'll jus' luv 'im ta death, she giggled to herself.

Chapter Twelve

Dolly bade the wedding guests, drunk on wine and food, a silent farewell. Once in the darkened coach she lifted her veil and immediately was engulfed in a clenching embrace which she returned just as ardently as it was given. There ensued much giggling and laughter for the balance of the trip. There was a small yelp of pain from Lord Fowler-Greene as he had his ear bitten soundly, but playfully.

"You little vixen," he laughed. For reply Dolly nibbled daintly on his other ear. Lord Fowler-Greene groaned in delight. He used his pearl-handled walking stick to pound on the front of the coach. "Faster, driver," he roared. When the horses picked up speed, Lord Fowler-Greene was thrown off balance and landed on the floor with Dolly on top of him. Dolly kissed him passionately, all the while tweaking his ear. Kissing his lips, his chin, and his neck, she whispered softly in his ear. While the words were not distinguishable, Lord Fowler-Greene whispered, "More."

Dolly turned her head from left to right and back again in an effort to take in her new surroundings as she was led through the darkened foyer and up the ornate staircase to his bedchamber. When she hesitated to admire a view from the gallery, Lord Fowler-Greene prodded her forward with an intimate pinch on the back of the thigh.

She smiled and playfully twitched the fold of skin beneath his chin. Lord Fowler-Greene blushed and pinched her again in an effort to disguise his embarrassment. He'd not had excessive experience with women, not even when his wife was alive. And to have his advances met with a friendly welcome was indeed a novel treat.

"Hurry, hurry," he breathed. "This way."

Dolly laughed and pleased him with a quickening of her step.

In his haste to reach the door, the lord tripped on the edge of her gown. Dolly quickly reached out a supporting arm and prevented him from falling. She gathered him closely to her, murmuring soft, winsome phrases. Lord Fowler-Greene found himself with his face tightly pressed against Dolly's soft, yielding breasts. The aroma of Tori's cologne wafted to his nostrils and set his mind reeling. Oh, give me strength, he prayed fervently, I hope I have the strength.

He regained his footing and opened the door. Glancing into the room, he saw to his pleasure that all was in readiness as he had requested.

Dolly stepped across the threshold and drew in her breath in a silent "oh" of wonder. Her eyes traveled from the giant bed, set on a dais and hung with heavy red velvet draperies, to the accent tables laden with fresh-cut roses. The rug beneath her feet was thick and soft and the candle glow illuminated the gold leaf pattern on the red damask wall covering. Everywhere she looked there was another bowl of fresh-cut roses. Where such flowers could be found in the late fall of the year staggered her imagination.

Lord Fowler-Greene stepped lightly over to Dolly and helped her to remove her purple velvet, ermine-lined cloak.

Dolly bent her head to facilitate its removal and Lord Fowler-Greene succumbed to the urge to plant a kiss on the nape of her neck. Dolly leaned back and pressed against him and he held her for a moment. Turning slowly, she allowed him to embrace her and feel the warmth of her body. Dolly smiled secretly when he whispered in her ear, "I promise to go slowly, my dear, but you're so lovely ... forgive me." He pressed his mouth to hers and she took the initiative. Slowly her lips parted, allowing him to search out the warm, moist recesses of her mouth.

Dolly remembered who she was supposed to be, and fearing to give over the game, drew back from him, a shocked expression on her face.

"Now, now, darling, I see I have much to teach you. 'Tis perfectly normal, a natural thing. Don't be frightened. 'Tis only because I love you so much." He panted as he pushed her toward the bed.

They fell together, the lord on top of her, squeezing the breath from her body with his immense weight. Oh, Dolly thought to herself, this'll never do.

"Milord," she gasped. "I'm only a small girl, forgive me." She pushed him from her onto the mattress. Extricating herself, she slid from the bed and whispered, "One little moment, milord," carefully trying to hide her cockney accent.

Slowly and deliberately, she unfastened her gown and let it fall to the floor. Gracefully, she stepped out from its wide skirt and removed her slippers, all the while looking into the mesmerized eyes of Lord Fowler-Greene.

Free of the encumbrance of her gown, Dolly hopped onto the bed beside him, cooing soft words of endearment. Sportingly, she began to undress him. First the buttons on his waistcoat, then his cravat. Lord Fowler-Greene allowed her to undress him, helping her with subtle movements, much like a child being aided by its nursemaid.

When at last all restricting garments were removed, Dolly sweetly told him he would have no need for his jewelry as she was afraid he would inadvertently scratch her. She removed his heavy rings, testing their size on her slim fingers and weighing their bulk before plunking them down on the bedside table. Lord Fowler-Greene reached out his arms and pulled her toward him, and she deftly escaped his embrace.

She stood up quickly, looking down at the wide neck of Lord Fowler-Greene's blouse that revealed his white, hairless belly. The sight of it reminded her of the mackerels she used to split when she worked at the fish market, and she almost hesitated, thinking, A girl does 'ave 'er standards. Then her eyes traveled to the bedside table on which rested his huge, jeweled rings and a new determination was wrought in her.

Before she could change her mind, she began to undo the laces of her camisole. Lord Fowler-Greene watched her, lust dancing in his eyes. A primeval bellow rose in his throat as he divested himself of his few remaining garments.

Dolly watched him through slitted eyes as she busied herself with ribbons and laces in an effort to free herself of her many petticoats.

Lord Fowler-Greene settled back against the velvet throw and dazedly watched the tableau she presented. The whiteness of her body stood out in relief against the deep reds of the room. The flickering candles threw lacy, dappled patterns on her lissome form. As she raised her hands to free her long flaxen hair of its pins, her uplifted arms displayed the clean, flowing lines of her breasts.

Lord Fowler-Greene's breath caught in his throat as she turned to him and stretched her arms out, reaching for him.

Lord Fowler-Greene lay next to Dolly, a quizzical expression in his eyes. Sensing his gaze upon her, Dolly lifted her lids and smiled at him. "Who are you?" he asked bluntly. "Surely you're not Victoria."

"Wha' makes ye think not, milord?"

"Victoria Rawlings has the eyes of a cat. Yours, child, are a willow gray. I ask you again, who are you?"

"When did ye first perceive th' difference, milord?" Dolly asked haltingly, fear in her eyes.

"Oh, no, be not afraid, child. I wouldn't hurt you. I love you," he said simply.

"Ye do?"

"Yes," he breathed. "I know goodness when I see it. But tell me, how did you come to be in this marriage bed? Where is Miss Rawlings?"

Hesitatingly, Dolly told him of the deception.

"That old fox Lord Rawlings is behind all this. He sought to embarrass me and still keep the purse, a double purse! I can see him now, laughing at me. And what recourse would I have? If I create a stir he puts me in the position of being the laughingstock of London. This way, he thinks to keep his daughter and my money besides." Anger welled up in him as he thought of the trick played. His impulse was to thrash Dolly and send her packing. His gaze lingered on her as she lay on his bed, her face pinched in concentration to read his intentions, her eyes tear-filled. The coverlet had slipped from her and disclosed a shapely thigh. Something instinctive tore through his chest and engulfed him. He opened his arms for her and she came to him, pressing herself against him. He held her gently, smoothing the silky skin of her back. Love flooded through him, a sensation he had never known. He could do worse, much worse. As he held her he murmured against her hair, "Methinks, dear child, I made the better of the bargain."

Dolly pressed closer, reaching out behind the lord to the bedside table. Picking up one of the heavy jewels she had so carelessly placed there, she buried her face in her husband's shoulder, smiling wickedly.

Tori trudged wearily into town and headed directly for the Rooster's Crown, stopping from time to time to remove pebbles from her shoes. She looked gloomily at her road-torn slippers and wondered how long they would last.

Quietly, she opened the door of the rooming house and started down the dark passageway. Dolly had said the fifth door. Cautiously, she opened it and peered inside. She gasped. This was where she was to stay? A small, narrow and lumpy cot was to be her bed. There was a crooked chest that served as a wardrobe, with a cracked mirror hanging above it. As if drawn by magic, Tori looked around for other comforts. There were none. Not even a rag rug. The only consolation was that there seemed to be no bugs, and sparsely furnished as the tiny room was, it was clean.

Tori opened the chest. There wasn't much, another tattered gown such as she had on, a frayed petticoat, and a pair of woolen stockings. There was a chill in the room and Tori wrapped her arms around herself as she closed the lid. Looking at the cot and the two skimpy blankets, she muttered aloud, "I'll freeze!" Tori looked around again and bent over to peer under the bed. The ermine-lined cloak! Where was it? That's what the little slut was carrying in the package; she hadn't even left the cloak! Tori grimaced. Dolly had a brain, she did. She didn't leave anything to chance. A girl after her own heart. Tori suddenly giggled, flinging herself down onto the cot to rest her aching feet from the long, unaccustomed walk.

Huddled there, Tori looked up as the door opened.

"Oi though' Oi would foind ye 'ere lazin' 'roun'. Get up, me girl an' 'and over th' ren'. Oi waited too long as 'tis. No 'one more day'! Cough it up, me girl!"

"Wha' . . . what?"

"Th' ren'!" the blowsy woman yelled. "Where izzit?"

Panic gripped Tori, "I . . . I don't have it," she whimpered.

"Oi though' as much. Well, ye won' get it lazing 'roun' 'ere. Get yer backside over ta th' inn an' clean an' scrub. An' tell Jake ta pay ye yer wages t'night an' ye best brin' th' coppers straigh' ta me. Otherwise," she added ominously, "ye'll be spendin' yer winter in Newgate!"

"Newgate? You can't mean that!" Tori said vociferously.

"Oh, an' don' Oi? Do ye think ye can stay 'ere an' no' pay me rent? Oi wan' wha's me due, do ye 'ear? An' th' way Oi sees, a month's lodgin's ye owe me!" The slattern moved closer, threateningly. Tori could see the cruel lines in her face and smell the rank odor of spilled ale and decayed teeth.

"But I can't go to work at the inn. I'm waiting . . . I'm waiting. Besides, I . . . I don't feel well. But I'll get it for you as soon as I'm better."

"Wha's all this 'orse dung, when ye're better? Didn' Oi see a gen'leman cum in 'ere las' eve? An do ye 'spec' me ta believe 'e didn' leave ye naught? Hah!" she shouted raucously. "Do ye now?"

Tori bristled at the onslaught against her character and then she remembered it was Dolly the landlady was speaking of. She also remembered Dolly's cockney accent. "Well 'e didn' leave me anythin'! An' when Oi'm better Oi'll 'ave th' money fer ye!"

The fat slattern moved closer for a better look at Tori. Picking up the candle from the rickety table, she lit it with a flint. Holding the candle higher, she peered through nearsighted eyes, squinting at the girl. Fear gripped Tori's innards and she involuntarily drew back on the cot. Undoubtedly, the landlady knew Dolly quite well, and Tori wasn't at all sure that the difference between the two girls' appearance would go unnoticed if one were looking for it. Tori averted her eyes, allowing the landlady to think the candleglow was irritating to them.

"Aye! Ye do look a little peaked at tha', Dolly. Oi can' place me finger on it but ye do look feverish. Poor lass . . ." Just as Tori was sure she was gaining the slattern's sympathy, a look of horror came into the watery, brown eyes of the landlady. "Look 'ere, ye've no' gone an' gotten yersel' ridden wi' plague, 'ave ye?"

At the mere mention of the word, the woman withdrew a few steps. If there was anything she feared more than the pox, it was the plague. Almost indiscernibly, she wiped her hand on her filthy apron, and then remembering the candle in her hand, dropped it back onto the table as though it had suddenly become too hot for her to touch. She spit on her hands and rubbed them again.

"Now look 'ere! Oi'll no' 'ave yer sickness in me 'ouse, Oi'll no'! Oi runs a decent 'ouse 'ere an' Oi'll no' 'ave th' loikes o' ye callin' in th' 'ealth authorities an' closin' me down. Now out wi' it! Do ye 'ave th' plague? Wha's wrong wi' ye?"

Tori immediately saw she had the edge so far as the landlady was concerned. "No, Oi don' 'ave th' plague. Oi'm simply no' mesel' t'day. Mayhaps Oi'll be feelin' mesel' by mornin'." And Granger had better get himself here by that time, she thought sourly. I'll not have his tales of drinking to excess at my wedding.

" 'Ere, wha's th' meaning' o' usin' tha' uppity talk wi' me? 'Mayhaps Oi'll be mesel' in th' mornin','" the landlady mimicked. Then she shouted, " 'Ave some respec' ta who yer talkin' ta, miss, or Oi'll 'ave ye thrown out on yer ear this minute!"

Tori bristled, about to rebuke the slattern. Then suddenly, she took another tack. "Why, missus, ye talk so much o' th' plague mayhaps yer th' one 'avin' th' vision, ye know, a 'eavenly warning'. Oi should be careful or 'twill be yersel'." Tori allowed a veil of horror to slowly descend over her face and then she feigned an enlightened expression. "Why, missus, Oi 'ear tha' a weakness o' th' eyes is one o' th' first warnin's an' then an achin' o' th' 'ead an' then a shortness o' temper. An' lastly, th' wretched black spots tha' mark its victims. 'Ow 'ave ye been feelin' lately? Oi mus' say ye don' seem ta be yer usual composed sel'."

A dawning of understanding fell over the puffed and gray face of the landlady. Tori thought the small, oblique, brown eyes would pop from her head. A heavy, hamlike paw was clutched to her thick neck as Tori continued her charade. "Also, they tell o' a dryness o' th' mouth among other thin's."

"An' 'ow do ye know so much abou' th' plague?" the proprietress said in a raspy voice. She was clearly stunned by the similarity of symptoms.

"Why, missus, at one toime Oi worked in th' 'ouse o' a family doctor," Tori lied, "an' along wi' learnin' th' symptoms o' th' plauge Oi also learned somethin' o' th' cures."

"Hah! There be no cure fer th' plauge!"

"Oh, but there is, if catched ear'y."

"Please, be a good child an' tell me wha' ye know o' th' cure. Fer Oi'll tell ye a secret, Oi've got a friend whose 'ealth concerns me. She's no' been 'ersel' o' late an' Oi'm dearly worried fer 'er."

Tori stifled a grin at the landlady's try at deception. "Well, a good strong, 'ot posset made from barley an' goose fat always wuz th' doctor's favorite remedy, an' lots o' rest. Why, 'e would make 'is patients lie abed fer weeks! 'E believed contact wi' other people at a toime when th' ebb o' life wuz so low would worsen th' disease an' mayhaps catch other sickness."

"Oh, yes. Oi can see where 'e could well believe tha'," the landlady said in a weak voice as she retreated another three steps away from Tori. "Well, it'll never be said th' Mrs. Coombs wuz a fool an' never took good advice when it wuz 'anded ta 'er. Oi'll jus' go tell me friend ta lie down. 'Ow long did th' doctor say ta rest? 'Ow much goose grease should be in th' posset?"

Tori breathed a sigh of relief as the slattern backed out of the room and hurried down the hall to her own quarters. Worrying about her own health would keep Mrs. Coombs busy enough to let Tori stay here until Granger would come and get her.

Then the reality of the situation hit her. Oh, why hadn't Dolly told her the rent was due? And food! Where was she to get food?

Tori slept that night fitfully, fighting the cold and hunger that tormented her. There she sat all the next day, dreading the return of Mrs. Coombs and anxiously awaiting the arrival of Granger. Her night was spent the same as the one before, and added to her tortures was the smell of food cooking, wafting from somewhere down the alley and seeping through the crack in the window. Tori expostulated with every oath she knew and cursed Granger with a vengeance. Worse than the hunger and the cold was the anxiety over what could have happened to keep him from coming for her. Lastly, she berated herself for not having had the forethought to bring a little money.

All sorts of situations crept into her unwilling mind in the long hours she spent in the draughty room. Was Dolly discovered? Did Lord Fowler-Greene kill her? Was Granger a victim of some unforeseen accident? No imagining was too wild, no prediction too dire. In her cold and weakened state every horror played itself to the fullest, until Tori was a shaking heap among the few rags which covered her cot of despair.

Finally, Tori could stand the hunger no longer. She had to come to grips with her condition. "Oi think, me girl," she scolded herself, imitating Mrs. Coombs, "ye'll 'ave ta work fer yer keep!" Tori's stomach commenced to rumble at the thought of food. Then remembering the greasy slop that was served at the inn, she shivered.

What had started out as a happy lark, had turned into something dark and gloomy, not to mention possibly disastrous. "Why, I could starve or worse yet, freeze to death. What am I going to do?" she wailed to the small, mean-looking room.

Full of self-pity, Tori let her mind wander to the wedding reception with its copious food and drink. Her thoughts kept going to the ermine-lined cloak. Blast the girl! Dolly was probably right this minute stuffing her mouth full of meat and sweets and was comfortable and warm. Then she thought of Lord Fowler-Greene and shuddered again. "Never!" she shouted. Well, she would have to move her backside as the landlady said, and get over to the Owl's Eye Inn. Even if she had to work all day, she would make enough to satisfy her hunger.

Her face a mirror of dejection, Tori trekked around the building to the servants' entrance of the Owl's Eye Inn. Hesitantly, she opened the door and entered. She was rewarded with a smart cuff to the side of her head. Stunned, Tori blinked back the tears.

"Ye be late, Dolly. Oi' don' plan ta warn ye again. Oi'll be dockin' ye a copper this nigh'. If it 'appens again, Oi'll be gettin' rid o' ye. There be others tha' wan' me generosity."

"Generosity?" Tori squealed; then she remembered her place. Lowering her furious eyes, she nodded meekly.

"Well, don' stand there. Get ta work! Sweep an' mop these floors, then take out th' slop an' get ta th' kitchen. Today'll be busy. There be a weddin' over ta' th' Jocelyns'. Some o' th' guests will be stoppin' fer some ale. Now git a move on afore Oi cuff ye again."

Tori scuttled away to the far corner of the room where she spied a broom. She held it clumsily, never having used one before. Still, she had seen the servants wield one and it looked easy enough. Gingerly she moved it back and forth across the floor. The dirt slithered here and yon.

"Th' slop pails, lass," the cook bellowed. "Get a move on afore 'is 'ighness takes 'is boot ta ye. Stop th' dreamin'. 'Tiz a poor pastime these days. 'Tiz only 'ard work tha'll give ye th' coppers ta fill yer belly."

"Oi'm 'ungry," Tori said pitifully.

The cook, eyes aghast, couldn't believe her ears.

" 'Ungry! Why ye know ye don' get no food till th' inn closes an' tha's almos' twelve 'ours from now. Wha' in God's name 'as gotten inta ye, Dolly? An' t'day it's only cabbage an' bread, 'is 'ighness said ta take ye down a peg fer th' sloppy work ye been doin' this mornin'."

"Oi detest cabbage," Tori said belligerently. "Dry bread!"

"Oi, but ye'll eat it when ye're 'ungry!" Tori yelped as she saw the cook upraise her hand to swat the sassy girl. Mollified by Tori's reaction, the cook headed back to the kitchen with Tori in her wake.

"Get after the slop pails, lass. Why ye be followin' me?" Tori looked blank. "Oi swear," the cook continued, "yer wits be addled this day. Get over ta' th' lodgin's an' get those pails!"

Tori walked on dragging feet over to the inn's lodgings and down the hall. As she grasped the handle of the chamber pot, her stomach somersaulted; she dumped the contents into the pail. God, how could she ever do this? Setting the pail down, she leaned against the wall and gagged and tried to stem the flow of tears. She had to do it! If Dolly could do it then so could she! Gritting her teeth, she picked up the pail and opened the door. She repeated her task with each of the other six rooms and walked around the side of the building looking for the pit which emptied into the middens. Staggering near to the edge, she near vomited from the stench.

Unable to go one step farther she leaned against the outside wall and gasped for breath. Her legs felt like jelly, her arms seemed as if they had been pulled from their sockets, her stomach muscles were drawn into a tight knot, and her neck felt like someone had tied a garrote around it. Again tears threatened to overflow.

She had to sleep. She needed rest. And she was so hungry. Tori knew if she stopped now she would never be able to move.

With a mighty heave she flung herself from the dank-smelling wall and stood upright on her trembling, quaking legs.

Back in the inn she spotted her tormentor in the process of emptying a tankard of ale. "There be guests

in th' dinin' 'all. Take th' orders an' serve th' food. An'
be quick abou' it. We don' need any yellin', bawlin'
customers."

Brushing the hair from her face, Tori entered the
dining hall. She glanced around at the customers—all
men who eyed her lecherously.

"Cum 'ere, Dolly, me girl, an' give me a kiss," one
bearded giant roared.

Tori paled at the request and walked hesitantly over
to the man. "Sir," she asked quietly, "wha'll ye 'ave fer
dinner?"

"Sir, izzit?" the man roared. "Ye be a tease, Dolly,
me luv, cum 'ere an' give me a kiss."

Tori's step faltered as the man reached a long arm
and brought her onto his lap. He gave her a smacking
kiss on the mouth and set her upright. Tori gasped.

"Now ye can get me my meat an' potatoes," he
laughed.

So this was the kind of game they played at the inn.
Dolly was a plaything of sorts. She worked like a mule
and then had to suffer these indignities! Through
clenched teeth, Tori told the cook the customer's order.
She carried it in shaking hands and placed it before the
bearded man. She smiled tremulously.

"Ye'll 'ave ta move faster, Dolly, me luv," a man
shouted. "Oi canno' fill me belly on pretty smiles."
Tori hastened to obey.

As Tori stood waiting behind the kitchen doors she
watched the cook dish out generous portions of lamb
and cabbage. The rough language and the hoots of the
men rattled her, and for the hundredth time that day
she pitied Dolly for the long, hard years she had
worked in the inn.

The cook pushed a tray of food at her and glanced
curiously into her face. " 'Ere, Dolly, lass, wha's eatin'
ye? Ye know if ye let them bullies get ye down they'll
stomp on ye! 'Ere, 'ere, where's tha' ole spunk o' yers?
Get out there, Dolly, and give them wha' fer."

So, Dolly was spunky, was she? And none too gentle
with the clientele's feelings, too? Well, perhaps that
was the way Dolly found to help her get through one
long day after another. Taking a deep breath, Tori

stepped out into the dining hall and delivered the tray. As she was bending over the table, she felt a hand reach up under her skirts and pinch the back of her thigh. Almost spilling a tankard of ale, she swung around and, not caring who was the recipient, slapped the reddened face of the man nearest her.

Shocked at what she'd done, Tori prepared herself to do battle. Instead she was complimented and cheered by laughing jeers directed at the man whose face she'd slapped.

"Tha' be more loike our old Dolly," a voice called from the far side of the room. "Brew and vinegar, Oi always says, eh men?"

When her tasks were finally finished, she looked at the cook in hope of food for herself.

The cook took a piece of boiled cabbage the size of an apple and a chunk of dry bread and handed it to Tori. Looking at the unappetizing meal, she shook her head. Her stomach turned and the bile rose to her throat.

Shaking her head, Tori walked into the taproom for her wages. Weary to the bone, she didn't see the booted foot of the bearded giant till it was too late. He caught her as she fell and started to paw her before the others. Tears gathered in Tori's eyes as she fought off the man with all her remaining strength.

"Cum on, Dolly, it'll be fun an' games. Stop th' blubberin'." Even though the tone was kindly, Tori was in no mood for the jeering and jesting at her expense. Seeing the tears, the man let her go. She walked over to the proprietor and waited patiently for her day's wages. He doled them out and held back several of the coppers. Tori looked at the meager coins and wondered if it would be enough to pay the rent. Eyes smarting, she turned to leave when someone grabbed her from behind and swung her into the air. Tori screamed in fright as the man tossed her to a companion. They tossed her back and forth and roared with laughter at her screams. Unnoticed in the mêlée the door opened and a cold, hard voice rang out, booming over the commotion.

"Leave the girl!"

Tori, crying openly, looked up at the tall man with the piercing black eyes. Someone hissed!

"Are you all right, Dolly?" the brusk voice demanded. Tori nodded affirmatively. "Come with me. I'll take you to your room to be sure you get there safely," he said, raking the occupants of the taproom with a threatening, pointed stare.

"Watch out, Dolly. Wha' makes ye think Scarblade's th' one ta make ye safe?" a voice jeered, only to be cut off by a black look.

The innkeeper called nastily, "An' don' return on th' morrow! Oi'll be havin' a new lass 'ere. One tha' can do th' work an' no' weep an' wail all th' day. It wuz only a l'il jest th' men were 'avin'."

Tori cast a frightened look at the innkeeper. "But . . ."

"Ye got yer wages, now take yersel' off!"

Tori was barely cognizant of the events of the past few moments. She was only aware of her gratitude to this tall dark stranger who had saved her from the rough handling she had suffered. Suddenly she realized the identity of her rescuer!

Chapter Thirteen

Once he opened the door of her room he looked at her and waited for her to speak. Tori, in a quandary, did not know if the man and Dolly were friends, or what to say. He solved the problem for her. Looking into the room, he let his eyes rake it from top to bottom. He saw no sign of the ermine-lined cloak. Also, Dolly herself seemed different somehow.

"Dolly, where's the cloak?" he asked coldly, making his voice light.

"What?" Tori managed to answer.

"The ermine-lined cloak that you said a gentleman gave you. Where is it?"

"Oh." Tori's thoughts raced. "Oi . . . Oi returned it ta th' gent since it seemed ta upset ye," she said, quietly. Evidently it was the correct response to his question, for the man looked pleased.

"So, you had a change of heart, is that it?" Tori nodded and watched him carefully. "You stole it, didn't you?" the man demanded. "No gentleman gave it to you. You just wanted to trick me into giving you something of equal value. Am I right?"

Not knowing what the correct answer should be, Tori merely nodded. "I thought as much!" Scarblade smiled, apparently pleased to have his convictions made valid. "Come here now and take those blasted pins from your hair," he said in a deep-timbred voice. "I'm in a mood for loving this night."

Tori blinked. Did he mean . . . could he mean. . . ? Her mind raced, frantically searching for some diversion to occupy him while she tried to think of a way to make her escape.

"And none of your wiles, my lass. I've come to

91

claim the gold guinea or what it was meant to pay for."
His eyes swept over her mockingly, dangerously. Tori
knew this was not a man to cross.

"What's it to be, Dolly? The money or the goods?
You'll not get off as easily as you did last night."

What did he mean? Had Dolly rejected his advances? No, somehow Tori could not believe that was
so. Dolly had an eye and an inborn appreciation for
the male sex. It wouldn't be like Dolly to have refused
this handsome rake anything!

A movement of his hand revealed he carried a bottle
of wine. "Surely ye'll invite me ta 'ave a sip wi' ye,"
Tori said coaxingly.

"Of course, I brought it especially for you, knowing
your taste for the grape. Get your cup, Dolly. We'll
have a little celebration."

"Celebration?"

"Aye! To mark the settling of the differences of last
evening. Go on now," he said as he worked with the
cork in the bottle.

She moved across the room. "Ye know Oi've not
much cause fer celebratin' now, wi' losin' me only
means o' livelihood this evenin'," she said, falling back
into Dolly's native cockney.

He gave a grunt as he pulled the cork from the
bottle, then gave a raucous shout of laughter and
seemed beside himself with the humor he found in her
words.

"Your only means of livelihood! Ah, Dolly love,
now you've no reason to play the grand duchess with
me. This is the Blade, remember? You'll make do
somehow, I'll count on that. A lovely young girl like
yourself and so . . . agreeable! Dolly love, an agreeable
female always finds her way in the world. Besides,
where's that hoard of coins you're so fond of reminding me of? Last I knew, you had a king's ransom in
gold sovereigns. Now you wouldn't be trying to connive
me out of my hard-earned cash, would you?"

So, Tori thought enraged, it seems Dolly carried
more than an ermine cape in the bundle she kept
clutched so close to her heart. The bawd! Leaving me

without a ha'penny and the rent due ... and Granger!
When I get my hands on his neck ...

But more immediate problems flooded her mind.
What was she to do with Scarblade? He truly believed
she was Dolly and what he expected of her brought a
hot flush of color to her cheeks. In a rush, the emotions she experienced while sitting atop the giant chestnut welled through her with all their vividness.

His dark, heavy-browed eyes with their hidden
depths of excitement and a thinly veiled passion looked
into hers. Again she felt herself struggling to keep her
breath from knotting in her throat as she had that September day when she had met the infamous Scarblade
for the first time. But to meet him again ... and in this
manner!

"Drink up, Dolly, is my wine not good enough for
your ladyship?" he mocked. He approached her and
Tori felt her knees weaken. If he touched her she knew
full well what effect it would have on her awakened
passions. She hedged, retreated a step, put the cracked
cup up to her lips, and took a hearty swallow, choking
on the raw brew. Scarblade put the bottle to his mouth
and partook deeply of its contents.

When he finished he put the bottle down and gazed
at her with heavy-lidded eyes. His white teeth flashed
during a quick smile and he called softly to her, "Dolly
love, will you take the pins from your hair now?" Tori
noticed the scar on his cheek become more pro-
nounced, and this, more than his burning looks, terrified her. "S for seduction" echoed through her
thoughts.

He spoke so intimately. Couldn't he see she wasn't
Dolly? Surely once a man slept with a woman he
wouldn't be so easily fooled. Dolly and Tori were very
close in looks and build, but there were definite differences. The eyes for example—how could he fail to notice Tori's tear-bright, cat-yellow eyes, so different from
Dolly's, which were a soft, willow gray? It occurred to
Tori that as far as Scarblade was concerned, there
was no discernible difference between women. He
could enjoy them, use them, and possibly profit by
them—and never take real notice of their dissimilarities.

Tori struggled to gain control of her shaking knees. Then in a brazen retort to his demand that she let down her hair, she removed a pin, gathered a curl, and returned the pin to hold it more securely.

Scarblade's eyes narrowed. In one step he was against her, holding her fast to his lean, hard body. His lips were hot and wine-scented as they pressed against hers. She could feel her lips part beneath his as she struggled to free herself, as if fighting for her life. Scarblade held her closer, enveloping her within the strong fold of his arms.

Weakened by conflicting emotions, Tori ceased her struggles. Scarblade's answer was a renewed ardor as he pressed long, passionate kisses to her lips. She felt his hands in her hair, on her breasts, on the small of her back, and reaching lower.

Tori felt her sensibilities leave her and in their place, from deep within, came an answering response. As though of their own volition, her arms sought the rippling muscles of his back, the narrowness of his waist. Her thighs pressed against his, feeling their strength through her skirts. He was no longer kissing her and she was aware that his breath came in sharp rasps that matched her own. Low groans of pleasure escaped his lips as he began to trail them along her neck and then down to the cleft between her breasts. Tori clung to him, welcoming him, pressing herself closer, and she was aware of his tumescence. Violently she struggled to free herself from him. What was wrong with her to acquiesce to his salacious, lustful advances? Had playing the role of Dolly become so ingrained in this short time that she was actually falling prey to that girl's loose morals?

Tori lashed out blindly, feeling the broken nails of her hand gouge and rake at his chest and neck. Fury inflamed her cheeks, and shame and humiliation at what she had almost allowed to happen brought hot, stinging tears of frustration to her eyes.

"You devil!" she shouted. "Keep your hands off me." She lashed out again with a clawlike hand aimed at the ebony eyes that burned through her, too furious to remember to feign Dolly's accent.

Scarblade sidestepped her flailing arm, caught it cruelly by the wrist, and pulled her against him, holding her there in an iron grip.

All the weariness of the past few days overcame her. Dry, wracking sobs of approaching hysteria caught in her throat. She was the vanquished and he the victor. Let him do with her what he would, then just leave her to sleep, perhaps to die.

Closely pressed one against the other, they held each other; Tori's lips were burning and bruised, and from time to time an involuntary trembling took hold of her.

Through the light material of her bodice he could feel the provocation of her breasts, and was aware that she could feel him swell with desire.

Feeling his lips part from hers, Tori opened her eyes and the flaming S on his cheek seemed to hypnotize her with its denotation of sexual arousal. He could read the desire in her eyes and his caresses on her breasts became more active. Again Tori surrendered herself, near to a faint, as though all energy within her was anticipating a most unsuspected pleasure.

The sound of shrieking laughter filled her brain and she felt the 'Blade move away from her. Slowly, her sensibilities returned, as though she were pulling herself from a dream. When Tori turned she was startled to see Mrs. Coombs filling the open doorway with her bulk.

The hag was watching Scarblade and taking note of the murderous expression on his face; her laughter died in her throat. Retrieving her composure to a degree, Mrs. Coombs made her excuse for her abrupt entrance. "It's me rent," she said harshly, defying Scarblade to dispute her right to be there. "Oi've cum fer it an' Oi wants it now!" Hanks of greasy hair hung over her bloated, swollen face, and she tossed her head with a jerking motion. "Well," she demanded, "do ye 'ave it er no'?"

Scarblade put his hand into a pocket, withdrew some coins, and tossed them to her. "Here!" he said in a deep voice that rankled with suppressed fury, "this should more than satisfy you."

Mrs. Coombs scurried to capture the scattered coins,

near losing her balance in her haste. When she had picked up the last coin she turned to Tori with hate-filled eyes that bore into the girl's being. "An' Oi'll thank ye ta take yer leave o' me 'ouse. Oi'll no' 'ave th' loikes o' ye scandalizin' me 'ouse. An' be quick abou' it or Oi'll 'ave th' watch on ye, an' it'll be more than jus' back rent Oi'll be 'avin' ye picked up fer. Oi'll tell 'em 'ow ye tried ta kill me, Oi will!"

Tori's obvious confusion was well marked by Mrs. Coombs. "An' Oi suppose ye'll deny ye tried ta kill me. Barley an' goose grease posset, indeed! Oi near passed me innards inta th' chamber pot, Oi did. Now out, Oi tell ye! This 'ere's a respectable 'ouse. . . ."

Scarblade had heard enough. This old harridan was going too far. The intensity of his passion was replaced with a scornful dislike bordering close on hatred. "You have your money, Mrs. Coombs, more than enough. Certainly more than this poor room is worth."

Mrs. Coombs drew herself to full height, and although Tori could see the faint twitching of her many-tiered chin, the landlady spoke with authority. "Out she goes, ye hear? Now!" came the sneering final edict.

Tori opened the small chest which served as a wardrobe, withdrew the meager items, and rolled them into a small bundle. Her step faltered as she walked past Scarblade and out the door. Where could she go? How would Granger find her?

There was a strange look on Scarblade's face as he watched her trudge down the filth-strewn alley. She was really going! This wasn't like Dolly! In fact, she had been acting strange these past two days. Normally she would have fought back and the landlady would be cowed by the tumult of Dolly's fury, terrified of her threats to have the old harridan's neck stretched by some of her rapscallion friends. He had seen her do it in the past. And then the business of the cloak! If she had been pressed for coins she could have sold the cloak and then had enough money for the rent. It didn't make sense! He watched the girl as she trudged down the road. She almost looked ill; where would she go?

The moon came from behind the clouds and lit up

the narrow street. She would no doubt sleep in some alley and be at the mercy of any slum ruffian.

Scarblade turned to the slovenly Mrs. Coombs and sent her flying down the hall to escape his murderous glare. Moments later, he mounted his huge chestnut and started down the road after Dolly. He wanted that girl as never before. He tried to fight the feelings that raced to the surface. She seemed different tonight. She had fought him like a tiger and struggled against him. On other nights, she had come to him willingly and lain in his arms. She had been soft and warm, yielding to him in her passion. This was a new twist. Suddenly, his arms ached to hold her again, to feel her flesh pressing against him as a few moments ago, exciting him as never before. He had been pleasantly surprised by the strength she displayed. He had enjoyed her resistance almost as much as her response.

Quickening the pace of his horse, he rode abreast of Dolly and pulled up on the reins. "Come here," he said, "I'll help you." Tori kept on walking, neither looking up nor to the side of her. Tired, she knew that if she stopped even for a second she would not be able to continue. When the highwayman was done with her, had his way, he would leave her to rot. She must walk!

Scarblade scooped her up with a mighty arm and settled her across his lap. Tori, taken off guard, went limp and almost slid out of his arms. She was reminded again of another time when she sat next to him and knew the wild beating of his heart. She felt oddly at peace and didn't want ever to move from his hard embrace. She raised her head and looked with soft, glowing eyes at the man who held her. Scarblade met the adoring gaze and drew in his breath. He bent to kiss her and pulled her closer, holding her securely, and the chestnut made its way through the quiet city streets. The only sound Tori was aware of was the horses' clapping hooves and her own wildly beating heart.

Minutes later, partly due to the slow plodding of the horse and partly to a feeling of security, Tori's eyes closed and she slept.

From time to time Scarblade looked at the dozing girl with the strange smile on her face.

They rode that way for close to two hours, the tall man with the carbon-black eyes and the sleeping girl.

Scarblade rode into the clearing of a vast wooded area where he was met with a soft query.

"All's well," the Blade spoke softly. "I didn't think I would be so late this night. I had a spot of trouble, as you can see."

"It be Dolly, guvner," said the deep, musical voice.

"Aye. She has been evicted and found herself homeless. And," the Blade said quietly, "she has been near beaten. Make a pallet for the lass and take her gently, Josh."

The burly, blond man lifted the sleeping girl from the Blade's arms. "Lord, I don't remember Dolly being this beautiful," he said, looking down at her.

"It's strange you should say that, Josh. I myself was thinking much the same thing."

The big man kicked his own pallet near a tree and spread the cover with his foot. Gently he lay the sleeping girl down and stood back to observe her. Having an eye for beauty, he grinned. Marcus was going to find he was about to have a few problems when the men spotted her.

Josh walked over to the fire where Marcus sat hunched with a cup of ale in his hands. "I fear there will be trouble if the girl stays," Josh said quietly, but with an ominous tone.

Marcus nodded soberly. "I know. But what was I to do, Josh? I couldn't let her walk the streets and fend for herself. She has not a copper to her name and only those rags she wears. If you had been in my place what would you have done?"

Josh nodded. "Much the same, me lad."

Marcus shrugged. "I think we best wait till morning and see how the lass responds. I'll give her a purse so she can start over somewhere. Is the watch yours this night, Josh?" At the other's nod, Marcus admonished him to keep a sharp eye on the girl and to wake him if she stirred.

Marcus peered up at the star-filled night and felt the cold air wrap itself around his body. He would have to find winter quarters soon. And the girl, what of the girl? She certainly could not last long out in the elements. Why did he keep calling her the girl? Her name was Dolly and many's the time her name came easily to his lips. Why not now? Somehow it did not seem like Dolly. Oh, she looked like her and she wore her clothes, but her manner was different. This girl was soft and warm and she had melting eyes when they weren't breathing fire. He shrugged. It was Dolly, who else could it be?

Finally he slept, a fitful sleep. A beautiful girl kept telling him to guard her ring while a girl in rags pleaded with him to hold her close. Marcus wakened as dawn broke. His eyes went immediately to the slumbering girl and to Josh. Josh nodded. All was well.

Marcus rose wearily to his feet and walked over to the pail. He dunked his whole head in the ice-encrusted water. Droplets glinted off his dark, wavy mane as he toweled himself and strode to the fire. Josh handed him a steaming cup of coffee, and a brooding look masked his features as he sipped it.

"There is something I think best you know," Josh said hesitantly. Marcus raised thick brows. " 'Tis the brothers, John and Charles. They were arguing last eve about things being divided more equally. They mean to make trouble. I heard Charles brag about the price on your head. He said they could turn you in and collect the reward. Then they could keep up with their plundering and keep all the spoils. And there wouldn't be anyone to share the loaf. I see no problem with Richard and Ned. They're good and loyal men, if you care for their ilk."

"Charles said that, did he?" Marcus asked thoughtfully.

"There's going to be trouble, Marc," Josh said soberly as he glanced about to see that no one was within listening distance when he used Scarblade's Christian name. It was an agreement between them that Marcus would only reveal his true identity to his band of men when all were aboard ship and safely bound for America. "I can feel it in my bones. And I think," he added ominously, "it's going to happen when we do the job you outlined."

Marcus nodded his agreement. "No doubt you're right, Josh. I'll just have to stay ahead of them all the way. If I have to, I'll dispose of them. I'll need your help, Josh. I want you to keep an eye on the pair of them."

Josh was seized with a violent fit of coughing. As he groped for a handkerchief, Marcus felt saddened at the condition of his friend. "We have to get you out of this torturous climate, Josh. Once in the warm air of the Carolinas your recovery will be rapid. This cold, damp air does no one's bones any good," he said as he rubbed his forearms briskly.

Josh nodded weakly, the spasm over. "I long to see all my friends there," he sighed. "While I don't approve of all of this plundering, I can see that it's the only way to save the colony. I just pray that God sees fit to spare me to make the trip back, Marc," he said sadly. "Each day I feel myself grow weaker; there's no sense trying to fool myself—nor you, either."

Marcus frowned. He, too, noticed the change in the big man's condition. Josh had been strong and robust, but he now had the appearance of a man who was wasting. While his ruddy complexion still had a rosy hue, it was an unnatural color. The color of fever. Still, the bearded man was held in awe by the other men. He towered by a good head over the others. His arms were like corded saplings and his hands like huge hams. He could fell a tree in record time and then haul it away single-handedly. His golden crop of hair and thatch of beard were the envy of all the men. He had gray eyes, soft as a morning dove, that sized the worth of a man in a moment's time. For this Marcus was thankful. His own judgment had not been too trustworthy of late. While Marcus had the wits and the ingenuity to carry out the daring robberies, he depended on the brawn and the muscle of Josh. That and the common sense he showed when needed.

"Did you carry out the task I assigned to you?" Marcus asked suddenly. He had to shake himself out of this melancholy and get down to business. Time was short and every day counted. He must have his work finished when the ship sailed.

"Aye, Marcus, me lad. I delivered the full cask of sovereigns to the ship. Cap'n Elias has his instructions. He'll not part with one sovereign unless it is to you in person. The money is well guarded. I paid him well, Marc. And the offer of a new home in the Carolinas was like a piece of cake for the man and his family. He just awaits your decision on the sailing day. Have no fear. He is trustworthy. And that speaks for his crew as well."

"We need more, Josh. That pitiful cask is but enough for a year on the black market. Then what? Time is short for us now, and traffic on the roadways is light." A wave of rage welled up in Marcus, constricting the muscles around his heart. "Damn the King!" he swore viciously. "If he would only lift the blockade, cancel the embargo, he would save himself the trouble of putting a price on our heads and allow his soldiers better use of their time than searching the highways and the byways for the likes of us. And if we do get caught ... hundreds of people will have lost everything—their land, their hopes, the promise of their children's future."

"If we can carry off the plan you have in mind we will be set for life. Do you think it will work, Marc?" Josh asked anxiously.

"If everyone does his job right I don't see how it can fail. It will be the most daring robbery in the history of England. And my conscience doesn't bother me a whit!" Marcus laughed.

"Imagine the look on the King's face when he finds out the covey of wagons bearing the taxes have been robbed. And it will all be in gold sovereigns. Only a short time to go and we can be on our way." Josh sighed. "I cannot wait to see America again. I've had enough of this land."

"The guard will be heavy," Marcus warned. "I wish I knew what to expect. And what kind of weapons they'll have."

"Have no fear, Marc. Before it is time to ride, I myself will pay a visit to the Wild Boar Inn. With a little gentle persuasion one can find out what color undergarments the King wears." He roared at his small joke and convulsed in a fit of coughing. This time, the handkerchief came away red, Marcus noticed out of the corner of his eye. As Josh tried to hide the telltale signs, Marcus felt a hard knot in the pit of his stomach. He could not, he would not, lose Josh! They had been friends for a lifetime. If he had to, he would blow life into the man's chest to keep him alive.

"And the girl, Marc. What's to be done?"

Marcus shrugged. "I see by the look on your face that there is doubt of her. Is it that you think she is a spy for the Crown?" he teased the burly, blond giant.

Josh nodded wearily, doubt lining his ruddy face.

"But Josh, you're not serious. You don't know the circumstances—" Quickly he told him the story and watched the big man's face.

"It would sound like a bit of playacting to me, Marc. This business with the cloak, that's what worries me. The Dolly we both know would never have returned something that valuable. I think it is a trap. And another thing," he said, wagging a huge finger, "she has the looks of Dolly and the hair. But the hands, Marcus, me lad. Did you see her hands. Lily-white and not used to work. Aye! Blistered and red, true, but all the same, the hands of a lady. Dolly had the hands of a workingman. Strong, useful, calloused."

"No, I didn't notice, Josh. You see why you are invaluable to me?" Quietly Marcus rose, walked over to the sleeping girl, and looked down at her hands. What Josh said was true. Her hands were grimy and some of the tapered nails were broken, yet Josh was right. They were not Dolly's hands. He looked carefully at her and felt again the odd sensation of recognition. Who was she?

He squinted his eyes and frowned. Now he had not one, but two problems. John and Charles and this wench calling herself Dolly. He walked back to the fires and accepted another mug of coffee from Josh. "You're right, Josh. I was a fool to bring her here."

"Don't feel badly, Marc," Josh laughed. "Just be careful and watch your step. That's my advice to you."

Marcus grimaced. "I'll watch my step and everyone else's, too," he grumbled sullenly.

"What are you going to do with her, me lad?"

"I don't know just yet, Josh. We'll just have to take it one day at a time. I can just see all our hard planning thrown in the air if she's a spy. We need that tax money, Josh; otherwise the whole trip was for nothing. Just a temporary reprieve. Our people will starve in a matter of months. We can't let anything happen. See," he said, directing a looming, portentous glance in Tori's direction. "She's wakening, Josh."

Tori raised herself on one elbow and opened her eyes. Where was she? Memory flooded her being, bringing with it a sharp rebuke. Lord, how she ached! Would she be able to move? Her muscles were sore and cramped. Her head throbbed viciously. She sighed and looked around. Her heart skipped a beat as her eyes locked with those of the highwayman who sat near the fire.

In the early-morning light the final difference between Dolly and this girl was evident. Her eyes were cat-yellow and fever-bright. What had he been thinking of not to have noticed them last night?

Tori tried to struggle to her feet only to fall to her knees. Both Scarblade and Josh watched. Josh had to hold Marcus's arm or he would have gone to her side.

Marcus relaxed. He watched the girl gain her feet and stand wavering in the cold air. She looked around the campsite and spotted the pail of water. Tori tottered to the rough plank that held the pail and wrapped her arms around the ancient tree. She swayed dizzily. Marcus jumped to his feet. Josh missed his coattails by a mere inch. Just as Tori started to fall, Marcus caught her.

"Best take it slow, Dolly, my girl," the Blade laughed. "It would appear to my men that you have taken to sipping or nipping, whatever the case may be."

Tori frowned at his words. Her head felt thick and full of cotton. Rubbing her hands over her forehead she felt uneasy at the warmness of her skin.

"Take your hands off me," she croaked in a hoarse whisper. "Leave me be. When I want your help, I'll ask for it." Again she swayed precariously.

"Then hurry and ask for it, for in another minute you will fall to the ground," Marcus snapped.

Tori fought an angry retort as she felt herself falling. "Help me," she pleaded, her eyes bright. Marcus caught her as she sunk to the ground and she knew no more.

Taking in the scene, Josh ambled over and felt the girl's hot forehead. "She is feverish, and look at her cheeks. Just what we need," he grumbled, "a sick girl on our hands. A sick girl who just might be a spy for the Crown," he emphasized.

Marcus nodded impatiently as he lowered the girl to the pallet. "Fetch more blankets, Josh, and make some kind of a poultice for her fever." As Josh made off to do his bidding, he saw Marcus carefully pull the rough blankets up to the girl's chin. Josh smiled to himself. He, too, could well remember the feel of a girl in his arms.

Tori opened her eyes and gazed into the sloe-black eyes of Marcus. "Am I sick?" she quavered. Marcus nodded. Tori closed her eyes as though there were lead weights tied to the lids. She felt to open them would take all the strength she possessed. Something deep in her mind told her this man would take care of her and let nothing happen to her. She drifted off into a feverish sleep. Tori felt gentle hands place something on her head and neck. A feeling of sudden warmth engulfed her as piles of blankets were heaped on her.

"The fever is high, Marcus," Josh said irritably. "She should have a physician look at her."

Marcus shook his head. "Just do the best you can, Josh. That's all for now. We can't risk moving her, and you well know that no physician can be brought here."

"But, Marc, she should be indoors. This cold, damp air will have her chest congested in no time. She has to be raised off the ground."

"Perhaps if we fashion a makeshift tent of some blankets and raise the pallet she will fare better."

There was much grumbling on the part of the men, but they hastened to obey Marcus's orders. Anyone who had ever seen Scarblade's temper once vowed never to be the one to raise it a second time.

Soon the improvised quarters were arranged and Tori raised on her narrow pallet well off the ground. Josh appointed himself her nurse and ministered to her like a guardian angel. He knew in his heart that this girl had some manner of hold on his friend, Marcus, whether Marcus admitted it or not.

Chapter Fourteen

"It's time! There should be good pickings tonight, men," Scarblade shouted, enthusiasm lightening his voice. "The wedding that was held yesterday will see the guests leaving today. Yesterday there was but a mere handful that took their leave. If we ride quickly and carefully we should be able to overtake close to a dozen before the night is over. Mount up, men, and follow the roads I've mapped out. Josh is staying behind with the girl. Remember my warning. There is to be no killing and no abuse." The men shouted their agreement and galloped out of the clearing while Marcus rode over to the makeshift tent and inquired of Josh.

"She's the same. She mutters but it's nothing important that she speaks. Ride safely, good friend, and take care!" Marcus turned and spurred the beast he rode.

Again Josh touched the girl. She appeared to be worse. If possible, her cheeks were more flushed. There was nothing else to do but wait.

All through the day Josh sat at her side and swabbed her head and arms. From time to time Tori opened her feverish eyes and saw a gigantic man with a golden beard watching her. She mumbled occasionally in her delirium. He tried in vain to catch the snatches of words but they made no sense to him. She spoke of "darling Granger, dear Granger"! Josh shook his large head like an angry bear and patted the girl's hand. "Sleep now," he said softly.

Josh kept up with the herb-soaked cloths, and several hours later, when he checked her again, she appeared to be awake and talking coherently.

"How sick am I?" she questioned hoarsely.

"Well, lass, a few hours ago I wouldn't have given a

ha'pence for your chances, your fever was that high. But now," he smiled, "I think it has broken and that you will be well in a few days' time. How do you feel?" he asked.

"Weak," Tori whispered. "My bones ache and my head throbs like a drum. Where am I?"

"With Scarblade and his men, lass. I am Josh. Surely you remember me?"

Tori looked puzzled; then memory returned in snatches. She nodded weakly. She must not give herself away.

"Tell me, Dolly. How is it you are in this position, sick and such?"

"I had not the money for the rent. The old hag threw me out and Scarblade helped me," Tori whispered, her strength almost gone. Her eyes closed and she slept. But this time it was a healthy sleep. Gone was the flush from her face, and her brow was cool to the touch.

Josh dragged his weary bones to the fire and helped himself to some rabbit stew. He washed it down with ale and immediately had an attack of coughing. The blood was coming up in greater quantities these days. He had hoped to hide it from Marcus but the younger man had seen this morning. He would have to make sure that nothing happened to himself till after the tax robbery. Marcus needed him, as did the colonists in that far-off place, North Carolina. God would give him the strength. He laughed at the irony of the situation, praying to God to let him live so he could help rob the King. "But to feed starving people," he defended himself. If there was a God, He would see to it that the task was carried out.

For hours Josh sat by the fire, feeding it from time to time so that the flames crackled and danced. He spread a mound of blankets near the fire and lay down. He dozed and woke as the embers sputtered and sizzled. It was but an hour to dawn when the sound of hoofbeats could be heard coming across the clearing. Josh stirred himself and placed the tall coffeepot on the flame.

There was much laughing and joking as the men tied

their horses and came near the fire. Josh poured the steaming brew and watched silently as the men drank. Marcus was the last to arrive. His eyes questioned Josh but he spoke not a word.

"The fever is down and the lass will be as right as rain in a few days' time. How did the night go?"

"Almost a king's ransom," Charles laughed loudly. "We made a pretty penny this night. All the fine ladies had their best jewels with them."

Josh watched silently as the men dumped their booty on the dirty rag in front of the fire.

"At least two hundred sovereigns," John laughed. "Right, Scarblade?"

Marcus let his eyes rake the pile of gleaming jewels. Tomorrow they would have to be redeemed for sovereigns. After dividing with the men he would have about one hundred sovereigns to give to Captain Elias to add to the cask he held for him. He sighed. It still wasn't enough. But there was no question of withholding the men's shares. He must be fair to them.

"Listen to me, men. I have warned you before many times. Don't spend any of the guineas or the sovereigns as yet. Bide your time and wait."

There followed a chorus of grumbling, but it was good-natured for the most part. They knew Marcus was right. All but Charles.

"Ah, Scarblade," he sneered. "Wha's th' good o' 'avin' th' money if we can' use it? Oi, messel', wan' ta do a bit o' wenchin' an' Oi need money an' this is as good a toime as any ta say tha' John an me ain't satisfied wi' th' way th' division on th' spoils go. Oi wants more! Oi takes as many risks as ye an' th' others. Ye get 'alf a share an' th' other 'alf is ta share among th' four o' us. 'Tiz 'ardly fair, Scarblade. Own up ta th' fact!"

Marcus had never liked the looks of Charles Smythe, and he liked his brother John even less. Were it not for the fact that they came highly recommended, he never would have engaged these two unlikely fellows.

Charles and John, of a like height, six feet tall at least, were both slim and light-haired. While John was the less attractive of the pair, being dirtier and more malicious-looking, both shared the same quickness and and furtiveness of eye. Marcus, when he looked at them, was reminded of two half-starved, mangy dogs, scurrying to a far corner with a much-prized bone, all the while casting nervous, watchful glances to see no one came near to deprive them of their booty.

Now Marcus was incensed because of their ever-encroaching greed. Ned and Richard, on the other hand, had endeared themselves to Marcus. Poor, beggarly street urchins, who in manhood had become petty thieves and pickpockets, they now rode with Marcus for the promise of a better life in Chancelor's Valley. Still, Marcus was leary of Charles's and John's influence upon them. They were not far removed from the street urchins they once were.

Marcus's anger toward Charles burst forth. "You agreed when we set out on the venture. I warned you then that I was not in this to make money for myself. It is for the colonists in America. Your share is your own. To a man you agreed. I also offered you land and a home in America for those of you who want to return with me. Ned and Richard are wise enough to accept my offer for a better life. You would be wise to consider it also. What more can I offer you?" Marcus said coldly, his raven-black eyes narrowed.

"An even split," Charles barked, his mouth slanted in a sneer.

"There's no way that the money will be split evenly. If you don't like it you're free to ride out of here. No one will be the wiser," Marcus growled threateningly.

"Ride out, izzit?" sneered Charles, "wi' th' biggest robbery yet ta take place? If we left ye'd 'ave all th' tax money fer those people o' yers. No, Scarblade, we'll stick ta ye loike a mustard plaster till after th' tax robbery. Then we'll decide."

"Then it'll be too late," Marcus said through clenched teeth. "For I sail the day after. Or were you thinking of turning me in, Charles, and collecting the reward and the rest of my share? Speak up, man, or I'll tie you to the nearest tree."

"No, 'Blade, Oi wuz jus' 'avin' a bit o' fun wi' ye. Ye be righ', tiz a fair arraingemen'. Oi gave me word

an' it's good. Oi speak fer me brother John as well."
Marcus didn't believe a word of the man's talk. He
knew him too well. He shot a knowing look at Josh,
who didn't believe him either.

Tori fingered the rough material of the breeches she
wore. At last her fondest dream had come true: to wear
breeches. Yet, now that she had her way she suddenly
longed for her own beautiful gowns. She didn't fancy
looking like a boy after all!

Tori watched Scarblade mount his steed with great
ease; she longed to do the same. She would miss the
men when she left. While they hadn't been exactly welcoming, they had treated her kindly. But now it was
time to leave. She was feeling better after her bout of
illness. If Scarblade would let her have a horse, she
could be on her way by first light of day. If not, then
she would have to walk. Where would she go? She'd
have to try to find Granger. Having made her decision,
Tori approached Scarblade hesitantly. Almost shyly,
she raised her eyes, for the man inspired fear within
her still, and flashes of that night in Dolly's room
flooded and ebbed within her. The man's powers had
thrilled her and yet filled her with dread. That he was a
man to be reckoned with Tori was convinced; she had
only to see the effect his commands had upon his men
to know this. She had witnessed his anger. Feet planted
firmly apart, S-shaped scar blazing on his handsome
face, black eyes scornful in his ominous rebuke of the
unfortunate object of his wrath. Now Tori herself
risked being the recipient of Scarblade's anger and she
trembled slightly with dread.

"Scarblade, it's toime Oi left," she said softly as he
swung around at her slight movement.

"Leave? Where will you go?" he asked, his eyes
cold, his mouth tight.

Tori shrugged. "Oi'll find a place fer mesel'. I can'
stay longer wi' ye. Oi truly appreciate yer kindness
while Oi wuz sick. Propriety makes it necessary tha' Oi
leave."

Scarblade smiled wickedly. "Propriety, is it?"

Disconcerted, Tori realized her mistake. Dolly

wouldn't care about propriety, let alone know the word. " 'Tiz a word Oi 'eard from a friend o' moine. Don' it sound nice when it rolls off yer tongue?"

"I'm afraid your wishes count for naught, my lady," Scarblade said coldly as he dismounted from his steed.

"Wha' d'ye mean?" Tori asked fearfully.

"Just what I said, dear lady," Scarblade said, his face all cold indifference.

Alarm caused Tori's eyes to grow wide. Panic settled over her like a pall. "Wha' kind o' man are ye, anyway?" she demanded. "If Oi choose ta put off yer advances, why don' ye take it loike a man instead o' some churlish lout? Ta keep me 'ere till Oi weaken will never 'appen, so let me leave an' Oi'll no' bother ye again."

"Dolly, my love," Scarblade chuckled, "it is Dolly, is it not?"

So that's it, Tori thought. Her mind raced. "Wha's in a name?" she inquired softly, her heart pumping madly.

"In your case, quite a lot, dear lady," Scarblade mocked. "For example, if you were really Dolly, the men would respect you for the life you lead, which is hard-working and fair. A day's work for a day's wages. A little frolic on the side and everyone is happy. Now for the other example, let us say that you were a lady of quality, and a spy for the Crown. That," he said coldly, "makes a new story. Why, the men would be most upset! I would find it hard to interfere if they decided to have their way with you. They would rape you, to a man. They could use a garrote on you, they could shoot you down like the spy you are. I see by the tears that are welling up in your eyes that you are about to deny the truth."

Tori fought them back. "So my name is not Dolly. That does not make me a spy for the Crown. For personal reasons I took Dolly's name, but I assure you that I am no spy. And if you think to frighten me with the tales you have just spun for my benefit, think again. I can ride as well as any man here. I can also outthink any one of you. To die is not so terrible, if what one believes in is worth dying for, is that not so, Scarblade?"

He measured the girl before him. Why did she make him feel like a schoolboy? He felt like hunching over and scuffing his feet in unison.

"I want to warn you, my lady. I have no control over the men. You will stay. There is to be no mention of your leaving, now or later. When it is time for you to make your departure I will give you notice, not a second before. Is that understood? For your sake I will try and keep the men in line and away from you."

"So you can have me to yourself?" Tori demanded. "The spoils to the victor?" Tori was instantly contrite for her unfair words. If anything, Scarblade had drawn a wide berth around her.

As she faced the truth behind her anger her face flushed a deep crimson and she knew her ire stemmed from Scarblade's obvious indifference. Almost insulting, when one considered the wild moment they had shared in Dolly's room.

Marcus narrowed his eyes and brought his face within inches of Tori's. "I shall be the victor, make no mistake. As to the spoils, I think not. You are too skinny for my taste. I prefer more flesh on my women. And I prefer to have them come to me. They appreciate me more." Marcus laughed mockingly as he reached out a long muscular arm to jostle her shoulder.

"You, you insufferable ... lout," Tori spat. "Don't touch me unless I give you permission!" she shouted angrily. "I am not some piece of merchandise to be pawed and passed from hand to hand! And furthermore, I will not give you my word that I'll not try to leave here. I will leave! You cannot keep me a prisoner here for your own nefarious pleasures. I won't have it! Do you hear?" Tori shouted as she stamped her foot in the dust. "I'll kill the first man who comes near me!" she said as she pummeled his chest with her small fists, eyes glittering angrily.

Marcus looked down at the shining, golden head as she pounded his chest. Suddenly he smiled as he grasped her arms; she was a handful, there was no doubt about that. He marveled at the soft feel of her through the thin material of the shirt she wore. Her cheeks flushed and her eyes sparkled. Marcus looked into the angry, cat-yellow eyes and felt a sharp longing come to the surface. Slowly he brought his face closer. Tori, reading the intent in his eyes, struggled to escape the strong hand which held her. She was unable to move; his lips touched hers and she continued to struggle, aware of her resolve slipping away. Tori felt warm all over, her blood coursed, she felt dizzy and light-headed. Unexpectedly, she found herself on her knees, her arms upstretched, reaching. Tori looked up into his somber, licorice eyes. What she saw there made her silent.

Awareness dawned on her of the picture she made there, kneeling in subjugation before this dark-haired, sun-bronzed giant with her arms supplicating his favors.

Tori hated him with every fiber of her being. What kind of devil was this who could rankle her to an hysterical fit of scratching one moment and then dissolve her sensibilities to those of a wanton.

And he, with booted feet spread firmly apart, the cut of his trousers clinging to the tense, steely muscles of his thighs. The wind-tousled dark head was cocked majestically, his expression uncaring and aloof. Only his hands, which were clenching and unclenching on his hips, revealed something of his embroiled emotions.

Suddenly he lifted his piercing gaze from her, his attention caught by something in front of him. Turning slowly, Tori came face to face with the sneering men who now stood in a semicircle behind her.

Lust distorted their faces. She looked to Josh for assistance. There was only kindness and pity in his eyes. Tori blinked as he bent to help her to her feet.

"Back to your tent, lass, before there's trouble," he cautioned. Tori stumbled and hastened to obey. The laughter that followed her undignified retreat stung her to the quick.

Chapter Fifteen

Curling herself into a tight ball in the corner of the tent, Tori pulled her legs up to her chin and closed her eyes, hiding her shame. Where was Granger? What had happened to him? Why hadn't he come to Dolly's room? What was to become of her if she stayed here? She had to find some way to leave! With Scarblade and Josh she felt reasonably safe, but she didn't trust the men. Ned and Richard were all right, she supposed, they seemed engrossed in the job they had set out to do, and seemed to respect her rights as an individual. But Charles and John made her very uncomfortable with their leers and blatant remarks about her morals. It was no secret that they thought they were entitled to her favors for a price.

Tori decided she would wait till Josh had the night watch. Several times she had lain awake and seen that when it was his turn he would doze and drop his guard. Tori knew he was ill, very ill, and she wished there were something she could do for him. Josh had tended her so gently when she had the fever, and she knew him to be kind, a gentle man in spite of the fact that he was in complete sympathy with Scarblade.

Someone approached, then stopped outside her tent. Tori listened as the men spoke together. "It's too risky to let Josh go with us tonight, Scarblade," Richard said quietly. Marcus respected Richard's and his friend Ned's opinions. They were tough and serious boys in their early twenties. Marcus felt he could rely on them because both wanted to better themselves. Whenever Marcus sat about the campfire talking of North Carolina, a wistful look would shine in their eyes.

"If he has a fit of coughing it would be our undoing." Richard continued speaking of Josh. "It's best that he stays and guards the girl and sees to the camp."

Marcus grumbled his agreement. Richard asked, "Have you given any thought to finding out who the lass is, Scarblade? We know to a man that she isn't Dolly. So who is she and why is she here? Are you holding her for a ransom? A little money in our pockets isn't hard to take. And she doesn't belong here, 'Blade. She's too soft for this kind of life; there's something about her, as though she's a real lady. But she's got a lot of spunk, I'll give her that."

"I'll decide what to do with her later," Marcus said loudly; "right now there's business to be decided."

"Ha!" jeered Charles, who had approached Scarblade and Richard and had heard the tail end of their conversation. "Now's th' toime th' decision's ta be made! If ye don' wan' ta 'old 'er fer ransom then let's 'ave a bit o' wenchin'. 'Tiz always yer decision, Scarblade. There wuz nothin' said in th' beginnin' abou' any wenches joinin' us. Ye made th' rules an' we all followed 'em. Th' wench is somethin' else. Ye denied me an even split so Oi'd 'ave some money in me pocket fer a bit o' wenchin' on th' town an' now ye mean ta deprive me an' th' men o' this 'eaven-sen' opportunity!"

There were loud mutterings from the rest of the men; they sounded to be in accord with Charles. Marcus cast an ominous glance in Josh's direction. The big man had his hand on the pistol which rested at his hip. From the look of things it would be two against the group.

"I said I'd decide later; there's business to be settled now," Marcus shouted angrily.

"Th' business can wait! Th' wench is ta be decided now!" Charles sneered ominously. The men behind him muttered their agreement.

Tori crouched in her tent, eyes wide, heart beating fast, waiting for the decision that was to come.

Josh stood tall and appeared to be coiled to spring; Marcus, his attitude contrary to the blazing scar on his cheek, casually rocked back and forth on his heels.

"If that's the way it is, then listen to me," Marcus spoke clearly and loudly. Tori could imagine the picture of night-dark eyes flashing bolts of lightning,

mouth drawn tight over strong white teeth, that pose of
authority so natural to him, the wind ruffling his dark
hair about his pantherlike head.

"The wench is a spy sent by the Crown. Now do you
still want to use her and whatever else you have in your
minds? Or do you want her where we can watch her
and have her sent back with our good tidings after the
tax robbery in the condition she arrived? In the end, if
I let you have your way you'll have to kill her. There'll
be no other way out for any of us. She can recognize
everyone. She can point all of us out and as for myself,
I much prefer to do my dancing on the ground, not on
the long end of a rope on Tyburn Hill."

Josh spoke, "Scarblade's right, lads. I don't want to
hang for a wench."

There was much grumbling on the part of the men,
but it appeared that Scarblade had won. Tori, a quivering mass of nerves, sat huddled in the tent and found
herself giving thanks to the tall highwayman.

Charles left the small circle of men and advanced on
the tent; entering, he seized the startled Tori by the arm
and dragged her into the clearing. "She's mine!" he
said as he held her in front of him. "Raise yer weapon,
Josh, an' ye'll kill 'er. We deserve 'er, we've ridden
long an' 'ard fer ye, Scarblade, an' we deserve a bit o'
frolic. Wha's it ta ye? An' all this blather tha' ye speak,
dancin' on th' end of a rope, indeed," he scoffed.
"Once we're on th' ship an' she's on th' wharf, wha'
could th' King do then? Or perhaps we could brin' 'er
along ta pass th' toime on a long sea voyage!"
Charles's hands tightened painfully, biting into her
arms abusively.

"Speak for yourself, Charles," Richard said, "I want
no part of it."

Ned chimed in with Richard, "I don't want to force
a woman to bed with me, count me out!"

Tori looked from Ned to Richard and breathed a
sigh of relief. At least they refused to go along with
Charles. But would they stand against him if Charles
won out? Tori felt a knot of fear grow within her.
Would Scarblade let Charles have her? Would he care

so little? Charles waited for Scarblade's reply but Tori knew he meant to have her . . . regardless!

She jerked her arms free of Charles's grasp. "Take your hands off me. I have nowhere to go," Tori hissed; "where could I run?" She stood tall and resolute and let her eyes go from Scarblade to Josh. Scarblade's eyes were cold and unreadable; if he thought she would beg he was mistaken. She had never begged in her life! Her heart beat rapidly, her breath came in heaves.

Scarblade watched a tiny smile play about the girl's mouth; she appeared unafraid and there was an alien glint in her cat-yellow eyes. He had to make a decision and he looked meaningfully at the girl, willing her to speak.

Reading the request in his eyes, Tori turned and faced the men. She drew herself up to full height and resought and found Scarblade's eyes. It was to him she spoke, her tone soft and feminine but each word encased in a sheath of steely assertiveness. She had their attention.

"Your men may have their way with me as you will. But, you were right, they would have to kill me when they're through. For I promise you," she said softly, "any man who touches me will be dealt with by me! I'll follow you to the ends of the earth if necessary! I'll wreak upon you a vengeance the likes of which you have never seen. When I have found you, and I will, I shall remove your ears with a dull knife; take one eye from its socket with my own fingers, remove your teeth one by one, and make a soup from these things. You will eat and retch on your own flesh! Then I'll use this same dull knife and without a second thought, I'll carve your manhood from your body! I shall sit on a tall horse and listen to your screams and laugh." She uttered a silvery tinkle of a laugh and Josh shuddered. He believed every word she said.

"Now which of you wants the first honor?" Tori asked softly, almost conversationally. Charles and John slowly backed away from her, hesitation and doubt evident on their faces. Charles moved closer to Tori as Josh came to stand beside her. Tori waited while Charles was still some distance from her; there was no mistaking the lust in his eyes even at that distance. Before Josh knew how it happened, Tori had the knife from his belt in her hand. She moved back several paces and looked with loathing at Charles. Letting a smile of satisfaction spread over her face, she saw Charles's step falter. Tori tested the weight of the blade in her hand and turned it so that she grasped its point. She hefted the blade experimentally as Charles advanced slowly toward her.

Scarblade drew in his breath as Tori raised her arm, the tip of the knife held secure. She drew back her arm and flexed her wrist. "Another step and your manhood is gone," she said quietly.

Charles stopped, a grimace on his face. " 'Ave no fear, little laidy, Oi've no thought o' ye this day. Bes' we ferget th' whole thin'." He watched anxiously as Tori continued to hold the knife by the tip.

With a fast and fluid motion she hefted and threw the weapon. It sailed through the air like a silver-tipped bird and found its mark in a daisy which had somehow escaped the ravages of the encroaching winter. Tori narrowed her eyes and looked where the knife rested. Satisfied, she walked to her tent and lowered the blanket that served as a door. Sitting down on the pallet, she succumbed to a fit of trembling. "Thank you, Granger, for helping me," she repeated over and over. "Thank you, God, for guiding the knife to where I aimed it!"

Tori was shaken from her show of bravado. Granger had taught her to throw a knife when they were children. But today her small skill had exceeded her greatest expectations.

Outside, Scarblade bent to pick up the knife. He looked at Charles. "Dead center, she hardly disturbed the petals." Charles's face was white; he felt played for the fool, humiliated.

Scarblade looked with concern at Charles's face. "This is the end of the matter, let the girl be! I've a feeling you're no match for her."

"Then she is a spy! Where else could she learn ta throw a knife loike tha'? It's a certainty it's no' th' accomplishmen' o' a laidy! She's a gypsy, Oi tells ye!"

Scarblade turned to Josh, who leaned against a tree, his huge arms folded across his chest. Scarblade grinned as he asked, "Did you see that, Josh?"

Josh joined him in his laughter, "A lass after me own heart. 'Tis a shame she's promised to another."

"What?" Marcus asked in a sharp tone.

" 'Tis true, Marc. In her delirium she kept speaking of 'darlin' Granger' and then just calling his name over and over," Josh said slyly.

Marcus did not fail to glean Josh's meaning. Calling for her lover, was she? Little bawd, dreaming of another while tempting him with her full, moist mouth.

Shooting Josh a reproachful look, Marcus stalked off in the opposite direction from Tori's tent. He was certain that if he should come across the girl he would take that long, white neck of hers and squeeze it till it snapped.

Why didn't he just let the men have their way with her? He'd like to see her taken down from her high horse . . . and yet . . . and yet . . .

The oval perfection of her face haunted him; her features were like Dolly's as was the color of her hair, but there the similarity ended. This girl's features were more refined. The delicate winged arch of her brows, the clotted-cream complexion, that petulant upper lip, so inviting to kiss, so tempting for a man to take it in his teeth and bite it!

A dull ache from the pit of his guts began to spread within him, warming him. He remembered her as she looked a short while ago. Down on her knees, her outstretched arms beckoning him, her round, high breasts heaving beneath the thin fabric of her blouse. It would have been so easy, so fitting to seize her and carry her off and satiate himself with her beauty. Scarblade stomped off into the woods, a glare looming in his black eyes.

Chapter Sixteen

"Are you ready to leave . . . Dolly?" Scarblade asked mockingly.

"I thought I told you that I would not be a party to any robbing or banditry," Tori spat, throwing back her head in defiance.

"Either you ride or I'll tie you to yonder tree and let the wolves take a choice morsel or two from your lovely frame. Make up your mind, for I'm rapidly losing patience!"

Tori looked imploringly at Josh. He shrugged his huge shoulders in resignation, but Tori thought she saw a glimmer of amusement on the giant's florid face.

"No!" Tori screeched, stomping her foot in the dirt. "I won't do it, you cannot make me do something which is against my will!" she added rebelliously.

"And I," Scarblade shouted derisively, "have very large hands, the better to whip you with if necessary. Now move!"

"I refuse," Tori answered haughtily. No sooner were the words out of her mouth than Scarblade was off his horse and standing next to her. His mocking eyes infuriated her to the point where she could no longer hold her tongue.

"Do you think for one minute I'll mount that horse and ride from this clearing to hold up some coach and steal from innocent people? Well, Scarblade, gentleman of gentlemen, I bid you think again. For you will have to give me a pistol—and I promise you I will use it. I," she said with contempt, "aim low, very low."

"Is that your final word?" Scarblade smiled.

Tori, taken off guard by the disarming smile, stammered, "Yes."

"Then you leave me no other choice but to seek out this friend of yours—you do have a friend named

Granger, do you not?" Tori could only stare blankly.
"We shall seek him out on the morrow and string him
from the nearest tree. The decision is yours; I give you
five seconds!"

Two seconds later came the soft reply. "You . . . you
. . . despicable creature, you loathesome vermin, you
. . . you . . . you odious highwayman!"

Tori mounted the horse he held by the reins. "Don't
touch me," she screeched, "you . . . insufferable desperado." Jerking the reins in her fury, the horse reared
on its hind legs. Deliberately, she yanked the reins to
curry in the beast and in her doing so the horse nearly
pawed Marcus as he hastened to get out of the way.

"So, you're fleet of foot also. You have many accomplishments, Scarblade," Tori said mockingly.

There was horror in Scarblade's face. "You'd have
let that horse come down on me," he said in awe, his
eyes turning into glinting carbon.

"My mistake, kind sir, you were too fast for me.
Yes, I would have let him come down on you and not
shed a tear."

Furiously, Scarblade mounted the chestnut. That a
mere slip of a girl could best him, and before his men!
He wondered if she knew how to shoot a pistol. Probably, he thought sourly, if she knew how to throw a
knife. What else can she do that I don't know about?
he wondered. The fine hairs on the back of his neck
itched. She was probably this minute casting some kind
of spell on him. That was it, she was a witch!

"Wipe that silly smile off your face, Josh, or I'll
wipe it off for you," Scarblade sniffed.

"Aye, lad, I was just thinking of a wild pig caught in
a net."

Scarblade shot him a venomous look. Josh continued
to smile. He knew the girl could have reined in the
horse in a second's time. She had the situation well under control. From his position in line he had seen the
smile on her face and the wicked wink she had
bestowed on him. Yes, Marcus had met his match in
this one.

"The girl goes with me. I don't trust the others with
her. We separate at the fork in the road. Let us pray it

is a good night; Lord Starling only invites the richest people to his intimate dinner parties."

"Aye, lad, we have the right of it. We separate in twos and meet back here at the fork."

The small party rode quietly in single file. When they reached the fork in the road they separated and Scarblade and Tori rode abreast. Scarblade handed her the pistol and Tori almost dropped it.

"It's heavy."

"Does that mean you don't know how to shoot? Somehow, I thought you would be an excellent shot. You seem to know how to do everything else," he said snidely.

Tori refused to be baited. She capitulated. "Remember the daisy? Well, I could shoot the petals one after the other and leave no mark on the next. Does that answer your question?"

She smiled in satisfaction, her eyes frosty. Never, until this day, had she held a pistol. In fact, this was the closest she had ever come to one. The lie had been worth it from the look on the highwayman's face. Truly, it appeared he had believed her when she said she would shoot very low. Suddenly she laughed, a silvery, tinkling sound.

Scarblade gritted his teeth at the sound, and once more the fine hairs on his neck prickled.

"This is the road to the Starlings' estate. Soon they'll be arriving. We'll just wait here in this rutted lane, you'll remain quiet and let me approach the coach. Just stay in the back of me and keep your eyes alert. If necessary, let the passengers see the pistol. I warn you, keep that tongue of yours still!"

"Yes milord. If I were not astride this beast, I'd be giving you a deep curtsey," she jeered.

" 'Twould not surprise me if that tongue of yours was forked."

"Why milord, see for yourself," Tori said prettily, then stuck out her tongue and wiggled it, laughing mirthfully at the expression on his face.

Scarblade closed his eyes wearily. Somewhere he had gone wrong. Everything had been fine till he had brought the girl to his camp. Now everything was at sixes and sevens. She had to be a witch! What kind of woman was she? Where had she been born and raised? He shook his head in defeat.

"Quiet now, I hear the beat of the horses' hooves. We'll let the coach get past us, then I'll ride to the head so the driver can see me and pull in. You stay behind the coach, and no tricks. Just remember, your dairling Granger hanging from a tree."

Tori wrinkled her nose and curled her lip. "Just remember Granger and the rope," she mimed him softly. "The things I do for you, Granger," she muttered under her breath as she affixed a black mask such as Scarblade wore over her face.

The ornate coach thundered by the small lane. Scarblade gave a start and headed out; she followed and rode behind the coach. She saw the team being reined in and pulled her mount to a halt. She sat quietly behind Scarblade as the door of the coach opened and four people emerged.

"Your money and your jewels! Best hurry, my fine friends, for it has the look of rain or snow," came the request.

Pistol in hand, Tori's eyes fell on his tall figure. *I should shoot his leg off,* she thought viciously.

One of the ladies, seeing Tori's lissome form astride the horse, exclaimed "It's only a boy!" The others took up her cry and seemed surprised. No doubt, the thought of a mere boy earmarked for a life of crime would upset these quality folk.

Well, I'll just teach this Scarblade a lesson, Tori thought viciously. *Force me to do this against my will, will he? Well, we'll just see about that!* For one fleeting moment Granger's face flashed before her eyes. She blinked, the vision was gone.

Tori inched her horse closer to the carriage so she could better observe the passengers and at the same time be almost abreast of Scarblade.

"Oh, my lady," she spoke pitifully, "you have noticed that I resemble a boy? 'Tis sad, is it not, to think of a mere boy taking to the open road with a band of outlaws?" The bewigged and powdered ladies shook their heads in agreement.

"What would you think if I told you that not only does this . . . this desperado use mere boys, but girls as well?" With a flourish she removed her cap and a mass of golden curls tumbled over her shoulders. There was shock and outrage written on the ladies' faces. The men were indignant, Scarblade was furious! Tori grinned impishly; she bowed low in the saddle, waving her arm in a wide salute. Pulling on the reins, she made the horse daintily step backward.

"You hellcat!" Scarblade hissed. "I'll tend to you in a moment."

"Throw your money and jewels in a pile by that rock," he said, pointing. "Be quick about it or I fear you'll all have a good case of frostbite if your coach should leave without you." Scarblade raised his eyes and pointed to a small trunk with a curving lid. "And throw down that trunk from the luggage rack. Be quick about it!"

A lady raised a cry of protest. "No, please, my best gowns!"

Scarblade silenced her outrage with a penetrating look from beneath lowered lids. He smiled approvingly at the woman, causing her to blush under his insolent gaze. "Milady," he said in a deep, intimate voice, "a beauty such as yours needs no artificial heightening."

The lady in question turned to her companions with a simper of delight on her lips. One of the gentlemen, most likely the woman's husband, sent her a stinging jab to the ribs.

Scarblade smiled and Tori did not fail to notice it. She yearned to rake nails across his handsome face.

With a quick movement he slapped the lead horse of the team and the coach lumbered down the corded road. "Be quick now, for you have a small journey ahead of you, on foot. Without a driver the horses will not travel far, and I'm certain you'll catch up with them soon."

The party from the coach started down the road, and the halted coach was within sight. Scarblade and Tori watched them hastily climb into the vehicle. The driver lashed at the team and they sped down the road.

Scarblade motioned to Tori to gather up the spoils. "Do it yourself, I'm not your lackey."

Infuriated beyond words, Scarblade wanted to wring her neck. "Do as I say," he thundered, "immediately!"

"No!" Tori held the reins and backed up slowly, the pistol held tightly in her hand. "Come one step nearer and I'll shoot," she added dramatically.

Scarblade sat and measured the girl. He knew she would shoot. The question was, would she shoot to kill, to wound, or to warn?"

"Damn your soul," he roared, knowing all the while that if he dismounted she would be gone in a flash.

Tori, sensing his thoughts, laughed. "It would seem, Master Scarblade, that we have here what is known as a stalemate. Would you not agree?" She leaned over the horse's mane, the pistol held loosely, the golden hair tumbling over her shoulders.

Scarblade drew in his breath. She was beautiful with the moonlight behind her making a nimbus about her golden tresses. Silently, Scarblade returned the pistol to his belt, straightened in the saddle, and spoke coldly. "You may leave now. You're on your own; you're free to ride out of here."

"You're lying through your teeth," Tori spat. "You won't let me go!"

"You're free to leave," Marcus repeated.

"You're trying to trick me," Tori said suspiciously.

"You think that only because you have a narrow, suspicious mind," Scarblade said coldly. "What are you waiting for? Ride!"

"Your word that I will not be stopped."

He nodded curtly.

Tori saw the handsome man astride the huge beast and tried to read his thoughts. It had to be a trick, but still, she couldn't be sure. She would have to try. Brushing the golden tendrils from her face she once more looked deep into the eyes of the highwayman; then, before she could think twice, Tori shoved the pistol into the waistband of her trousers and spurred the horse. She dug heels into its flanks over and over again, and rode as if the devils of hell were on her heels.

She glanced behind her, her hair flying wildly in the wind. She was right, Scarblade was after her!

She should have known all he wanted was the pistol out of her hand. He knew that she could not ride and brandish the gun, let alone fire it. Again she dug her heels into the horse and risked a glance behind her. He was gaining on her. She whimpered as she lowered her head to keep the biting wind from stinging her eyes. Suddenly, with no warning, she felt herself being lifted from the saddle and sailing through the air.

"Let me go!" she screamed. "Don't you dare touch me! Put me down!" she ordered. "You gave me your word! Let me go!"

"Gladly," came the reply. She felt herself falling through the air, and landed awkwardly in a drift of snow.

"How dare you . . . you . . ."

"The words you are no doubt looking for are odious, insufferable, despicable, loathsome, and vermin. I think that covers it," the man laughed.

"How dare you laugh at me?"

"Why not?" Scarblade asked, unperturbed.

"Because . . . because . . ." The S-shaped scar on his cheek deepened in color and Tori was torn between excitement and dread. "Damn you!" Tori spat.

"Tsk, tsk," the bandit said, mockingly clucking his tongue, "such language, and you a fine lady and all."

"Shut up," Tori snarled.

"The fun is over," he said emotionlessly. "Come over here; we'll have to ride double."

"I'm not riding double with you, Scarblade; get that through your head. I'll stay here and freeze."

Scarblade slid from the saddle and stalked over to the girl. He looked down at her and held out his hand. She made no move to accept his offer. He grasped her thin wrist and pulled her to her feet.

"Take your hands off me," she spat as she struggled to free herself. He grasped her other wrist and held her prisoner. She lashed out with her foot, giving him a forceful blow to his shin.

"If you want to fight, I'll give you a fight, you hellcat." He locked his leg around both of hers, forcing her to lean against his hard-muscled body.

Tori, caught by surprise, leaned for a moment against his broad chest. She could feel the wild beating of his heart, or was it hers? Weakened by his nearness, she allowed him to hold her firmly as he looked down into her eyes. The aching desire for her fast became a turbulent squall.

Scarblade observed her soft mouth and her wide, gold-green eyes. He longed to kiss them and her downy cheeks. He wanted to smother this lovely girl with passion, to feel her respond to him as she had that night in Dolly's room.

Tori, caught in his unrelenting embrace, her heart beating like that of a small creature caught in a net, suddenly went limp. Her eyes were misty and her lips parted as she looked into the depths of his smoky orbs. She felt lost in them and could not have moved if her life depended on it. Warm lips met and her head reeled. She brought up her hands and gently held his face and . . . felt so warm, so safe, so wanted.

Scarblade pulled away from her, a mocking, infuriating smile on his lips. Tori felt tremor after tremor of humiliation shoot through her. The man was of the devil's own making, her mind roared. To stir her this way and have her yielding to him, only to be cast away and to read the glow of victory in those jeering ebony eyes. There had been fire and passion in that brief kiss—was the man, who found it so easy to put her aside, made of steel?

Chapter Seventeen

Tori sat inside her tent reviewing in her mind how she had been thrust into a den of thieves. It had occurred to her once or twice before that it was her own deviousness that had put her in this predicament. But not caring for the implications of the truth, Tori ignored the facts and bemoaned the fates. Sitting there quietly, she heard Scarblade approach Josh and say in a low tone, "Josh, the time has come for Marcus Chancelor's visit to England to end. I'll go into London this evening and take care of that little matter."

"Have you decided how you're going to go about it?" Josh asked hoarsely. He had lost a good deal of his strength in the past few days.

"Not quite," Scarblade answered, "but I think the more people who know this is to be Marcus's last evening in town, the better. I'll go to the lodgings and dress myself in something more suitable for an evening visiting a playhouse and some of the more respectable inns."

Tori pricked up her ears. Somehow the name Marcus Chancelor seemed familiar to her although she couldn't place it. She could no longer hear what Scarblade was saying to Josh, for the men had moved away from her tent. Her eyes sparkled and her heavy heart lifted. To go to London and a playhouse and possibly even Covent Garden. Her mind boggled at the idea; it seemed ages since she had worn a dress and sat in refined company.

Peeking out from under the flap of the tent, Tori saw she was quite alone. She didn't try to fool herself into thinking she could escape, for surely she would be detected, but it was only a few steps to where sat the trunk that Scarblade had taken from the last robbery.

Quickly, she crept out of the tent and grasped the

heavy ornate handle on the side of the small trunk. In less than a moment she had the luggage inside the tent. She struggled with the straps that secured the lid, silently praying the clothes inside would fit her. Self-recrimination stung her when she remembered Scarblade bringing the trunk to her and telling her to make use of the contents. Winter was upon them, he had said, qualifying his concern for her by adding that they hadn't time to care for a sick woman. How foolish she had been to rebuke his gift, however ungraciously offered.

When at last she opened the straps she lifted the lid excitedly. Please make them fit me, she prayed. Beneath the thin, blue paper which covered the contents lay two gowns, one of blue and the other of iridescent green. Beneath the gowns were slippers, chemises, shawls, ribbons, and assorted toiletries.

Holding the blue gown to herself, she saw it was slightly large, but a few pins here and a ribbon there, and it would be better than she could have hoped for.

Hastily, she placed the blue silk next to the shimmering green. There was really no choice. The second matched her eyes perfectly.

As Tori rummaged through the trunk to find more ribbons, Scarblade stepped under the flap and stood watching her, an amused expression lighting his features.

"I thought you wouldn't have the trunk if it were lined with gold?"

Her first inclination was to spit a stinging retort; then, thinking better of the idea, she turned to him and smiled her sweetest smile.

"But that was before I had an occasion to wear these gowns. Now that we're going to Covent Garden this evening, you'll have to agree I must look my best."

"We're going . . . where?" Scarblade asked incredulously.

"Why to the playhouse, of course. You don't want me to look shoddy, do you?"

"See here, I've no intention of bringing you to London with me! Wherever did you get such a daft idea?"

"But I heard you telling Josh you're going to London to see Master Chancelor."

"You can just get that idea right out of your head. I must hand it to you, you're an accomplished young lady in the areas of knife-throwing, horseback riding and . . . ahem . . . eavesdropping. Not to mention lying, stealing and . . ."

"Save your breath. I've no desire to be embarrassed by your effusive praise," Tori answered lightly, flashing him a bright smile.

"Why, you little minx!" Scarblade exclaimed, making a threatening motion toward her.

Tori screeched loudly as she tore from the tent, Scarblade close on her heels.

"Here, now," Josh shouted as he suddenly stood in front of the breathless Tori. "What's doing here?"

"This little . . . our 'guest' fancies herself accompanying me to London."

"Hmmm . . . that mightn't be such a bad notion. Master Chancelor might prefer to have a lovely lady on his arm when he makes his farewell to London society. Besides, a beautiful woman always attracts considerable attention, and I assume Master Chancelor wants his farewell to London to be noted."

Marcus took his friend's words well, considering Josh's good advice of the past. "Very well, then. Josh makes good sense. But I want your word you'll not make a scene or try to escape. If you do, I'm not above killing you." Marcus's eyes measured her, awaiting her promise. "And it will not be as last time you made a promise to me. This time you'll keep it or suffer the consequences." The raven-colored eyes turned to stone, causing Tori to suffer an involuntary shiver.

"I swear to you," she said earnestly, "I'll not try to escape, nor will I make a scene. But I do need some time away from this camp and from Charles."

"Aye! The lass speaks the truth. I've seen him watching her. If you take her with you, 'twill give me a good night's rest. So weary am I of protecting her from the devil."

Tori threw Josh an appreciative smile. "I'll be with

you as quick as I can," she said to Scarblade. "An hour at the most."

"An hour! Surely you can get your things together more quickly than that? Besides," he added, "I'd say the lady could use a bath. Get your things together now. I'm sure Master Chancelor will allow you to use his rooms to make yourself presentable for the opera."

Tori couldn't believe her luck. Going to the opera and a bath! She was ready in short order, her gown and accessories bundled in a roll strapped to the back of her saddle.

On the ride into the city, Scarblade was sullenly silent, wondering how he had gotten himself into the situation of taking the girl with him. What a fool he had been to listen to Josh and believe the girl's promises. Who would watch her and keep her from escaping when he paid his visit to Lord Fowler-Greene?

When they approached the outskirts of the city, Marcus rode beside her, his thigh occasionally brushing hers. He seemed poised, as if to grab her should she be so bold as to try an escape.

"Don't you think people will find it rather strange to see you riding so ... shall we say, intimately with another of your own sex?"

He drew away from her as though his thigh had touched fire. He had completely forgotten she was dressed in breeches and that a cap covered her long golden hair—to all the world she appeared like a young man.

Within the hour they had ridden to a wide, tree-lined street facing a small, triangular park. "Master Chancelor has rooms in the end house," the highwayman said, so suddenly she was startled.

Then it all came back to her in a rush. She was sitting in the dining room at home having dinner with her parents, Granger, Lady Helen, and Lord Fowler-Greene. That was where she had heard the name. Lord Fowler-Greene was telling them about a gentleman from America who came and pleaded with the House of Lords to convince the King to help his colony. The details were vague after all this time, but she remembered her father had been favorably impressed, in fact, so favorably impressed that Lord Rawlings had pleaded the man's case and because of that lost favor with the Crown.

"So," she said aloud, "I've this Marcus Chancelor to thank for my present predicament!"

Scarblade led the horses around the back of the house where a stableboy came out to meet them.

"See that they're fed and rubbed down," he ordered, tossing the boy a coin. Then he turned to Tori and led her back to the house, entering the three-story structure by the back door.

"I think you'll find all you'll need in Master Chancelor's rooms. I believe there is a housemaid who will help you ready yourself for the evening. I'll arrange to have a bath drawn for you immediately. While you're bathing I'll take the opportunity to see to a matter of business." He spoke so softly, so kindly, Tori almost forgot the conditions under which she was visiting Marcus Chancelor's rooms. Certainly, anyone hearing him speak to her thus would find it hard to believe he wished himself rid of her.

Scarblade walked up the flight of stairs and opened the door with a key. She found it surprising that a gentleman like Marcus Chancelor would give a highwayman access to his living quarters. With a start she suddenly realized she hadn't contemplated the implications of Lord Rawlings' upstanding Master Chancelor consorting with a rogue like Scarblade. Perhaps Lord Fowler-Greene was correct in saying Lord Rawlings was foolish to defend the stranger to the House of Lords.

Tori had never been in rooms which were let to respectable boarders and she found herself pleasantly surprised that they should be so clean and well kept. They were furnished simply and yet stylishly, seeming to reflect quality more than obvious wealth. They were certainly better than Dolly's quarters!

She went to the window that faced the street and looked down into the park across the way. It was empty of people, owing no doubt to the snow, but she could imagine that in fair weather it would be buzzing with activity.

"Planning your escape?" came a deep voice from behind her.

"Indeed not, at least not until I've had my bath!" She turned to face him and was startled by the presence of a stranger in the room. It was a full moment until she realized she was looking into a mirror and the strange young man she saw was none other than herself.

Marcus watched her and realized the reason for her amazement. "Why, with your appreciation for men, surely you approve of your appearance?"

Tori faced him with more than her usual grace and femininity, as if trying to compensate for the boyish figure she cut. "Sir, I'll not argue with you while I'm so unfortunately at a disadvantage. After my bath and toilet I'm sure you'll find I have the edge."

With a churlish grin Scarblade thought, The knights had their armor, the redskins their war paint, and women their own particular battle garb.

A shy knock sounded on the door and he bid the person to enter. The housemaid stood there, dressed in her blue-and-white-striped muslin apron and snowy white mobcap. "The water for the bath, sirs," she meekly volunteered, stepping over to a screen that hid the gleaming copper tub. Three footmen entered the room and hastened over to the bath and poured in great pails of steaming water which they conveyed on a wheeled cart. When the bath was full, they left, pulling their forelocks in salute to Scarblade. When the maid attempted to leave he stopped her. "You'll be attending the young lady to her bath."

The young maid looked around the room inquisitively, then looked back with a question in her eyes. "This young lady, Emmy. Take off your cap."

Tori pulled the cap from her head, her golden hair falling almost to her waist. A slight gasp escaped the maid's lips, but so well trained was she that she asked no questions.

"The lady and myself have had a long, hard ride, and in this murderous snow. The lady felt it best to don the warmer clothing of a young man."

Another glance from the bright, intelligent eyes of

Emmy told Tori that Scarblade's story seemed plausible enough to her. As a housemaid she had seen many strange things, and a lady dressed as a boy did not head the list.

"I have faith the lady will have no further use for the costume, Emmy," Scarblade said congenially, "so I'll wait outside the door, and when she disrobes you can hand me her clothes." He produced the bundle that included Tori's gown and handed it to Emmy. "Have the laundry maids press these and make them presentable."

"Aye, sir," Emmy answered. And if she were puzzled by the strange request to relieve Tori of her clothing, she said nothing.

Once Tori was submerged in the hot water of her bath, she cleared her mind of all her worries. She had resented Scarblade leaving her without a stitch to wear, but she saw he had come to a solution to his problem of her trying to escape. Now he could go about his business without fear. Where could she go for help if she were stark naked? Certainly Emmy would be of no assistance.

Emmy returned with the iridescent green gown and its voluminous petticoats freshly pressed. In the maid's absence, Tori had washed her hair, and now she requested Emmy to pour fresh water over her head so she could rinse it free of the soap. The water in the pail had cooled and Tori shrieked with surprise.

The two girls found themselves laughing in delight, and from there the conversation went easily. Tori listened to Emmy as she spoke of the young man she hoped to marry. "I suppose, miss, that you and Master Chancelor are planning to marry. I saw the gleam in his eye when he looked at you," she giggled. "I wish me Jimmy would look at me tha' way."

"Oh, no, Emmy we're not . . ." Tori stopped in midsentence, a look of astonishment on her clean, scrubbed face. "Who did you say, Emmy?"

"Why, Master Chancelor! If I may say so, the kitchen maid and laundry maids are all agog over 'im. Oooh, I wish me Jimmy had some o' his looks, I do. Just t'other day I wuz saying to me mum . . ."

Tori withdrew into her own thoughts, trying to set the pieces right in her mind. Could it be? Was Emmy correct? Tori knew the girl had no reason to lie to her, and certainly she wasn't stupid. Scarblade was Marcus Chancelor, the man responsible for her predicament! She laughed aloud, seeing the humor in her situation. Marcus Chancelor, because of him her father had lost favor with the Crown. Because of him she had been forced into that impossible match with Lord Fowler-Greene. Because of Marcus Chancelor she had sought out Dolly and arranged to play out the deception on Lord Fowler-Greene. And now, because of Marcus Chancelor, she was being held a prisoner in a camp of highwaymen!

Her laughter bordered on hysteria and Emmy became alarmed. "Oh, miss, what's wrong? What can I do for ye?"

Regaining her control, Tori said sharply, "Hurry, Emmy, get me the towels. I must make myself ready for Master Chancelor when he arrives. I want to 'surprise' him!"

Emmy hurried to do the lady's bidding. The miss was certainly upset about something! And Emmy hadn't liked the way she had said the word 'surprise'!"

As Tori dried her hair she sat on the chair near the window looking out at the falling dusk. When the footmen came to empty the copper tub, Emmy had shielded Tori from their view with the screen.

"I hope I didn't upset your ladyship by anything I said," Emmy said apologetically.

"Not at all, Emmy. If anything, you've put my mind at ease about a number of things."

"Well, I wouldn't like to think Master Chancelor would be displeased by your ... er, surprise, him being such a nice gentleman and all."

"Have no worry, Emmy, the surprise I plan for Master Marcus Chancelor will certainly please him. You see, I plan to be at my best this evening. I shall dazzle him with my charms, entertain him with my wit, and flatter him with my attention. Why I daresay the man will be beside himself with pleasure!" Tori smiled wickedly to herself.

Behind the screen Emmy shrugged her shoulders in bewilderment. Somehow she was terribly glad she and her Jimmy were not of the gentry. Being quality folk must complicate one's life.

Marcus dismounted and tied his great chestnut to the hitching post outside Lord Fowler-Greene's home. He took the steps up to the door two at a time, his heels making a clicking sound on the recently shoveled porch. As Marcus was about to touch the ornate brass knocker, Lord Fowler-Greene's manservant pulled open the door.

"Milord, Lord Fowler-Greene awaits you, he's in the library."

Marcus wasted no time in getting to the library. He threw open the room's heavy oak doors to find Lord Fowler-Greene sitting in what Marcus supposed was his favorite chair, leafing through an old, dusty volume from the shelves. Immediately upon seeing Marcus, the lord rose and approached him, extending his hand in welcome. "Marcus, this is indeed an unexpected surprise."

Marcus smiled and returned the hearty handshake. "I came to tell you I'll soon be leaving England. I want to thank you on behalf of Chancelor's Valley for all you've done for us."

" 'Twas hardly enough; the pleasure was mine, I assure you." In truth the lord had taken a great liking to Marcus and was exceedingly sympathetic to the needs in the colonies. Marcus brought Lord Fowler-Greene up to date on his activities, omitting any mention of the girl he kept prisoner.

They shook hands, and Marcus, sending him one last salute, left the library, closing the doors behind him.

He was eager to get back to his rooms. He knew the girl well enough not to give her too much leeway. He heard a sound behind him and turned, stunned to see Dolly tripping lightly down the stairs.

"Scarblade, Scarblade!" she cried, hurrying toward him to throw herself into his arms. "Ain't it wonderful?

Imagine me here in this place! The gods have surely been kind to yer old friend Dolly."

"Dolly," Marcus asked incredulously, "is it really you?"

"Aye. Look at me, have ye ever seen me looking so grand? Did you know I'm now Lady Fowler-Greene? Can you imagine?" Marcus noticed Dolly's speech seemed a bit stilted, but he also noticed that her diction had certainly improved from the heavy cockney.

"Are you now Lady Fowler-Greene? I'd heard the lord had married, and a love match at that, but I'd not heard he'd fallen for a serving wench from the Owl's Eye Inn. I'd no idea the lord even frequented a hole such as that."

"Shhh!" Dolly cautioned. "I'm being kept under wraps, at least until I've learned the manners of a lady and can speak like one, too. Oh, 'Blade, 'tis long hard days Oi—I—" she corrected herself, "I put in learning how to act the lady with Lady Helen as my teacher." Her lip curled with she mentioned her sister-in-law.

"But how did you come to find yourself married to a lord?"

"You'll think me daft," Dolly laughed. "Come into the breakfast room and I'll tell you all about it."

Tori, looking resplendent in her gown, was standing before the mirror when Marcus strode into the room. He stopped for a moment as he caught sight of her. The wide, low cut of her neckline revealed her smooth, white shoulders and accentuated the curving fullness of her bosom and long slim throat. The color of the dress turned her freshly washed hair, which was artfully arranged atop her head, to a paler shade of gold. Emmy, experienced housemaid that she was, had deftly used a curling iron to produce thick, glossy ringlets over Tori's left ear.

Marcus found himself bewitched by the amazing difference in Tori's appearance. Tori shivered under his scrutiny. Gallantly he reached to the bed for a rich velvet cloak and deftly draped it about her shoulders. Nuzzling her ear, he said in a low, throaty tone, "What a bewitching bandit you make, Dolly, a vixen in velvet."

"Don't you approve, milord?" Tori asked, a ripple of delight singing through her. Her thoughts were becoming muddled. Must he stand so close?

"Oh yes, madam. I approve heartily!"

"Good! I most want to please you!" she answered waspishly, her sarcastic tone bringing some semblance of composure to her.

Seeing her fully dressed, Marcus was disconcerted. His business with Lord Fowler-Greene had taken longer than expected. He hadn't thought to tell Emmy not to bring in the lady's clothes until he returned. "You had your opportunity to escape, why didn't you?"

"I promised, milord," Tori replied sweetly. For the moment she was shaken. What was wrong with her? She hadn't even thought of escaping! It wasn't her promise that kept her here, she realized; it was her determination to 'surprise' Marcus Chancelor. Fool! she rebuked herself, too besotted with your scheme to take advantage of an ideal opportunity!

Coming further into the room, Marcus spied the copper tub refilled with steaming water. Angrily, he realized he didn't know what to do with the girl while he himself bathed.

Seeing his glance at the bath, Tori guessed what was on his mind. "We can set the screen up around the tub, milord, and I can sit in the far corner of the room whilst you bathe."

"I assure you, Dolly—" he said the name mockingly— "it wasn't my modesty I was thinking of; in fact, I may decide you should scrub my back!" Marcus cast her a distrustful look. What would prevent her from running out of the room while he was so conveniently indisposed?

"I promise I'll not try to run away," Tori sputtered, a little worried that he might actually be uncourtly enough to strip and bathe in front of her. "Haven't I already had my golden opportunity?" she argued, then insisted, "I didn't take advantage of it, did I? I've given my word as a lady, and I mean to keep it."

In actual fact, Tori played the idea over in her mind, mulling the possibilities of a successful escape. But all the while carbon-black eyes swam before her and she admitted the horrible truth to herself that she did not want to be free of this Marcus Chancelor. She would rather ride the roads with a band of thieves than deny herself ever seeing Scarblade again, ever feeling his strong arms about her and his lips pressed hard against hers.

Quickly turning away from him to hide the blush suffusing her face, she sat meekly in a far corner of the room while Marcus hurriedly bathed and dressed. When he stepped out from behind the screen, Tori was pleasantly surprised by the handsomeness of his appearance. The dark stubble of beard was cleanly removed, as were the dirty garments he had worn. Here before her stood a gentleman dressed in fine evening wear. The black of his coat was set off by the blue brocade of his waistcoat and the pristine whiteness of his cravat.

Her eyes raked over him and she saw him smiling strangely at her, the scar on his cheek giving him a rakish look.

Quickly she hid her admiration and busied herself with her ribbons. Marcus came and stood close behind her, putting his hands lightly on her waist. "You're lovely, really." Inhaling deeply of her womanly scent, he kissed her warmly on the shoulder.

Tori turned to face him. "How kind of you to say so, milord. And may I say you also cut a fine figure. It would seem we are quite a stunning pair," she teased, "I being the better, of course."

The shared laughter eased the strain between them, and after seeing to a few details, they left for an evening at the opera.

Marcus had hired a coach for the evening. Once settled within, Tori braved a question. "When am I to meet your friend, Master Chancelor?"

He did not honor her with an answer, if indeed he had one. He merely sat across from her, his knees occasionally touching hers with the rocking of the carriage, and stared at her.

Knowing when to give over, Tori sat silently for the remainder of the trip to the inn where they were to have dinner.

Sitting in a secluded corner of the dining room, Tori looked across at Marcus with a penetrating gaze that made him uncomfortable. He would not forget the impact their arrival had on the other patrons. Several gentlemen seated in a group had turned and stared pointedly at Tori when she entered. A low murmur of conversation swept the room, and soon it was apparent the gentlemen were very envious of Marcus's position as Tori's escort. The ladies present also turned to appraise the charms of this woman who could create a stir among their men.

Tori had also noticed the stir their arrival had created. She swelled with pride at being the envy of the other ladies who had to content themselves with pasty-looking, nondescript suitors and spouses. She knew they would have gladly traded places with her to be in the company of a handsome, rugged, well-dressed gentleman with licorice-black eyes.

Marcus gave his order to the servant and turned his full attention on Tori. "Have you ever been to the opera . . . Dolly? It seems odd to call you by that name; it's certain you are anything but a tavern wench, much as you would have me believe otherwise."

Tori looked up at him through her long, thick lashes, noting the effect this wile had on him. "I think, since we are to be friends, we must know each other's true names, Marcus Chancelor. I am Victoria Rawlings. My close friends and family call me Tori."

He raised an eyebrow. "So . . . Miss Rawlings, is it?"

Now that he knew the elegant Miss Rawlings was no spy, the following day's tasks would be much easier. And that witch Dolly . . . Lady Fowler-Greene. The two of them, Miss Rawlings and Dolly . . . birds of a feather. Still, he tried to control the shock he felt at her words. He had not expected that she would learn his identity. "I might have expected Emmy would mention my name. Yes, it's true, my name is Marcus Chancelor." Before she could utter the question which came to her lips, Marcus leaned forward and told her the reason for assuming a pseudonym. When he had completed his story, he was touched by the sparkle of tears he noted in Tori's eyes.

"So now you know the reason for my robbing and plundering, as you so aptly refer to it. But Tori," he cautioned, the sound of her name on his lips giving her an unexpected thrill, "you must always refer to me as Scarblade, at least in front of the men at camp. Not even they know my true identity. It's much safer for the plan; the less they know the better the chances of getting the money back to North Carolina. Only Josh, who has known me since I was a boy, knows the truth."

Tori agreed, although why she could not say. She should be furious with Marcus Chancelor. Were it not for him, she reasoned, she would not find herself in her present circumstances. But something had touched her, his face when he had spoken of this far-off colony had lifted and brightened. His voice had filled with a tenderness and yearning. No, Tori wouldn't give him away, if for nothing else than to protect him from that animal Charles. Somehow Tori felt Charles might someday be Marcus's undoing. Josh seemed to believe in Marcus's cause, and that was sound enough reason for her.

After a delicious dinner, Tori and Marcus again climbed into their hired coach and rode the short distance to Covent Garden. The immense ornate doors of that famous theater stood open welcomingly. Tori had visited the Garden on numerous occasions with her parents and Granger, but this night seemed special. Now she was on the arm of a most attractive gentleman and she shone brightly under the envious glances they received.

Once or twice Tori saw recognition in the eyes of an acquaintance. At first she thought one of them might approach her till she remembered that to all concerned she was now the wife of Lord Fowler-Greene and under no circumstances would anyone call attention to the fact that the lord was being cuckolded for a gentleman so much younger and far more handsome.

Seated in a private box, Tori and Marcus listened to the ethereal strains of the music. With the lights low and the players on stage, Marcus observed his companion. She certainly was a many-faceted girl, he found himself thinking, at home here in the most popular theater in England as well as upon a horse or throwing a knife. He could not help but admire her vitality, her onward rush to meet life and enjoy it to its fullest. The candlelight played soft shadows on her face and shoulders, and he once again tasted the freshness of her skin beneath his lips. Although she was composed and sophisticated at the moment, he perceived a hint of the wildcat beneath the surface and found it fascinating.

After the opera, Marcus suggested they partake of a brandy at a nearby tavern. When she looked at him questioningly, he mentioned it was a very fashionable place to go after a performance at the Garden, and many of the society matrons went there.

"I'd really rather not, Marcus. The long ride into the city and the interminable cold has gotten the better of me, I'm afraid. Couldn't we just go back to your rooms and have a brandy there? I noticed a server on the table by the window."

Marcus smiled, the first genuine smile she had ever received from him, and Tori found herself breathless under his warm gaze. "I'm so glad you suggested we return home. I'm not very comfortable in places of fashion. I much prefer quiet and intimacy."

Tori glowed when he called his rooms "home," and wondered how it would feel if it were *their* home. All the way back Marcus and Tori sat looking out the grimy windows of the trap, marveling at how the snow could make a wonderland from the dirty city streets.

Once back in the flat, Marcus poured brandy into little tumblers. He handed her the burnished liquid and made a toast, "Farewell, Scarblade and Dolly, good cheer Tori and Marcus." Tori drank deeply, stirred by the quiet depth of his voice and the poignancy of the toast.

"I'm afraid you'll not get much sleep tonight, Tori; we must be back at camp by the morrow. But, why don't you try to get some rest? I'll wake you when it's time to leave."

Tori eyed the wide bed longingly; how long had it been since she had tucked herself under a real feather quilt? Her eyes felt heavy and she stifled a yawn. "Go on, Tori," he urged. "I'll just make myself comfortable here on the chair."

Tori smiled her agreement and stepped behind the screen in the far corner of the room to remove her gown. As she was taking down the minute hooks which fastened the gown's back, she wondered how it was that it seemed so natural to be preparing for bed with Marcus in her room. When she stepped out of her garments, she realized for the first time that she had no nightdress to wear and the billowing petticoats which had stiffened the skirt of the green silk certainly were far from suitable.

It was then that she spied one of Marcus's dress shirts hanging from the corner of the screen. A bit self-consciously, she donned the fine lawn blouse, aware of the fact that it didn't even come down to her knees.

Peeking out from behind the screen with the intention of instructing Marcus to close his eyes while she jumped into the high poster bed, she saw that he had slid down in the chair, feet outstretched, and had fallen asleep.

He looked so young, almost boyish, as he lounged there, the lines of worry gone from between his heavy, dark brows. Quietly, she stepped over to the mirror to remove the pins from her coiffure. Picking up a heavy brush from the dresser top, she stroked it through her hair, the shimmering, golden locks cascading to her waist. Pulling the brush through the last stubborn snarl, she caught a glimpse of Marcus's reflection and realized he was watching her. The image of his face as he studied her was disconcerting, and she turned her attention to removing the last few snarls, conscious all the while that his eyes were upon her.

Marcus, used to dozing lightly due to long nights on watch at the camp, had awakened to find the light from the nearby candle outlining Tori's slim woman's body through the gossamer thinness of his lawn shirt. As she lifted her arms to her head the shirt shortened to reveal lean, rounded haunches and betrayed the darker crease that separated her buttocks from her thighs.

A cascade of golden waves fell to below her waist, drawing his attention to honey-colored, lissome, smooth legs ending in neat, delicately shaped ankles. A smile played about his lips as he noticed the tightening of the muscles in her legs as she stretched herself on tiptoe to view the unrelenting snarl that defied her brush.

Tori replaced the brush on the dresser and turned to find herself locked in a warm embrace. His mouth came crashing down on hers, his arms surrounded her, pressing her closer, tighter, hurting her.

She clung to him, more for support than out of passion, the pressure of his lips forcing hers to part. Instinctively she began to draw away ... but he would not let her.

The scar deepened in color, as if burning his cheek. Marcus lifted his mouth from hers and they stared into each other's eyes. His dark gaze smouldered, penetrating into her wide, yellow-green eyes. Her face filled with wonderment and she slid into his embrace and kissed him, soaring with the glory of her passion.

He tightened his arms around her and returned her kisses with tender touches of his tongue. His hands strayed to her breasts and she welcomed his advances. Her heart pounding violently, thighs pressed against his, she became aware of his arousal.

Tori was melting, dissolving, becoming a part of him, kissing him with more and more abandon. Overcome by the passion and desire she felt for him, Tori caressed him with infinite tenderness and let the tide of her own desire carry her.

Marcus looked down into Tori's humid eyes with a questioning tenderness. With an answering look from her, he lifted her into his arms and carried her across the room to his bed.

Chapter Eighteen

"There's no other way, Josh! The girl comes with us!" Marcus's voice was unyielding, a tone he had never used with his old friend.

"She's got you bewitched, Marc. Leave her behind. I don't understand you." The giant's worried, pale-blue eyes penetrated Marcus's anger.

"I'm sorry, Josh," Marcus was contrite, "there isn't anything I wouldn't do for you, but I cannot go along with you on this. We all ride together, and that means the girl. You know as well as I do what's at stake. We can't afford any mishaps now—sailing time is too close—they already postponed the tax delivery, and I think that was due to the last robbery we committed. There's been a leak somewhere."

Marcus lifted his eyes in earnest to his old friend. "We are now well behind on the sailing. I can't afford any more delay. In four months it will be planting time, and I feel that the lives of all the people in the valley hang on my head. It's a grim business, Josh."

The bandit's eyes became hard and cold. "The snows are already here, what then? There's no place for us to winter, we have to make haste!" In a somber tone he stated again, simply, "The girl rides with us."

Josh saw the hard set of Marcus's face and knew he had lost. It was the first time Marcus did not pay heed to his advice. "Oh, the gods be with us, Marcus. Who's to tell her, you or me?"

"I leave you the honor, Josh." Marcus had no wish to gaze into those melting eyes. He needed time to keep his senses alert. Whenever he came near her he remembered the feel of her in his arms, her soft, moist mouth beneath his.

Josh nodded morosely. "First, I best ride on to the Boare Inn and see what I can smell out."

Marcus asked, "Are you well enough, Josh? You must keep your strength for what's at hand."

"Aye, I'm well enough," Josh answered, heaving himself to his feet. "If I ride now I should be back by sundown. Watch Charles, Marc. He had his eye on the girl and he means to have her one way or the other."

Marcus let his eyes go to the sleeping Charles and his brother John. Marcus, too, had seen the way Charles looked at the girl, and it rankled him more now than ever. If Charles dared to touch her he'd find himself at the business end of Scarblade's knife!

Still, Marcus could not set Tori free; too much was at stake, and he found himself reluctant to part with her. Somehow she had penetrated his reserve, inched herself beneath his skin, and he was aware of the void her leaving would create in his life.

Josh mounted his sorrel and rode quietly out of the clearing. Once on the road, he flicked the reins and the animal broke into a fast gallop, bearing the weight of Josh's huge frame with ease.

The day crawled by. The men took turns chipping wood and keeping the fire roaring. By late afternoon the skies clouded over and there was a sharp drop in the temperature. The men gathered around the fire and talked in low tones. "I think we should build a ring of fires," Marcus spoke. "If it snows—and I think it will—we're in for a spot of trouble. Let's heave to, lads, and get at the wood. No stinting now, put your backs into it. If I don't miss my guess the snow will start by nightfall."

The men muttered and grumbled but fell to the work. They had no wish to have the blood freeze in their veins.

Tori sat huddled by the fire, shivering; the thin rags she wore were no help from the cold. She wrapped a moth-eaten blanket close about her and drew her legs up to her chin. She felt hot tears sting her eyes. She longed for her bed and a warm cover over her, but most of all she wished to be far away from Marcus Chancelor—Scarblade!

Earlier in the day, Tori had watched Scarblade bending to the task of chopping wood for the fires. His

leather tunic strained over the bunching muscles in his
back, the knotted tendons in his forearms glistening
with a veil of sweat as he brought up the axe and
swung it down with a force that bit into the frozen
wood and split it with a shattering crack. The power in
his muscled torso and legs gave her a thrill of remembered intimacy.

Softly, she approached him, driven by the need to
touch him, to feel once again the hardness of his body
against hers. The shabby cloak slipped from her shoulders, the wind tumbled her hair about her head. She
reached out and touched his arm, and startled by her
coming upon him so quietly, he turned toward her. His
ebony eyes took in her full, parted lips, lids half closed
over the yellow-green eyes.

Abruptly, he pushed her away from him with such a
violence her teeth rattled. His eyes avoided hers; the
pain of rejection pricked her eyelids. In a gruff voice
he commanded her to go to her tent.

Humiliation prevented her from coming forth with
an oath. Not remembering how she had fled his accusing eyes, she lay there in her darkened tent forcing
back the tears. He had used her and she, God forgive
her, had helped him, enjoyed it, loved it! And now he
was through with her as though she were some cheap
doxy.

Oh, how I hate him! she cried silently, I hate him!
But realizing the truth for what it was, "God help me,
I love him, I love him!"

Now, when she thought of him, the name Marcus
came to her lips. But she had sworn to think of him
and refer to him as only Scarblade. This was a promise
she had no intention of breaking. Foolish and fast of
tongue she might be, but she had no stomach for being
responsible for the lives of those people in North Carolina.

Tori knew she was to ride with the men; she had
heard Marcus and Josh talking. Suddenly, for the first
time in days, she felt warm. Looking around, she saw
the fires flare up. There were eight of them spread in a
wide circle, and she could still hear the sharp ring of the

men's axes as they continued to chop wood. There
must be enough to last the night.

Marcus carried the bedrolls and deposited them inside the circle. Her breath came in quick gasps as he
sought for and found her eyes on him.

"The least you could have done, Scarblade, in your
plundering, was to steal me a fur wrap. I'm freezing,"
she said petulantly. "Do you care?" she cried. "If I
wake up frozen, I'll be on your conscience," she spat.
"That is, if you have one! What kind of man are you?
Be honest!"

Marcus stood still, his eyes glowing like coals in his
bitter face. "What do you know about honesty? You
used the name of another and have the effrontery to sit
there and tell me what I should and should not do. But
for my intervention you would be six feet under the
hard, cold ground."

Tori was undaunted. "I can take care of myself,
Scarblade. I didn't ask you to interfere in my behalf. I
didn't ask to be brought here! In fact, I tried to leave."

"So you could go straight to the sheriff's men and
turn us in. Did you expect to collect the reward?"

"Yes!" Tori snarled. "I would betray you in a moment if I believed I could get away with it. I owe you
naught! You're keeping me against my will." She
jumped up from the ground, her eyes blazing. Oh,
God, when will I learn to keep my mouth shut? she
thought. Why do I seek to hurt him? I only blacken
myself in his eyes. "Scarblade, give me a horse and I
give you my word I'll ride out of here and you'll hear
no more of me. I won't go to the sheriff, my word,"
she pleaded. He had to agree, he had to set her free, to
be away from him, to put him out of her mind if she
could.

Scarblade snorted as he stretched out his hand as if
to grab her. Tori, sensing his intention, backed off,
stumbling slightly. "Don't lay a hand on me, Scarblade!"

"I wouldn't think of it, Dolly," he mocked. "Actually I had no intention of touching you. I merely put
out a hand to feel the snow. It's started," he said as he
raised his eyes.

"So it has," Tori said quietly, knowing the hardship the weather would bring to his task.

Scarblade and the other men joined Tori in the center of the ring of fires, enjoying the blazing warmth. The hours crawled by, and Tori dozed off several times only to be awakened by the surging chill in her extremities. Her feet were colder than the snow that continued to fall in great fluffy flakes, and she was certain she could sense the beginnings of chilblains on her fingers.

Scarblade often left the warmth of the ring to walk out to the edge of the encampment, no doubt to listen for the approach of Josh. It had been too many hours since he had left to attend to his mission, and it was clear that Scarblade was sorely worried. Tori, too, was apprehensive about Josh's safety. His condition had worsened due to the cold and lack of substantial food.

Darkness had long since fallen and Scarblade could wait no longer for Josh. Arousing the grumbling men with the toe of his boot, he commanded them to ready their horses to make a search for his friend.

"Wha' o' th' girl?" John asked. "Are ye goin' ta take 'er wi' ye?"

Scarblade turned and noted the expression of worry in Tori's face. "What of it, Dolly?" he asked, his concern masking the challenge in his eyes. "Will you wait here for Josh's return, for it would seem he met with a mishap along the way. He'd never be so long in returning if something hadn't happened, and if I don't miss my guess, he became too ill to continue his journey. He just might need the tender touch of a woman when we bring him back. What say you, can you be trusted?"

Tori saw the silent pleading in Marcus's eyes and felt the sharp stab of concern for Josh. "Yes, I'll be here waiting. He saw me through my illness, and I'll not run off and leave him to the rough hands of you and your men. Go and find him, Scarblade, and bring him to me."

Marcus, relieved at hearing her promise, flashed a smile. "We'll not be long, for there are only two ways to travel to where he was going." Without further words, Marcus hurried off to mount his chestnut and to begin the search.

At their leaving, Tori began the chore of stoking the fires and warming her own blankets and bedroll in expectation of Josh's arrival. He would need a warm bed and hot soup, she thought, as she began warming a kettle of beef broth. So busy at her task was she that she failed to hear the stealthy sounds of someone stalking her. An arm shot out from behind her and knocked her to the ground. She struggled in vain against the wiry strength that held her fast, forcing her over onto her back and fumbling with the wide belt she wore. Shaking the masses of hair from her eyes, she saw her attacker—Charles!

Numbly, Tori protested against the wild cruelty in his eyes, and when she struggled to gain leverage to fight him off he sent her a stinging blow to the head. Blackness threatened to engulf her and a dizziness upset her equilibrium. She felt herself swooning and vaguely thought that if she must be raped then let it be when she was unconscious and unaware of the horror that faced her.

Suddenly Charles had her by the shoulders and was shaking her, rubbing cold snow over her face. "Nah ye don', me 'igh an' mighty wench. Ye'll no' pass out an' deny me th' pleasure o' yer struggles. Cum to!" he demanded, his coarse voice raging in her ears.

Terrified, Tori gathered all her strength and frantically tried to put him off her. If she could only get to her feet she might be able to hide from him in this blinding snowstorm.

But it was not to be. Charles held her fast with the weight of his body and tore her clothes from her in a frenzy. Her shoes had come off in her struggles, and Charles had torn the shawl and thin cambric shirt from her shoulders, leaving her reddened flesh exposed to the ravages of his lips. Having no patience for her camisole, he ripped it from her while one arm was pressed against her throat, leaving Tori to gasp for air.

Shifting his weight and imprisoning her legs beneath his own, he fumbled with her belt buckle again, this time succeeding in loosening it and tearing down her trousers. His greedy, lascivious eyes shone with triumph as he proceeded to undo his own trousers.

Tori swore and cursed, words she had not known she knew. She was fighting, struggling to gain a grasp on her attacker, aiming with clawlike hands for those horrible glittering eyes.

A sound behind her and Charles ceased his attack, a fearful, terrified expression like that of a trapped animal on his face.

Slowly, he backed off her, his fear so great that Tori imagined she could smell it. Pulling herself away from Charles, she looked off to where he was staring. Scarblade!

"So, Charles! It wasn't until we were well off in the opposite direction that I remembered I had left the girl here alone and unprotected. It would appear that I was correct in my concern for her!"

"Oi wuz jus' 'avin' a bit o' fun, Scarblade. Oi didn' mean no 'arm, Oi didn'. She loikes it, Oi tells ye, don' ye, Dolly, tell 'im 'ow ye loikes it!"

Charles's face was a study in terror as he begged her for aid. Seeing he was whipping a dead horse, he changed his tune. "Go on, tell 'im," he demanded. "Tell 'im 'ow this ain't th' firs' toime, 'ow there's been plenty o' toimes afore this. An' tell 'im 'ow ye loikes it rough! Won' ye tell 'im now!"

For an answer, Tori spat, her face wrought into lines of disgust and hate. Scarblade pounced on Charles, bringing a heavy fist into his face. Tori watched, mesmerized by the violence of the scuffle. Charles didn't have a chance, Scarblade was too big, too strong.

The deep-ridged scar glowed with malevolent portent as Scarblade grabbed Charles's tunic with both hands. Quickly, viciously, Scarblade drew back his right arm, his knuckles white and stark against the eerie fire's glow. There was a lightninglike blow to Charles's terror-drawn mouth, and Tori stepped backwards as the rotted stumps of Charles's teeth splintered and shattered beneath Scarblade's force.

As Scarblade whipped his hand back for a second blow droplets of crimson rained upon the flames. Tori was revolted by the sound of the spitting and hissing as the blood boiled in the fire.

Panting from the exertion of the fight, Scarblade turned to Tori, concern written in his eyes. She sat there, numb with horror and trembling with cold. She did not seem to notice Marcus as he adjusted her clothing into a more reputable state, moving her arms and legs as needed, as though she were a wooden doll.

"Tori, Tori," he called to her softly, trying desperately to break through her daze. Slowly she turned to face him, great tears falling from her wide, staring eyes. Choking sobs escaped her parted lips, deepening to wracking heaves.

Tenderly Marcus picked her up and carried her close to the fire and held her on his lap, stroking her head and whispering soft and tender words, trying to keep her from becoming hysterical. He realized how deeply affected she had been by Charles's cruelty. This was a woman who would give herself totally to a man she loved, willingly give the pleasures of her body, as he well knew. But by the same token, to be touched by someone she could not love was indeed a fate worse than death.

After a time Tori came around, her heavy, quaking sobs abating to a mild hiccoughing. "Will you be all right now?" Scarblade asked, his voice heavy with emotion. "I should have killed that bastard son of a . . ."

Tori put her cold hands to his lips and held them there. "I'm glad you didn't kill him, I wouldn't want you to have the blood of a man upon your hands for me. I promise you, I shall be fine."

Marcus could see that she spoke the truth. The color was returning to her cheeks and her lips had lost their whiteness. But her eyes were still blazing and widely staring.

"Marcus, I want you to go and look for Josh, he needs you more than I do right now. I promise you, I'll be fine." Her eyes strayed to the place where Charles had crept off, and she gave an involuntary shiver. Marcus knew it cost her much to think of Josh and be left alone.

Reading his thoughts, Tori said, "If you would leave me your pistol I'll be more careful that no one creeps up on me."

"You're a brave girl, Tori," Marcus said, his voice husky and his eyes dark and tender. Tori caught her breath and felt herself melt into his arms, but stopped herself just in time. No matter how grateful she was to Marcus for saving her from Charles's attack, she would not put herself in a position to be rejected and humiliated by Marcus still another time.

Chapter Nineteen

Marcus jumped to his feet when a sound of rushing horses entered the encampment.

It was John and Richard, leading Josh's horse with the huge man tied to the saddle. There were icicles encrusted onto his eyebrows, and Tori was sure the man's eyes were frozen shut.

Marcus grasped the big man around the shoulders as Richard held his feet. "Get him wrapped in blankets and I'll get coffee and broth into him," Tori said. "If he has a coughing spell now . . ." She didn't finish the sentence. Marcus knew what she was about to say.

Carefully he lowered Josh to the ground and quickly wrapped him in blankets which Tori had warmed by the fire.

An hour later, due to Tori's careful ministering, Josh felt his strength returning. "I feel better already, darlin'," Josh said, attempting a smile. "Let me get my breath and I'll tell you what I found out at the inn. You'll be much surprised."

The thin, swirling snow continued to fall in heavy, wet flakes. The wind howled ominously as the flames crackled.

"It will be a bastard of a storm," Scarblade said, looking thoughtfully at Josh.

"Aye, so it will," Josh murmured drowsily. "But it'll be to your advantage, Scarblade. Wait till you hear what I have to tell you."

"When you're rested, Josh. There's no hurry. There's nowhere to go this night. I want to stoke the fires and get the logs inside the circle before the snow gets too heavy. You will see to Josh, won't you . . . Dolly?" he asked in his old mocking tone.

Tori's eyes filled with tears as she looked at Josh's

still form, and for an answer to his question she raised her glistening, golden eyes to Marcus.

Josh dozed from time to time and Tori kept herself busy changing the hot rocks and pulling the worn blankets up around his neck. Soon the men had a stack of logs near each of the burning fires. They came stomping cold feet to stand next to Josh and silently wish his speedy recovery.

Some time after Tori had made Josh as comfortable as possible, she was aware that Charles had crept from the frozen woods close to a warming fire. His brother John was tending the wounds he had suffered from Marcus's battering fists. The brothers cast menacing looks in Marcus's direction, and John, being the bolder for not having met Marcus in open confrontation, was intoning whispers to Richard, who had obligingly melted snow to bathe Charles's face. Richard and John engaged in a brief difference of opinion, Richard no doubt defending his leader Scarblade.

Spitting into the fire and scowling at John, Richard rose to his feet and moved to another of the crackling fires to join Ned.

Tori experienced a sense of shame to be fought over like some bitch in heat, and she quickly reviewed her past actions, wondering if somehow she had given justification for Charles's attitude. Instinctively, she knew he was not finished with her and that Scarblade too had not yet felt the strength of his revenge.

Later Tori ladled out the hot broth to the men, John taking a bowl to Charles, and refilled their cups with strong coffee. Marcus observed the four small rabbits on the stick as they roasted. It would have to be enough.

The skimpy meal over, the men retired to the fires, wrapping themselves in blankets and huddling together. The snow had now turned to blinding swirls as the wind howled. "The wolves will be out soon," Scarblade said to Tori. She raised her startled eyes to meet his. "They won't come near the fires," he said reassuringly. "I've seen them make a ring outside a fire, though."

Tori shuddered. There was no hint of mockery in his tone and she believed him. Tales of the wolves Tori had heard came spiraling back to her in full horror.

The firelight dealt kindly with Josh's features, and he appeared less ravaged. Tori admired this kind, wise man. It wasn't really anything he said or did, it was the man himself. He most truly believed in what he was doing. She had caught snatches of his conversations with Marcus about the people in America. "My people," Josh had said. His and Marcus's people. Tori knew their people were starving.

When Marcus had spoken of the small children going hungry her stomach had heaved as she remembered the elaborate banquet that must have been served at the wedding feast. Half the food would have been wasted. To think that small children were starving made her want to cry. With this heavy thought she dozed off.

Suddenly Tori was awakened by some strange sound. Peering out past the fires into the darkness, Tori found herself staring at diminutive winking lights. It was a full moment before she realized they were the eyes of animals reflecting the blazing fires. Low, whining, grumbling sounds filtered by the falling snow and howling wind fell on her ears. Her flesh crawled and she shivered with fear. The wolves, she thought, terrified. Then, remembering Marcus saying they would never go beyond the outer fires, she calmed. Odd, she thought, how much I trust him.

Leaning over Josh at dawn's first, feeble light, Tori cradled the great leonine head to her bosom and removed the sweat-soaked rags from beneath it. The cold was making them stiff with frost and they cracked in her fingers as she exchanged them for dry ones.

"Pray tell, lass, why do I find myself in this compromising position? What will the men think?"

Tori flushed a bright crimson and her eyes sparkled. "Ah, Josh, by your tone I can tell you're feeling better. I'm so glad," she said sincerely. "What do I care about what the men think? They think the same thoughts regardless. They're a pack of jackals, the lot of them. How you and Scarblade ever became mixed with them is beyond me. Lay still, Josh, I'll get you some hot coffee."

"Scarblade! Come here!" Josh called, and when Marcus was near, said, "I best be telling you the news

I picked up at the Boare Inn yesterday. I'll be speaking softly, so listen carefully."

"Do you want me to leave?" Tori asked hesitantly.

"There's noplace to go, lass," Josh said as he looked at the swirling snow. "Stay. You might as well hear now as later." Marcus agreed, and Tori settled herself next to Josh and sipped her coffee.

"While at the Boare I heard the men talking about the taxes being collected. Did ye know, Marcus, that this year they were doubled?"

"Doubled?" Marcus exclaimed in surprise. "Why?"

"It seems our good King George has left boyhood behind him. It's amazing how the price of wenching doubles and triples in those advanced years."

"I see," Marcus laughed. "So we shall find ourselves that much richer. Good!"

"A little after the noon hour two of the sheriff's men who collected the taxes stopped for some ale. I listened quite openly. They didn't seem afraid to speak. Right cocky they were. One of the men, evidently not used to drinking ale, got in his cups sooner than the other and they began to argue about the delivery. The sober one kept saying they prayed for snow so that their route would be disguised." Marcus looked perplexed.

"I couldn't figure it out at first myself," Josh laughed. "Seems they know if it snows no one will be able to keep up with the wagons. They say the wagons are to be drawn by a team of six horses, the King's own horses. I tell you, Marcus, me lad, I found it hard not to laugh in their faces. The wagons, carrying heavy loads, will have to move slowly. We'll have all the speed on our side." He craned his neck. "And they won't be able to see us for the swirling snow. In minutes we'll be covered with snow ourselves, and we'll blend in with the landscape. The wagons, on the other hand, will leave deep ruts. What d'you think?"

Marcus shrugged. "How much of an armed guard is there? Do you think they're expecting any trouble?"

Josh answered, "Aye. They've one man to ride point. John can overtake him at the bend by Cutters' farm. There's to be the driver and an armed guard waiting atop the coach. Crack shots, both of them!" Josh added gloomily. "There's to be four wagons in all. That makes a total of twelve men and the one riding point. There're only six of us, counting the girl, seven."

"And the route, Josh? Which is it? Is it the one we marked on the map?"

"Aye, one and the same. And I know the route and lanes like the back of me hand. There's not a place for a one of them to sidetrack us."

"What of a trap? Could there be more of the King's men waiting in the ambush anywhere along the way?"

"I think not. If so, the men were not told of it. They couldn't wait to tell how carefully this route had been set up. No, they would have bragged of it. I think you have the inside track. 'Tis a daring deed we do, and if caught . . ." He drew his fingers across his neck in a slicing gesture.

"There's no other way, Josh. Let's have no second thoughts now. What time are the coaches to leave?"

"Right now! Dawn! That gives us three hours till they hit Cutters' farm. We have to make our move then and be quick about it. From there it's another hour's ride in normal weather to the wharf. We load the casks, and that's the end of it. But it may take two, three hours if this weather keeps up. Best be prepared!"

Marcus sat hunched against the weather, his face cold and unreadable. Josh and Tori sat silently watching him.

"It sounds too easy, Josh. I feel there is a trap somewhere."

"Ye be wrong, Marc. In this weather how could there be? Ye can't see your hand in front of your face."

"If there is a trap, we'll just have to take over the wagons and assume the positions of the guards. I have an idea swimming around in my head," Marc said, glancing at Tori. "But we'll only use it if necessary."

Tori, noticing Marcus's look at her, shuddered with fear—was she to be the decoy?

Chapter Twenty

The snow swirled and spat above the dancing, roaring fire. Tori sat huddled by the blaze and watched the emotions flicker across Marcus's face. He looked terribly worried.

He rose to his feet and walked over to replenish the smaller fires and to stir the men.

"I feel a bit like a newborn babe," Josh said with a wan smile. "Or else I'm developing sea legs in anticipation of our journey." He pulled his cloak close around him and rubbed his hands together. Tori stood shivering and tried to wrap the thin blanket securely around her sparse frame. Finally, with much tugging and struggling, she had it wrapped to her satisfaction. Her thoughts went to the ermine-lined cloak, and for a second she could almost feel its warmth and the softness caress her body.

Marcus led the horses to the outer circle of the fires and directed the men to tie ropes securely from one saddle to the next. They would have to ride in a straight line so as not to get lost in the snow. It was blinding. It would be almost impossible to keep one's eyes open. He felt a momentary twinge as he watched Josh and the girl mount the horses. Josh's great sorrel snorted and pawed the ground. Josh would ride the lead, as he said his horse could make the trip blindfolded. Marcus hoped he was right, this had to go off as planned, time was so short.

Tori cast a backward glance at the small ring of fires. For a second she felt a pang at leaving the clearing. I must be mad, she thought to herself. I'm on my way home! Still, somehow she felt an aching loss.

For close to two hours the small band headed into the wind and the heavy snow. Josh rode with his head hunched in his cloak. Everyone followed blindly. Sud-

159

denly the sorrel halted and Josh called back to Marcus, " 'Tis the fork. If there is to be a trap, it will be over the rise. What is it to be, Scarblade?"

"Keep going," Marcus shouted to be heard over the wind. "If they're camped there, they'll have to have some kind of fire."

"You'll see the smoke and smell it," Josh called back, "the winds will carry it to us."

"Keep going!" was the command Josh shouted as he prodded the sorrel gently. The snow was getting deeper by the hour. Progress was almost at a crawl.

The small party rode silently, each busy with his own thoughts. Tori let her mind wander to happier days when she was a child and had nothing to occupy her mind but flights of fancy.

Marcus prayed silently that Josh would be fit enough to make it to the ship alive and well.

Josh had thoughts only of trying to fight down the ache in his chest. Warm climates and sunshine loomed so far away on the horizon that he felt he would never see them again. "I will," he said determinedly. "I have to!"

Charles rode behind the hunched figure of Tori. Soon as they made the camp this night, he would satisfy his want of her once and for all. Josh would be too sick by then to interfere. He would kill Scarblade if he had to. He shrugged deeper into the cloak and felt warm at the thought.

John and Ned and Richard had no thoughts other than how to spend the gold they were to have as their share.

The sorrel came to a stop and reared on its hind legs. He pawed the ground and snorted fearlessly. Marcus slid from the chestnut he rode and trudged to Josh.

"You were right, Scarblade. There's a camp over there, beyond the hill. How many, lad?"

"Probably a dozen. They know we ride only six. They probably figure that two to one of us. The odds are not good, Josh. I have a plan." Quickly he told Josh, who shook his head vehemently. "They'll kill her. They wouldn't be feeble-minded now! What would a lone girl be doing out here in such a storm? Use your head!"

Marcus shook his head stubbornly. "I am using my head. It's the only way. She has to be the bait! She's a fair-looking lass. Their first thoughts will be to have a little fun. 'Tis too cold for anything else. When she has them all around her we'll just have to make the best of it, and from what I've seen, she'll manage. There's no other way, Josh. You know that. We can't have come this far to lose now."

"What if the girl wasn't here?" Josh asked stubbornly. "What then?"

"There's no time to worry about what might have been. This is now, Josh, we must act now! I'll get the girl."

Back hunched against the wind, Marcus sought Tori. His heart thudded dully within him, the cords in his throat constricted into tight knots. Harshly, he accused himself. He was a man used to enjoying a woman's charms and not suffering a moment's conscience. But Tori was different, she wasn't a woman to be used and cast carelessly aside. She was the kind of woman a man marries. And I'm not a marrying man, he rebuked himself, remembering the conversation he had had with Myles Lampton and Samuel before he left for England. To find a woman who contradicts all I've said about her sex. One to offer a great sacrifice for another. To snatch her up and carry her off to the valley.

With these thoughts, Marcus trudged back to Tori and, quickly and in cold tones, outlined his plan. To his surprise, she accepted readily. "Can you do it?" His ebony eyes bore into hers and a shadow of regret dimmed their brightness. He hated having to entreat her to do this, but he knew no other solution.

Tori recognized the shadow in his eyes for what it was and lowered her gaze, not daring to probe deeper into those night-dark mirrors, not daring to listen to her heart which was beating a tattoo of *He cares! I know he cares for me!* Lips trembling and choking back tears, Tori nodded her agreement.

What difference did it make what she did? Sometime within the last hour she had become convinced that she would never get home alive. If she could in some way help the people of Chancelor's Valley, she would.

Marcus untied the rope tethering her horse and led her to the front of the line. "There is one thing I must tell you, Tori." He hesitated for a second.

Tori looked across at the man who sat next to her astride his own steed. She saw the look of hopelessness that was beginning to cloud the handsome looks of the notorious Scarblade. "They may shoot me down," he said.

She held in her tears. "I knew that the moment you explained the situation to me. I pray that you succeed in your mission. And if it is not too forward of me, would you perhaps do me one last favor?"

Marcus swallowed back a lump in his throat and nodded.

"Take care of Josh and see that he gets to that ship of yours." Before Marcus could reply Tori had spurred the horse and was off, leaving Marcus squinting into the driving snow that concealed her as effectively as the damask curtains surrounding a marriage bed.

Anger coursed through him with such a red-hot fire that he gasped. To have to be put in such a position that he sent a mere girl out to do a man's job and probably to be killed. He couldn't think of that. There were hundreds of lives that depended on him. Other young girls and small children. He could not let her color his thinking. Josh sighed mightily as he brought his steed abreast of Marcus.

"Don't think, Marcus! You were right! There was no other way." He could not resist adding, "You were wrong, Marc, only about the girl. Too long you have carried the worries of that young colony on your shoulders; and while they are broad, there is always someone willing to help. The girl has proved that!" He motioned with his hand and the men dismounted, their pistols drawn. Slowly they crept forward in the deep snow.

A shot rang out, splitting the frozen silence with a crack. Josh forcibly restrained Marcus while Charles whispered quietly to the men.

"Easy does it, lads. Not a sound now. We form a

half-circle. Fire quick and fast. There will be no second chance."

Vehmently clutching Charles's arm Marcus whispered, "No killing."

" 'Tis too late for that, Scarblade!" Charles muttered through his swollen, broken mouth that bore the mark of the brutal beating he had received the day before. "It's either kill or be killed!" The other man nodded.

Marcus knew he was outnumbered. He tried again. "Then try to wound only, I want no killing on my soul."

" 'Tis your soul ye be worryin' about, izzit, Scarblade? I'm not!"

Josh crawled back to the small half-circle of men. "There be eight of them, Scarblade, and the girl is sitting by the fire. What do you think? I swear she has them bewitched." Suddenly he chuckled at the expression on his friend's face.

Within minutes it was over. Charles, with the stealth of a cat, had two heads together and gave them a vicious crack. Josh had one man's neck in the crook of his arm. Ned, Richard, and John stood silently with drawn pistols. The five Royal guards surrendered and laid down their weapons.

Scarblade, heaving a sigh, thanked God there had been no killing. "Quickly now, bind them and leave them by the fire," he ordered John. "Before we go have one of the men replenish the fire and bind them loosely enough so they can free themselves after a time."

Scarblade looked into the cold, hostile eyes of Victoria Rawlings and felt a strange emotion rise up in his chest. The gold-green eyes appeared sleepy and feline in the firelight. She lowered her eyes and struggled to her feet.

Well done, Tori, she said to herself. What had she expected? A pretty "thank you," perhaps? Perhaps just one kind word. She waited. There was some strange look on the man's face, a look she could not fathom.

Josh shouted to be heard over the roaring flames and the driving snow. "This man," he said, jabbing a huge hand at a trussed form by the fires, "says that if we ride south we should overtake the wagons in an hour's time." He lowered his voice so that only Marcus could hear. "Then we would be at best another two hours' ride from the ship."

"If it is south, then we ride north," Scarblade said suddenly. "I had a feeling they would change the route. Persuade him, Josh, gently that is, for the truth."

" 'Tis the truth," Josh roared. "A smashed nose and a few missing teeth were all it took to convince him. We ride south. It'll still be only an hour's ride. 'Tis an uphill grade and the wagons will be heavy."

"Change horses with these men; ours are worn and we have many more hours of travel." Scarblade's voice boomed, and the small band of men hurried to obey their leader.

Josh shook his head and patted his sorrel lovingly and said the horse could ride for days. He would never leave her behind. " 'Tis the only thing I've left," he stated simply.

In the confusion of leading the string of horses to be changed no one noticed Tori as she struggled, her left arm hanging limply as she tried to mount the beast assigned her. She gritted her teeth and gave a great lunge and sat slumped over, breathing heavily, eyes glazed with pain.

Tori had followed Marcus's plan to the letter. She had trudged through the snow toward the guards' encampment, brazenly allowing the twigs and roots which lay beneath the snow to crack under her weight. Marcus had instructed her not to come upon the King's men suddenly—she was to give them some warning of her approach. But Marcus had not known the conditions of the guards. He could not have known that they were frozen with the cold and starved from lack of provisions and frightened for their lives, owing to their solemn responsibility for the tax shipment.

Tori hadn't even heard the report of the pistol. She was only aware of the young, half-starved, terror-stricken face of the guardsman, who in his panic, had shot blindly into the brush. When the small platoon of soldiers came to their senses they flushed the underbrush and found Tori. Roughly, they pulled her to her feet and dragged her close to the fire, where they forced her to sit. They began an interrogation and were waiting for her answer when Marcus and his men broke into their camp.

Carefully, she placed her hand inside the worn blanket she used as a cape, and it came away red and sticky, as she had known it would. She felt faintly sick and a little dizzy. Again she gritted her teeth, thinking, hoping, it was only a flesh wound.

Again the small band rode into the driving snow. Tori felt her arm going numb and gratefully admitted the absence of all feeling was better than the pain.

The string of horses plodded onward. From time to time the snow would let up and one rider would be able to see the rider in front of him. Then the swirling snow would come faster, blinding the men and the lone girl. The cold crept into their bones, locking their joints as they sat huddled on the slow-moving horses.

Tori sat her beast and suffered moments when she had to fight mightily to keep from slipping to the ground. She swayed dizzily as a violent gust of wind almost knocked her from the horse. Her breath seemed to freeze in the very air. The horse halted, and she sat silently and waited, cold and frozen, praying no one would ask her to dismount.

Josh sat slumped in the saddle. Marcus slid from his horse and plowed through the knee-deep snow. "What is it, Josh?"

"The wagons are ahead of us, at a dead stop. See the ruts? Methinks one of the wagons has a broken hub. I've been watching the tracks and I can see the way it weaves. The only thing I'm not sure of is which wagon it is; if it's the middle one then it will be all right. 'Tis hard to tell, but I know from the way their tracks freshen that they're at a standstill."

Marcus, eyes narrowed in the driving snow, said, "Then we'll have to go on foot."

"I don't know, Marc; I'm frozen fair. If it comes to a fight the men will be no better than I. We may come out second best," Josh murmured.

"Aye, Josh, but on the other hand, those men are just as cold as we are. Their arms will bend just as use-

lessly as ours. We'll do the best we can; we'll creep up
and take the last wagon and work from there. Silence
is the keyword. Let the girl stay on her horse."

The men trudged in a tight group to the stalled wagons. Scarblade waved his arm to the men as a signal to
follow, then drew his pistol. "We have surprise on our
side; by now they are no doubt sure that there will be
no trouble. Easy now."

For a man of his height and bulk he crept with
phenomenal grace through the deep snow. The men
followed in his tracks.

"Look, Josh," Scarblade whispered. "The canvas
canopy is frozen over. They can't see outside. Just pray
that the hatch at the rear is not frozen shut. That will
give us the most trouble. If it is, then I'll have to shoot
off the latch. You'd better be there with drawn pistols
and," he added ominously, "be prepared to use them if
necessary."

The men crouched low in the deep snow and advanced slowly to the wagons. Josh, in the lead, was the
first to approach the door. Crouched low, he peered at
the latch. He bent closer; the ice was encrusted over
the whole frame. Cautiously, he tried the handle: it
didn't move. He crouched silently and thought for a
moment. There was no sound from the coach. He held
one large hand up in warning and suddenly gave the
lock a vicious crack and at the same time grasped the
handle. The King's men inside, sitting near frozen all in
a huddle in a vain attempt to keep warm, were taken
by surprise.

Josh had the pistol aimed at the men in a second.
There was no time for the men to try for their own pistols.

Marcus, entering the coach behind Josh, dragged the
men from their positions and shoved them into the
snow toward Charles and the men.

"Bind them well, but leave enough slack so they can
free themselves later. Quietly now," he whispered. "A
sound from you and you'll get a bullet for your reward." The men looked with glazed eyes into the cold,
hostile ones of the man with the blazing scar on his

cheek. One of the King's guards was heard to gasp in fear, "Scarblade!"

Once the guard was bound and securely locked within the coach, Scarblade's men advanced on the next coach. It lurched in a sickly way to the side. It was the one with the first wagon. The guards were in a near stupor. They offered no resistance. "They'll be dead in another few hours," Josh cautioned to the men. "So will the others. You cannot last in this bitter cold with nothing to warm your bones. Tying them will make no difference. There's no fight in any of them. There's nothing we can do for them. They have taken an oath to stay with the convoy and cannot leave; either way is death to them. Otherwise they would have untied the team and tried to make it to shelter on their own.

"Once the monies are gone from the coaches they can then safely untie the team and leave if they want. But," he admonished, "they have neither the strength nor the will to do it. They will lie there and die. 'Tis not our fault, Scarblade."

The third wagon held only three men, all dead. They advanced to the first and Josh drew his pistol and shot off the lock. The door swung drunkenly and he looked inside. The men lay on top of each other for warmth, their bodies covered with the fine snow that had seeped in around the canvas hood. Marcus prodded a still form on top. It rolled to the side and lay still. "He's dead. So are the others," he said as he nudged each in turn. " 'Tis a sad business. They gave their lives for the Crown. You have to admire them for that."

"Try telling that to their families when their bellies are empty," Josh almost snarled. "What will the Crown do for them then? They'll starve just like your colonists!"

"Charles," Marcus called suddenly, "untie the men from the first carriage and offer them the use of the horses. We have to do that much for them. If they reach the authorities the game will be up. But I think they will choose to stay and die. The disgrace alone would make the rest of their lives a living hell."

"All right, Scarblade," Josh spoke. "What is it we do now? How do we transport the monies to the ship?"

"We have to use the first wagon, we could never get the others free of the snow. With a mighty effort this one may be pulled free. I'll drive it with Ned. The rest of you will have to load your saddlebags and carry what you can on horseback. We take as much as we can. The rest we have to leave behind.

"I think the bulk of it may be fitted into the wagon. They only used the four wagons for protection, not so much for the weight. Let's see to it," Scarblade called. "The faster we work, the warmer we'll get. Soon we'll be sweating and then we can be on our way." Suddenly he looked upward. "The snow is letting up! Look!"

"Right you are, lad," Josh laughed. " 'Twill be easier if we can see what we are about. Let's go, lads. What do you think?" he asked, looking at Marcus. "Should we take the pouches out of the casks? 'Twill make a lighter load, and we have to use the pouches when we ride the horses."

"The lighter the load the better. Pray, Josh, that we make it. This snow is mighty deep and the horses are cold and tired."

"Aye, lad. We all best pray," Josh said soberly. "And while you see to it, I want to check the girl," he added as he turned the huge sorrel around. He looked with pity at the near frozen girl in the saddle. "We'll be moving again, lass. Do you think you can make it?"

Tori nodded wearily. She had to fight to open her eyes. "It's stopped snowing!" she said in amazement. "Were you successful, Josh? How did it go?" she asked anxiously.

"The men in the wagons are all dead or near dead."

"Then why is it we're still alive, Josh? We've been riding as many hours as the coaches."

"Ye be wrong, lass. The convoy must have started last night sometime to have gotten this far. Don't forget we did not start out till midmorning this day. Must have been all the praying I did," Josh joked.

Tori, unable to make her mouth move, just nodded. God, she was so cold, so tired and so very hungry.

Josh looked with concern at the weary girl in the saddle. "We will stop at the first station we come to.

There will be one in a short ride. Do ye think ye can last, lass?"

Tori forced her jaw muscles to work and said through clenched teeth, "I'll be all right, Josh. Shall I move up to the coaches?"

"Move the horse, lass, and shake your arms to keep the blood moving."

Tori almost laughed aloud. Move her arms! The wound must have started to bleed again; she could feel a warm stickiness inside her sleeve. "Yes," she murmured, "I'll move my arms. Gently she prodded the horse and sat numbly and cold in the saddle as the huge beast plowed through the high snow. Once by the wagons, she reined in the animal and sat watching as the men loaded the casks into the lead wagons.

Tori looked at the high snow and then at Marcus Chancelor. Feeling the girl's eyes on him, he looked up, his arms full, and almost faltered at her appearance. She looked near death's door.

"Are you all right?" he asked, concern on his face. "I wish there was room in the wagon for you, but the casks will be stacked to the very top."

Tori heaved a sigh. She could never have dismounted. She clenched her teeth and made a tight fist with her hand. Please God, she murmured silently, just help me. Let me get through the next hour and then you can let me die.

Chapter Twenty-One

"There be the inn, lads," Josh called. "We made it," he cried happily.

Marcus reined in the team and climbed down. "Let us settle in the inn before I make my way to the ship. I must warm my bones and get some food in my belly or I won't be going anywhere. We best watch our words now and be careful," Marcus admonished the men. "Bring the saddlebags into the inn and the men can have their share before I leave."

Tori sat rigid while the men dismounted. She knew she could not do it on her own. She felt strong arms lift her free of the saddle. Josh held her gently but, even so, the grip he had on her arm almost made her cry out. The color drained from her face. She swayed and would have fallen except for his hold.

" 'Twill be all right, lass. Just a few more minutes and ye'll be warm and cozy. And all the food you want. Lean on me, lass." The big man half carried her, half dragged her into the warmth of the inn.

Tori looked around as the heat struck her like a blow. The huge room was empty except for a burly man. He watched silently and suspiciously as Josh led the girl to the fire and laid her down gently. "Soon ye'll be warm," he said with a smile. "I have to help the men now. Rest."

Rest! With this throbbing arm? The pain was starting up again. She looked up and saw the innkeeper. There was something wrong with him. Narrowing her eyes, she saw he had a pistol ready. Seeing his intent, horror gripped her. God in heaven, to have come so far to have a miserable innkeeper ruin it all! Pulling herself to a sitting position, knocked her shoulder against the fire tongs.

"You can do it, you can do whatever you must!"

170

Who had said that to her? Granger? He was always telling her she could do the impossible things he outlined for her. All right, Granger. I'll do it! she thought as she gritted her teeth. The innkeeper, his eyes on the open doorway, paid the girl no heed. Tori clutched the heavy instrument in her good hand and tried to get to her feet. She managed to get herself up, but her head was spinning.

From where she stood she had a clear view of the door. She knew that the first person through it would get a bullet in his heart. She hefted the tongs with her good arm and mentally weighed her chances and those of the person entering the room. She drew her eyes from the door to the innkeeper, then back to the door, and almost fainted.

Marcus and Josh were carrying a cask between them. God in Heaven! She swayed and swung in the direction of the innkeeper. Marcus, seeing her about to fall, dropped his end of the chest and pushed John out of the way as he raced for Tori. He saw John fall to the floor, the innkeeper lifting his hand to his head and crashing down in a heap.

Marcus reached Tori just as she herself slid to the floor. Josh roared as Charles pushed him out of the way. "Oi seen it! Ye killed me brother!" he cried hoarsely. "Ye pushed 'im inta th' line o' fire ta take th' ball. Oi seen it! Oi seen it!" he kept repeating over and over.

"Ye've lost yer wits, man," Josh bellowed. "The cold has numbed yer brain. Be still till we get the right of it. What happened, Scarblade?"

Marcus, his mind in a turmoil, could only stare at the still form he held in his arms. "She tried to save us, Josh. The shot went wild and John got it. Look by the man, there's the tongs she threw. See with your own eyes."

"That's the way of it, Charles. Be still now. These wild ravings will not help John."

Charles pushed Josh out of the way. "Oi seen 'im," he said stubbornly.

"Aye! I did push him, but it was because I saw the girl about to fall," Marcus explained. "I feared she would hit her head on the hearth. It's the truth, Charles. The man shot wildly when the girl threw the tongs to save your brother and me!"

"Take the bodies into the kitchens," Josh said to Richard and Ned, who had come running into the room. "We can't give them a decent burial in this heavy snow. Cover them," he added kindly.

"Oi need no 'elp, Scarblade," Charles said sullenly, "Oi can take care o' me own, an' some others," he added softly to himself.

Josh's eyes questioned Marcus. "I don't know the why of it, Josh. Who knows what that man was thinking. We did him no harm, and from the looks of this place there's nothing to steal," Marcus said, lowering his eyes to the slight, inert form in his arms.

"She saved my life, Josh. But for her the ball that rests in John would be in me. Help me make her comfortable, then see if you can find something warm and dry to wrap her in. She doesn't look well."

"Aye lad, I was thinking the same thing myself." Soon he lumbered back to the fire, his arms full of quilts and blankets. "They be good and clean. No vermin in any of them," he said, smiling reassuringly at Marcus. Gently they lay Tori by the fire and tried to unwrap the blanket that she had wound about her.

" 'Tiz stuck to her arm, somehow," Josh said as he gave the wet blanket a tug. "Mother of God," he roared to Richard, who had come to stand by the fire. With the cloak soaked and the knife in readiness, Josh cut the caked cloth from her arm. Staring at him was a large, angry, swelling, bleeding wound. Josh gulped in sympathy. "The pain must have been unbearable," he said softly to Marcus. "We must staunch the flow of blood. Already she has lost more than can be good for her. I don't mean to be sounding cruel, Marcus, but you best be on your way. I can take care of the girl. Like you said, time is short and you're burning it. She's weak, but once the bleeding is stopped and we get something warm into her, she'll be on the mend. My word, Scarblade, she'll be fine."

Slowly Marcus rose to his feet, his eyes on Tori. His head whirled, his thoughts followed a maze. Why did this have to happen? Pain shot through him and clouded his eyes. Slowly he nodded. "Take good care of her, Josh. There is much I have to speak to her about."

With Richard's help, Tori's wound was cleaned and a dressing applied. She was swathed in blankets and laid by the fire. Josh ordered the men to find food. "Hot food and no slop," he roared.

Tori laid next to the blazing fire, dozing fitfully at first, eventually drifting off into a deep, dreamless sleep. "I tell you, Josh, there'll be trouble. Charles has gone for the sheriff. When he sneaked out, I have no way of knowing; 'twas John's death that set him in a fury!"

" 'Twas an accident, not Scarblade's doing." Josh defended the highwayman.

"Aye, Josh, we know. Still, if the authorities come here—what then? How do we explain John's body and that of the innkeeper?"

"I've been thinking, lads, we have to hide both the bodies. I hate to ask you, and I would do it myself, but with this chest of mine I fear another stint in that cold air would finish me off. Ye'll have to dig out to the storehouse and wrap the bodies and put them under the piled snow. 'Tiz the best we can do for the moment. When and if the authorities come I'll pretend that I'm the innkeeper. And ye'll be my help and the lass will be me ailing sister. It may work. If not," he shrugged elaborately, "best put the pouches alongside the bodies."

Hours later, their grisly task completed, Ned and Richard sat hunched by the fire. Josh stood with his back to the men, his heavy face a mixture of worry and fear. "Scarblade should have been back by now. 'Tis almost six hours. He would have been riding alone and making better time on the return trip. 'Tis worried I am," he said, rubbing his jaw.

Ned and Richard nodded, their own faces creased with worry.

"Tell me now, the two of you. Did ye make a decision as to whether ye'll sail with the ship on the morrow?"

"Aye, Josh, we sail with ye," Ned said quietly.

"Good lads. I was hoping that would be your decision. What do ye think, lads? About Scarblade, I mean."

Richard frowned. "He should have been back hours ago. I suspect that Charles had his finger, if not his whole hand, in the pie somewhere."

Josh nodded worriedly. "The only thing that will be safe will be the money. Scarblade was right in not telling anyone where the ship is docked or its name. But Scarblade could have been waylaid coming back by either Charles or the authorities—or both, for that matter! I think," Josh said, rubbing his large hands together, "that Charles will not make mention of the money at all but try to get Scarblade strung up for what he thinks is murder. The Blade will have a hard time trying to prove he had no part in the shooting."

Hours passed, with Ned and Richard finally giving up their frantic pacing. They now slept in a corner of the room. The door was thrust open, and four burly men entered the inn, pistols drawn.

"Easy does it, lads, what's the meaning of this intrusion? What we have is yours, there's no reason for drawn pistols. Step lively, men," he roared to Ned and Richard. "Get these gentlemen some food and ale!"

" 'Tis not food or ale we be lookin' for, 'tis the band of Scarblade!"

"Why do ye come to my humble inn? There be no henchmen here, as you can see," Josh said, waving his arms around the room. He affected the speech of the intruders, making himself seem one of them. "What makes ye think they would be here? Nary a soul has set foot in this inn since the snows come yesterday. Sit yourselves down, men, and let's talk."

" 'Tis not talking we want," said one of the men, brandishing a pistol.

"Aye lads, I can see tha'. Well then, search if ye want. Whatever it is ye'll not be findin' it here. 'Tis nothing here that don't belong."

"Search the inn," the man with the pistol ordered. "Every inch of it, miss nothing!"

"Ye look like a man with a keen mind," Josh smiled, "tell me what's the trouble and why are ye here?"

" 'Tis a wild tale we heard this day," the man said, slightly mollified by Josh's tone. " 'Twas a man named Charles Smythe," he said, "claiming that Scarblade's men and Scarblade killed his brother, and the innkeeper, too."

"Scarblade, is it?" Josh roared with laughter. "And why would he be making use of my humble inn? And I'm the innkeeper, as you can see. Methinks this man Charles was havin' a bit o' sport wi' ye. 'Tis a shame makin' ye ride in this foul weather for a jest. I hope ye find him and string him high," Josh said virtuously.

The three men came back. "There's nothing, sir, no sign. I think tha' scoundrel was makin' sport wi' us."

The first man nodded slightly. "Then," he said, fixing his eyes on Josh, "ye'll be tellin' me yer name as innkeeper."

Josh roared with laughter. It was lucky he had seen the small wooden sign in the taproom that proclaimed one Andrew Simpson was the innkeeper. " 'Tis Andrew Simpson, lad. Tha' me name, the same one me old mum stuck on me the day I crawled from 'er belly."

"And who is the lass by the fire?"

" 'Tis only me sister, dim-witted at that," he said, tapping his forehead. " 'Tis only Nellie. Look smart, lass!"

Tori gasped. Dim-witted! A sharp retort came to her lips, but she bit her tongue and the pain brought tears to her eyes. She then let the eyes roll back in her head and made a small mewing sound.

" 'Tis worse than most I've seen," the stranger said in sympathy. "They should be locked away someplace or shot."

"Aye," Josh laughed. "She fair saps the strength of even me. I've been thinkin' of late she gets worse. There be days she just muses and rolls her eyes. I tell you it makes me fair sick. Still, she is me own sister."

On cue, Tori rolled her eyes again and made the

same catlike noises. She worked the saliva in her mouth with her tongue and let it trickle from her mouth.

" 'Tis sickening," the man said righteously.

"Pay her no heed, man. Sit with your back to the fire if she offends you."

Josh ordered Richard and Ned to fetch some food and ale, then sat down at the rough table, his eyes alert. The man was no fool and for the moment he was satisfied, but what about after? He had to convince him and get him out of the inn.

" 'Tis some blizzard we had yesterday," Josh said conversationally.

"Aye," the man agreed. "There's armed guards crawling the area from here to the fork down the Cutters' farm," he said, watching Josh carefully.

Josh looked properly blank. "Why?" he asked bluntly.

The man's eyes narrowed as he looked at Josh. "I guess there's no harm in telling you; sooner or later the men will be here for some food and ale. The convoy of wagons with the tax money did not reach its destination."

"What?" Josh barked, a look of shock on his face.

Satisfied that the shock was genuine, the man, who said his name was Simon, continued. "They say that Scarblade and his men robbed it."

"In that blizzard?" Josh asked, his voice incredulous.

"Aye, that be about the right of it, man."

"More likely, the wagons got stuck in the heavy snow," Josh scoffed.

"Not that convoy. They had the best horses to be had, and those were special wagons. A blizzard wouldn't have stopped them. No, they were probably held up by the highwayman."

"If what ye say is true, man, I wouldn't give ye a hair for the life o' that madman, Scarblade."

"Have no fear, the man has been caught."

"What?" Josh barked, a look of shock on his face. "They actually caught the scoundrel ... Scarblade?" he asked, his voice shaking.

"'Tis true he was empty-handed and denied the knowledge of the robbery. But they have him for the other crimes. 'Tis just a matter of time before we have knowledge of the tax money."

"If what you say is true, what did he do with the gold if he was empty-handed?"

"Who knows? Probably passed it to some accomplice."

"I still can't believe it," Josh said incredulously. "They captured Scarblade, did you hear, men?" Ned and Richard nodded, their faces unreadable.

"Did they hang him?" Josh asked him, his voice suddenly cold.

"Not yet, but they will," Simon laughed.

"And you say he had no money on him. Perhaps he didn't rob the tax convoy?"

"'Tis no matter at this time." Simon smiled wickedly. "He'll hang for the other robberies. Well," he said, wiping his plate clean, "we'll be thanking you for the food and the ale. Best be getting on the road. If ye see or hear of anyone looking like Scarblade's henchmen, notify the authorities. And," he said, looking in Tori's direction, "best see about the dimwit."

As soon as the men left, Josh slammed the heavy bolt on the door and looked around the bare room. He resembled a stallion held at bay.

"You heard, lads. We best be making plans right quick, too."

Tori struggled to her feet. "What can we do, Josh? They'll hang him!" she almost wept.

"Not yet, they haven't. And until that day we have hope."

"We'll stay with you, Josh," Ned said softly. "We'll be back."

Josh once again slammed the bolt. He looked at Tori and frowned, saying nothing.

"Where will they have taken him? Do you have any idea?"

Josh shook his head. "Wherever it is he has no hope of escaping. Someplace where only the most trusted can get to see him."

"Like who, Josh? What do you mean, 'the most trusted.' "

"For instance, Lord Whimsey, Lord Starling, and Lord Barclane, probably Lord Fowler-Greene."

"Who?" Tori gasped. "Lord Fowler-Greene, did you say?" Tori's eyes held shock and disbelief at the name. "Are you saying that they are the only men who would have access to Marcus?"

" 'Tis safe to assume so, lass. Why do ye ask?"

"Oh, no," Tori wailed, "oh, no!" She lowered her shaking body to the rough plank bench and looked at Josh with tear-filled eyes. "Of all the people in this whole world!"

Chapter Twenty-Two

A loud, insistent knock on the door startled them both. Tori glanced at Josh with a question in her eyes. "It's dim-witted ye be, lass, remember that," he said as he went to throw open the bolt.

A man entered, his hat low over his eyes and the collar of his cloak turned up against the cold. He stomped his feet and rubbed his hands briskly. "I seek shelter and food," he stated in a breathless voice. "I've been riding for days and am fair near to death for hunger." Slowly he removed his hat and threw the cloak to the floor.

Tori gasped, "Granger! Is that you, Granger? Merciful God," she said, rushing over to him and throwing her good arm around him. Abruptly she pulled back. "Damn your very soul, Granger, why didn't you come for me to Dolly's? Where have you been?" she demanded of him.

"Tori, is it really you? Do my eyes deceive me? Tell me it's you!"

Josh stood to the side, eying the tableau. So this was Granger! "Darling" Granger of the girl's delirium. He snorted in disgust. A poor specimen of a man if he ever saw one! Tori must be dim-witted!

" 'Tis I, Granger. Oh, Granger, what has happened? How are my parents? Come sit, you look ill. Are you ill?"

"Well, if I'm not I will be if you don't shut up, Tori. That mouth of yours never stops! My head throbs," he said pitifully, "and I'm so hungry I could chew this tankard."

"Josh, fetch me some food. Granger is hungry," Tori commanded.

"Is he now?" Josh smirked. And that's not all he is, Josh thought, wrinkling his nose. He wondered when this dandy had last had a bath. Tori must have wondered the same, for she blurted, "You smell, Granger!"

"You'd smell too if you'd slept with a herd of goats," Granger snapped defensively. "Fearing a stranger, no one would give me a place to roost. Being penniless, a goat herd was the only place I could find to keep warm!"

"Oh, Granger, you didn't?" she said with a tinkling laugh.

"I had too much to drink at your wedding," Granger admitted shamefaced. "I went off with Lord Fowler-Greene's sister, Lady Helen, and I might add, when I had tired of her she held me a virtual prisoner!" Granger shivered slightly, remembering those few days in Lady Helen's service. "Then, when I had more time to think of what Lord Fowler-Greene would do when he discovered Dolly in your place, I . . . I was afraid of what he might do. You know, Tori," Granger admonished hotly, "you never gave one little thought to me in your little plan! You were off safely somewhere and I was left holding the bag!"

"Safely somewhere! Why, you ungrateful . . . lily-livered . . . stupid . . . safe!" Tori shrieked. "Let me tell you something, you . . . Tori stopped in midspeech, noting the glitter in Granger's eyes. The glitter became a gleam and they both broke out in rollicking laughter. "You tease!"

Abating his laughter, Granger went on with his story. "I set out at last to find you at Dolly's rooms. When I didn't, I struck out on my own, following my ever erroneous instincts. One evening shortly afterward, I was accosted and left penniless, which is to say near to death in this uncaring world. When I appealed to your father he told me this was the perfect time for me to begin to fend for myself. I was on my way to throw myself on the mercies of an old school chum. Then I happened here."

Josh came back into the room and plunked down a heavy plate piled high with food. Granger tore at the meat like a starving man. Over his head Josh looked questioningly at Tori.

"He's the answer to our prayers," she said with

a glance toward Granger. At Josh's doubtful look she hastened to explain. Quickly, while Granger devoured his food, Tori told the story of her near-wedding and the deception, and the following events. Josh now looked at Granger with a glimmer of an idea. "Let me finish our story, Josh," Tori said, "then we can tell him what he must do for us."

"Whatever it is, the answer is no!" Granger said between mouthfuls. "I wouldn't be sitting here now if it weren't for you, Tori. And I wouldn't be smelling like a herd of goats, either!"

"Tell me of my parents, are they well?" she asked to divert his attention. Swallowing a great mouthful of food, Granger threw Tori a considering look. Noting his reaction to her question, she pressed further: "Tell me, Granger, are they well?"

"For a moment I forgot you didn't know," Granger said softly. "They sailed for America a month past. It appeared due to some mysterious influence; your father regained favor with the Crown and was offered the opportunity to take the mayoralty of a new settlement in America."

"They have really gone, gone to America?" Tears rolled down Tori's cheeks at the thought of never seeing her parents again. "Did you tell them, Granger? Do they know of the deception I played?"

"No, Tori. I think Lord Fowler-Greene was the mysterious source that helped your father gain favor. They left with the thought that you were all married and happy," Granger said quietly. "But they didn't know you're with child," he said, grinning.

"What?" Tori gasped.

Granger nodded. "Our mutual friend Dolly has been instrumental in making Lord Fowler-Greene very happy."

Marcus awoke hearing a steady drip-drip somewhere close to his head. At first he had no recollection of where he was or how he came to be here in this dark, stinking hole. Slowly, the past came back to him, each memory flashing through the cold facts of reality.

On examination, he accepted the fact that there was

not much to remember. He had been discovered, pursued and captured, and thrown into the stinking dungeon somewhere in the bowels of Newgate.

He could feel the oozing slime on the stone walls and the scratches cut into the mortar between the stone blocks. He pushed back thoughts of the hair-raising stories of men gone mad, left to rot here in the dungeons. He wondered what human hand had etched those scratches, clawed in desperation into the imprisoning walls.

His cell was furnished with a long plank along the back wall. It was here he had found himself when he awakened from resting his weary bones. There were no windows or portals to the outside; and only air he breathed filtered through the bars in the door. The stench was sickening—rotting flesh, decayed food, bad water, sewage, and human offal assaulted his nostrils.

A light scraping sound caught his attention and he sought out its source. A young rat crept out from a crevice in the wall. It scurried by in panic, as though it, too, desperately sought release from this wretched hole. It ran from one side to the other attempting to climb its way free, but the walls were so slimy the animal could not get a grip. Finally, as though dreading the thought and resigning itself, it scurried back through the crack from which it came.

Marcus sat on the edge of the plank, despair weighing down upon his broad chest.

An echo of tinkling laughter struck a chord in his reverie, and the image of yellow-green eyes danced before him. He lay down on the thin plank, the splinters of the chewed wood biting into him.

He laughed, at first shortly then more rollickingly. How ironic! He thought back to the quiet evening in Chancelor's Valley when his father first announced that Marcus was to go to England to beseech the King. It was then that he first promised that if he should find a woman who offered a great personal sacrifice he would snatch her up and carry her back.

And hadn't Tori done just that? Offered her life by going among the King's guard where she was shot and, further, knocked the innkeeper with the fire tongs, thereby committing a murder to save him? Beauty, compassion, spirit, and courage, and now that he had at last found the woman he wanted, he was powerless to claim her. Instead of snatching her off to Chancelor's Valley he would rot in the stinking bowels of Newgate and the next bit of sky he saw would be from the long end of a rope on Tyburn Hill.

Tori watched Granger sitting nonchalantly on the rough bench opposite her. "You'll help us, won't you, Granger?"

He nodded wearily. He had searched these many days for Tori. Now that he had found her he almost wished he hadn't. He should have known that she would be in trouble. "It's a wild tale you spin, cousin. Unfortunately, I believe every word of it. Nothing else would make sense, knowing you. You actually participated in the tax robbery? I'll wager the whole scheme was your idea, wasn't it?" he asked suspiciously.

"Say anything, think anything, I don't care. I'm that happy to see you. Are you warm enough?" she asked solicitously. "You are? Good! Get his cloak, Josh, he must ride now! This minute! You'll go to Lord Fowler-Greene."

Granger nodded from time to time as he listened to her instructions. Josh, too, added what he thought should be said and done. "Get back as soon as ye can, lad. We'll do what we can from here."

After Granger's departure, Tori and Josh sat at a table, each busy with private thoughts, Josh moving only to replenish the fire. Tori sat huddled, her mind in a turmoil. What would become of her, she wondered. With her parents gone to America and Granger, at best, good for nothing, how could the two of them survive?

"Why not come to America with us, lass? 'Tis the least we can do for ye."

"America," Tori gasped. "What would I do in America?"

"Well, for one, your folks are there. You could go to them and start a new life."

"Are you sure it would be all right?"

"Aye, lass. I'll personally make sure 'tis all right."

"And Granger, could he come, too?"

"Aye," Josh agreed sourly, "providing he takes a bath!"

"I'll personally see to it," Tori laughed. "Won't Mother and Father be surprised when we both walk in." She giggled at the thought of Lord Nelson's face when he laid his eyes on Granger.

With the gelding, his last personal possession, Granger plowed his way through the deep snow. As he lurched in the saddle he thought of the coming conversation with Lord Fowler-Greene. Would he help Tori? Would he help Tori's bandit?

Probably, Granger snorted, since the lord was so in love with love he would no doubt agree to anything.

Startled, Granger looked up at a commanding voice which ordered him to halt. Cold, numb, weary, Granger waited for the onslaught of questions.

"Have ye seen any men on horseback riding this way?" the voice shouted.

"Not a soul have I seen these many hours," Granger lied.

"Where are ye headin', man?"

"To the home of Lord Fowler-Greene. What seems to be the trouble?" Granger asked fearfully.

" 'Tis none of yer concern. Ride on, man." With this command the snow-covered figure herded his men in the opposite direction.

Granger heaved a sigh of relief and spurred his gelding forward. The next posse might head for the Boare Inn, and with the way his and Tori's fortune had been running of late, one of the men would know that Josh was not the innkeeper. Suddenly a vision of Tori swinging from a rope in a gentle breeze appeared before him. He gulped and again spurred the horse. He was almost there.

Every bone in his body ached for attention. A warm bath, some wine, and a soft woman. Ah . . . since these pleasures were to be denied him, temporarily at least, he continued to ride to the estate of Lord Fowler-Greene.

The gelding approached the wide, corded road that had been cleared of snow and wound to the fine house nestled in a grove of trees. Granger blinked at the beauty of the surroundings. The trees were covered with the gleaming snow and ice. He rode under their boughs, thinking it was like an arched shelter for a bride. He could almost see himself and the lord's sister Lady Helen, walking under these same bowed branches not so long ago. His stomach turned and he banished the thought from his mind.

Dismounting proved to be more of an ordeal than Granger had anticipated. His foot caught in the stirrup and he fell to the ground. Cursing under his breath, he lay for a moment on the drive. His foot free, he grasped the stirrup and regained his posture. Clapping his hands together to restore their circulation, he mounted the stone steps on shaky legs. He pulled the bell and listened to the deep sound of the gong.

The heavy door opened and a small woman peered out at him. "What can I be doin' for ye?" she questioned.

"Granger Lapid to see Lord Fowler-Greene," he said imperiously, not forgetting how to deal with insolent servants.

Cowed by his commanding tone, she softened her approach. "Aye, come in and warm yerself. I'll announce ye."

Granger stood by the roaring fire and held out his frozen hands to the welcoming warmth. Praying silently, he looked around the huge room. Wealth! Ah, to have such a lovely home and no pecuniary worries. Perhaps one day he, too, would have such a room.

Shaken from his silent prayers, Granger looked up at the sound of heavy footsteps entering the room. "Ah, Lord Fowler-Greene, how are you this fine day? And how is Lady Fowler-Greene?" As an afterthought, he then asked after the health of Lady Helen.

"Fine, just fine," boomed the lord. "And yourself, Granger? How are you bearing up under this storm we have just witnessed?"

"Fine, fine," Granger mimed him. "My Lord, I've

come here on a matter of extreme urgency and to implore your aid."

Lord Fowler-Greene looked puzzled. Suddenly, his
expression changed to fear: someone had found out
about Dolly. "What?" he almost shuddered.

"It is the highwayman, Scarblade. He's been captured."

"Are you sure, man? How have you come by this
knowledge?"

"From Josh, the Blade's first-in-command." Quickly,
breathlessly, Granger recounted the story that Josh and
Tori had told him.

Lord Fowler-Greene rubbed his jowls thoughtfully.
"And what is it you want from me, Granger? How can
I help? I've no connection with this highwayman!"

"My Lord, Josh feels that you would know where
they have taken the Blade."

"Did I not make myself clear? I had no idea they
captured him? Perhaps Lord Whimsey would know,"
Fowler-Greene said thoughtfully. "And if I find out
where the man is, what then?"

"We need your help, Your Lordship."

"You're asking me to go against the Crown. My
boy, what makes you think I would be a party to such
an escapade?"

" 'Tis not my idea, your Lordship. It was Josh's. He
seems to think you would help." Granger could read
the indecision on the man's face. Would he help?

"You know what would happen if I were found to
be aiding Scarblade?"

"Aye," Granger said sadly, "how well I know."

Lord Fowler-Greene paced the floor. He nibbled on
his knuckles and watched Granger through slitted eyes,
quickly considering the alternatives. To deny help for
Chancelor he risked a greater chance to be discovered
in his friendship with the man. On the other side, he
might show his hand in trying to help. Still, the risks
were greater were he to refuse his services.

"Very well, I shall send a rider to Lord Whimsey
with a note. That's as far as I'll go. The rest will be
yours to do on your own. I warn you now, the man
will be under a heavy guard. And I doubt if you can

bribe the guards." He shook his head. " 'Tis a fool's errand you come on, Granger. I fear there is no chance to save Scarblade."

"My Lord, when one is in these ... circumstances ..." Granger said delicately, "would one be permitted a visitor? Say a dear sister?"

" 'Tis happened before; depends on the time and the place. It would be worth a try."

"And the chances of a bribe, you say it won't work?"

Lord Fowler-Greene shook his head. " 'Twould be worth the man's life to accept a bribe, and so it would have to be a large one. Gold, hard gold, I'd say would be best."

"I hesitate to ask this of you, Your Lordship, but we are desperate? There anything that you could contribute?"

"You go too far, man," the lord said heatedly. "You ask me to contribute when Scarblade has stolen a year's taxes from the Crown? The man is far richer than I!"

As the two men waited for a response from Lord Whimsey, they sat silently lost in their own thoughts. Lord Fowler-Greene rang the bellpull and a maid appeared presently. "Fetch some wine and perhaps some honey cakes. My guest looks in the need of some refreshment. Tell me, Granger, what do you hear from your dear cousin, Victoria?"

Granger gulped. He was in no mood for cat-and-mouse games. He blurted out Tori's story, omitting nothing. Lord Fowler-Greene nodded sadly. "I helped all I could," he said softly. "I pleaded Lord Rawlings' case as best I could. Seems I was a little too hasty. What will become of the child now? And you, Granger, what will become of you?"

"My Lord, do not concern yourself with the likes of my cousin or myself. Somehow, we will manage."

"Have you given any thought to sailing on the ship with your ... er ... friends to America?"

Granger looked stunned at the question. He shook his head.

"I will pay your way, the both of you, if it is what

you desire. 'Tis the least I can do for the happiness you have found for me. Aye, Granger," he said, noting the disbelief on the man's face, "I have found such happiness! I never thought it possible to love one as much as I love Dolly. But," he said, holding up a plump finger, "I would rest easier if all the perpetrators of that little deception were somewhere far away. A place like America," he said smiling.

Granger smiled knowingly, conveying his agreement.

"I would even be willing to throw in a handsome purse to make sure that it is a happy occasion. One that you want, of course."

Granger was quick to note the lord's eagerness in having himself and Tori a long distance from England. "My good Lord, you are too generous. But I'm afraid Tori would not think of leaving her lover, Scarblade, behind. Even if it were only to place flowers on the poor man's grave."

The havoc that Tori could wreak on the lord's plans for Dolly's social debut rankled Lord Fowler-Greene. If he wanted Granger and Tori where they could do no embarrassment to him it was clear he would have to do all he could to help Scarblade and see that the American was safely escorted out of England.

Granger soon held a heavy leather pouch in his hand. " 'Tis a most generous thing you do, milord. I'll never be able to repay you."

"My dear boy, I've been rewarded enough!" The lord spoke lovingly of his wife and the happy event that would transpire in the summer. "A son, I hope," he laughed, "to carry on the name. 'Tis wonderful, beyond belief!" Granger listened to his happy talk with half an ear. So it ended happily; whoever would have thought that Tori would have been an instrument of happiness. He still found it hard to believe.

The sound of the closing door jarred the lord from his happy thoughts. " 'Tis your answer, Granger." He accepted the stiff paper from the rider and dismissed him. He weighed the letter for a moment. "Are you sure that this is what you want? From this moment on, there will be no turning back for you." When Granger did not respond, Lord Fowler-Greene broke the seal and said quietly, "Very well." His face blanched; he looked at Granger with worried eyes. " 'Tis the dungeons of Newgate!"

Chapter Twenty-Three

Tori gazed at Granger with tear-filled eyes. "The dungeons, we'll never get him out." She looked imploringly at Josh. "What are we to do?"

The big man was at a loss for words. "I wish I knew, lass."

Granger, noting the anxiety on both faces, quickly told them of Lord Fowler-Greene's thought.

"You'll be able to pay him a visit as his sister, and you, Josh, as a friar. I took the liberty of procuring a friar's robe from the village monastery. It might be short in the hem for a man of your height, Josh, but I'm sure it will do, though to what end, I have no idea." His heart was heavy in his chest as he watched tears well in Tori's eyes.

"What do you think, Josh? Should we leave now? Is it worth a try?"

"We have nothing to lose, lass. Bundle warm, for it will be a good ride."

"Here then is the letter from Lord Fowler-Greene granting you permission to visit the prisoner."

"Thank you, Granger," Tori whispered, and within minutes she and Josh were dressed to leave, Tori wearing the iridescent green gown she had worn to the opera with Marcus. When they left Scarblade's encampment, Tori packed all her belongings into her saddlebag. Could it have been only a few days ago she had sat next to Marcus listening to the ethereal strains of music?

They rode silently, and when they reined in their horses they were before the tall gray-walled prison. Tori wailed, "It looks so like death!"

"Aye, lass. It is a house of death. You understand they will hang Marcus? There's no pretending, lass; it's a fact."

Tori nodded solemnly as she followed Josh up the worn stone steps. They entered a dim, dark hall and waited for one of the jailors to come to them.

The man who approached them sported a huge circle of keys and limped heavily on one leg. He was a coarse, burly man with a shock of matted, sandy-brown hair. One side of his face was distorted by a long scar pulling down his upper lip. Just seeing his cruel, ugly expression sent a chill of horror through Tori's body.

Josh presented the sealed letter from Lord-Fowler-Greene and stood with a bowed head, correct for a holy friar.

"Ye be in toime, th' thievin' bandit is ta be 'ung as soon as them orders can be signed. Owin' ta th' snow, it migh' be longer'n we 'ope fer. An' ye be good, Friar, pray fer 'is damned soul." The jailor laughed raucously, muttering something about what a sight it would be to see the great Scarblade getting his comeuppance on Tyburn Hill.

They walked for what seemed an interminable time, down one rancid, filth-infested corridor after another; down stairs so steep and dark, Tori reached frantically for Josh's supporting arm. The deeper into Newgate they went, the worse the smell, and Tori fought the retches that threatened to choke her. Finally, the jailor stopped and withdrew a large key ring. The clanking of the metal against the bars seemed to echo and thunder in Tori's ears.

"Highwayman!" roared the voice of the jailor, "there be a friar and yer sister ta visit ya. Look smart now!" He withdrew a safe distance and waited, his pistol held loosely in one hand, the ring of metal keys in the other.

Tori, eyes for naught except the tall figure that stood by the bars, his hands clenched, looked into raven-black orbs and felt herself sway with remembered feelings. She could not bring herself to speak.

"Marcus, lad, what is it we're to do? What can we do to get ye out of here?" Josh whispered.

"There is no way, good friend. This is the end of the road for me. Have you followed my instructions?" he asked Josh, all the while keeping his eyes on Tori, drinking in her beauty and remembering the feel of her in his arms.

"There has to be a way," Tori said suddenly as she raced to the bars and grasped Marcus's hands. "I won't let them hang you, I won't!" she cried as the tears fell down her cheeks. "I love you, Marcus," she whispered, "I love you!"

Marcus stamped the sight of Tori on his memory. "You'd best go now," he said, his voice cracking with emotion. "I don't want you to see me this way." Looking at Josh, he said commandingly, "Promise you'll not allow her to be on Tyburn Hill! Take her away from here! Away from me!"

Tori's head throbbed dully. How could he do this to her? Cast her away as though she meant nothing to him, as though there had never been anything between them. To deny her this one last comfort, a kind word, a kiss, a hint that she meant something more than just a woman who had warmed his bed one night. A conquest, nothing more, and once conquered to be done with, not even leaving her the comfort of dignity.

Tori had blurted out her deepest emotions to a prisoner in the mouldering, foul-smelling dungeons of Newgate and he wanted none of her. She heard the echo of her words. "I love you," she had cried, and he ordered her taken away.

Staggering beneath the blow of his command, Tori shrank back into the shadows, despising herself for her weakness, then exulting in her strength. She loved him, this man called Scarblade, and she knew she would love him in spite of his indifference to her until the day she died.

Josh's voice broke through to her. "We can try bribing the jailor, Marcus. Surely somewhere, someplace, there must be something that could be used as a bribe. I know ye won't permit us to touch the tax money, lad, but perhaps . . ."

Suddenly, Marcus's eyes lighted. "There is one thing. I don't know if it would work. Once, not long ago, a young lady entrusted something to my care. Actually, I pilfered it from her in one of the robberies. A valuable ring. She said I was to guard it, the little minx, and one day return it to her. Perhaps it could be used," he said, a faint ray of hope in his eyes.

"Aye, lad. Where is this ring you speak of?"

"In my saddlebag atop one of the spare horses, wrapped in a pouch. Try, Josh. There's nothing to lose!"

Tori almost fainted. She knew what he spoke of, that stupid glass trinket he had taken from her. Did he really think it valuable? She cursed the day Granger had given it to her. Only a piece of glass. Looking deeper into the black eyes, she saw there a faint ray of hope. She could not take it from him; there had to be some other way. Her mind raced as she noted the jailor lumbering toward them.

Josh followed her eyes. " 'Tis time to leave, lad. I'll see to the task you gave me."

Tori looked longingly at Marcus, her heart in her eyes, a smile on her lips. She wanted to say something, but his glance at her was forbidding and the words died in her throat.

"If I do not see you, Tori . . ."

"But I shall see you, Marcus, I promise you."

On the way out of the dungeons, Josh asked the jailor the question bothering Tori. "Tomorrow, may we return?"

"I see no 'arm in this," the jailor laughed, eying Tori lewdly, "as long as ye 'ave that letter of admission."

Outside in the cold, bracing air, Tori gasped deep breaths. So disheartened was she, she had not the heart to tell Josh of the glass ring. He would know soon enough when they got back to the inn and removed it from Marcus's saddlebag. What would he say then? That this was the end? What else could it mean? A glass ring was not the answer! She doubted seriously if the jailor could be bribed at all.

Having no other safe accommodations to go to, the dejected trio returned to Marcus Chancelor's rooms. Huddled before the blazing fire, Tori sat next to Josh while he fingered the fake jewel. She told him the story haltingly. Granger tried to comfort her, to no avail.

"Then 'tis truly the end; for the gold is already

aboard ship and cannot be touched. Cap'n Elias would sooner part with his head than go against Marcus's own orders and part with a shilling of the booty," Josh said pitifully. "After all he has done there is naught to be done to free him."

"Not so quick, my friend," Tori interrupted; there may be a way. Listen to me carefully. Did I not do a good job of convincing the sheriff's men that I was a dimwit?" At Josh's nod, she continued, "Then why can't I play the harlot? What else in the world would distract the jailor? If you had seen him look at me you'd know what I speak of."

"My God, Tori," Granger gasped, but Tori ignored his outburst.

"What do you think, Josh? Will it work?"

Hope sprang into the big man's eyes. Till the meaning of her words penetrated his brain. Still, the hope remained, glowing feebly.

"Lass, Marcus would have none of it. Ye cannot sell yourself to get his freedom. He'd never forgive himself."

"Just answer one question, is there any other way? Is there, Josh?" Her voice became shrill as she saw Josh shake his head. "It's my body and I'll use it as I see fit! Are you telling me that if I go through with my plan that Marcus will turn against me? Is that what you're trying to spare me? Well, save your breath! He is already done with me, he ordered you to take me away, he can't bear the sight of me."

Josh shrugged his shoulders dejectedly.

"The decision is mine, regardless of the outcome," Tori said quietly. "Besides, Marcus has made it very clear what he thinks of me, and I've nothing to lose. If he dies, Josh, I die, too!"

"Tori," Granger asked hesitantly, "are you sure this is what you want? That this is the only way? I'll do whatever you ask if you're sure in your heart that this is what you want." He looked into her beautiful eyes and did not need to wait for an answer.

Tori sat before the fire, her arms clasped about her drawn-up knees. From time to time she glanced at Josh and winced inwardly at the expression on his face.

There was no other way! Hour after hour passed, and dawn slowly crept upon the sullen trio.

Josh stirred himself and stoked the fire which had burned almost to the embers. "We must all have something to eat before we set out." The effort of talking brought on a fit of coughing. It was Granger who helped the weakened giant to a seat, his eyes full of concern as he noted the condition of the handkerchief Josh held near his mouth. The spasm lasted longer than the others, and Josh looked weak and drained. He forced a smile for Granger's benefit. "Don't worry, lad, I can do me part. You make me a promise, though," he gasped weakly. "If I fall behind you're to leave me. Your promise, lad, swear."

Granger murmured his agreement.

Tori nibbled on a cold piece of meat and washed it down with warm ale. She coughed and sputtered; she couldn't eat. Not now! Not ever!

Granger paced the room while Josh rested. "Look!" he exclaimed, "it's snowing again!"

"No," Tori wailed, "not again!" She looked at Josh and her heart lurched. Good God, he had never looked this bad; perhaps Granger could take his place.

Josh answered her unspoken question: "The weather will help us just as it did the day of the robbery. Get dressed, we leave in ten minutes."

"This robe will have to suffice, Granger. 'Tis the best I can do. Since all we friars are in poor straits it'll pass muster. Here," Josh said, "slip this pistol into your boot like me and be careful. They'll search us this day." He slipped a knife similarly into his own boot with shaking fingers.

Tori watched the trembling hand and placed her hand on his shoulder. "Josh, would it not be better if you stayed behind or went ahead to the ship? Granger and I can do what has to be done. If we're killed it'll make little difference. Please, Josh, return to the ship; you may stand a chance that way."

" 'Tis good of ye to think of me, lass, but I'll be having none of it. Me days are numbered as ye know. I must be a party in this, for Marcus is me friend. I couldn't go to me Maker without at least trying to save him."

Tears welled in Tori's eyes. "All right, Josh, I'm ready."

The cold made Tori gasp, and her arm throbbed as the bitter wind seeped in under her cloak. She ignored the pain; her thoughts of Josh and the coming task she must perform occupied her mind. Could she do it? Of course, she could do anything she had to. Are you prepared to die? Tori questioned herself. If I must, came her quiet reply.

Cold, numb, weary, the small party dismounted and climbed the snow-packed steps. The jailor looked at them with suspicious eyes. Tori took the initiative with a slight wave of her hand to Josh and Granger.

"Sir," she said boldly, extending the missive written by Lord Fowler-Greene. She watched the jailor covertly, her gold-green eyes lackluster. She extended her arm in what she hoped was a languid gesture and patted the jailor's filthy cheek.

"It's fortunate that you're indoors in this weather. When I leave here I fear I may get lost in the storm. The good friars are headed in another direction," she cooed softly, the cat's eyes half closed as she watched his reaction. He was only too happy to talk.

"If'n Oi'm any judge a worse storm than th' other day. It's brewin', Oi tells ye. Lucky Oi am tha' Oi've comfortable quarters ta go ta. A fire, a bed wi' a little ale an' some meat an' cheese. Wha' more can a man ask?" He leered at Tori.

"Why, sir, you left something out—a woman to warm that bed of yours."

"There be no women in th' dungeons an' Oi've no jurisdiction over th' ones on th' debtors' side," the jailor smirked.

Josh was the first to proceed, then Granger, the jailor, and finally, Tori. She suddenly clutched the keeper's ragged arm and asked anxiously, "Are you the one that'll hang my brother?"

The jailor laughed. His foul breath reached Tori's nostrils, and she fought a retch. "No' Oi, th' 'angman does th' job. Bu' Oi plan ta watch," he laughed gleefully. "Oi loikes ta 'ear th' snap o' th' neck!"

Tori blanched but didn't falter. "Well, I shall not be here to hear it," she sighed. "I shall be lost in the snowstorm. Remember to look for my body in the spring," she laughed.

As they continued down the labyrinth of passage-ways, the air became more stagnant and mephitic. Tori could hear Granger gulp and Josh plodded ahead, his mind on other things. Tori stepped lightly, her flimsy slippers soaked from the numerous scummy puddles she had trod in.

The jailor walked abreast of her, glancing at her now and again, his murky eyes appraising her know-ingly.

Tori fought the urge to draw away from his foul-smelling body but had only to see Marcus's face flash before her to make her stay close to the ugly, wretched jailor.

As a tendril of moss hanging from overhead touched Tori's cheek she cried out and moved closer to the jailor. Taken by surprise, he was quick to take ad-vantage of her movement. He laughed as he caught her, and she lurched against him. Tori felt a large hand cup her breast and heard his in-drawn breath. Boldly, she looked into his murky eyes, not objecting to his ad-vances, feeling his hand tighten as she stood shivering in the cold. The jailor opened his mouth to smile, and she saw stubs of rotted teeth and a white, coated ton-gue. The sight was so repulsive she closed her eyes and willed herself to stay close to him.

The jailor, taking this as a sign of acquiescence, slipped his hand inside her gown, his rough, scaly hands scratching the soft skin of her breast.

"Not here," she whispered. "Later. I must see my brother first." He was reluctant to let her move from his side and grasped her breast tighter. His fingers found her nipple and he ground it between his fingers. Tori's eyes teared with the pain, and with one quick movement she was free and leaning against the wall. "Wait here, I must see my brother; then if you want for the rest of the day I'll stay with you," she said, turning from his ugly face.

The jailor, overcome with the promise, slouched against the wall; he watched Tori move to the heavily barred cell. His breath came in short gasps as he anticipated the outcome of the day. There were still a good many hours till he would have to take the next watch, and then, he thought hotly, he had the rest of the night.

His hands were on fire; never had he felt flesh so smooth and warm. He longed to cover that soft breast with his mouth while his hands did other things. It had been a long time since he had had a woman. He would have to make up for lost time today. The lust in his loins couldn't be fought any longer; his body was an inferno.

Tori glanced at Josh, who refused to meet her eyes.

Granger was busy talking to two watchmen who stood outside the barred door. Both, Tori noticed, had pistols in their belts. Marcus's cell was within sight now.

The jailor's hoarse voice called, and Tori looked at Granger. "I'll not be long, Friar, perhaps five minutes," she croaked meaningfully. The jailor advanced on her, not waiting for her return.

She looked in horror at his glazed eyes and his drooling mouth and clenched her teeth as she saw him lay down the key ring and the pistol on the sweating stone floor. His torch rested precariously against the wall and he appeared a specter in the dim orange glow. Pray God that Granger's hand would not slip and there would be no outcry. She worked her face into what passed for a smile and advanced toward the jailor. Impatient with her slow progress, he reached out an arm and roughly pulled her to him.

Her body taut as a spring, she fell against him. One of his knees parted her legs. Hot hands fumbled at the wide neck of her gown while his wet mouth assaulted hers.

Abruptly, one of his arms dropped and she tried to grasp it and put him away from her. Surely he would not take her here with the others! She was aware of him lifting her skirts and his hot breath scorched her face. He was like a rutting pig! His other hand dropped and she was free for a second; only his legs pinned her against the wall, his knees holding the voluminous skirt to her thighs. Then she was thrown against the wall, and the last she knew was a loud *whack* mingled with the outraged roar of some wounded animal.

Marcus had seen Josh and a young man approach his cell, but his attention was drawn to a chalk-faced, bloodless-lipped Tori as she spoke to "Friar" Josh. What was going on here? Why did Josh look so constrained? What was Tori doing here?

He had heard a harsh voice that he recognized as the jailor's and dimly realized he was calling Tori.

From where Marcus's cell was located he could barely make out the jailor leaning the torch against the sweating wall and saw Tori walking slowly toward him.

Rage exploding within him, Marcus witnessed the attack the jailor was making upon Tori . . . his Tori! And she was allowing it!

Anguish squeezed his heart, burst his lungs, and escaped his throat in the roar of some primeval animal losing its mate to an ancient enemy.

Seeing Tori's collapse onto the slimy, stone floor, Josh bellowed oaths mingled with threats, advanced on the grotesque jailor, his hand fumbling inside his boot for the pistol. He failed to see the man's upraised arm and the knife that was held tightly in it.

Stone-faced, Marcus watched as Josh's life's blood seeped out, spreading through the rough, dark-brown monk's cloth.

"Get the girl out of here," Marcus barked, repressed sorrow tightening his jaw, his scar burning dully on his whitened cheek. White-lipped anger hoarsened his voice. "Get Tori out of here!" he called to Granger, who was bending above her, attempting to lift her into his arms. "Now! Get her away before she sees . . . !"

Even as Marcus spoke the words, Tori's lids fluttered open. Bewilderment furrowed her brow as she looked upon the passageways filled with guards. Then her eyes fell to the form beside her. "Josh . . ."

Granger pulled her to her feet. "Don't look Tori, there's nothing we can do for him now."

"No ... no ... it can't be ... it mustn't ..."
Granger lifted her into his arms, but she fought him;
she had to get to Josh, her friend, Marcus's friend. ...
Arms outstretched, agony inscribed on her features,
she reached to his still form, refusing to believe he was
gone.

Granger dragged her away, but for one moment her
eyes locked with Marcus's. She saw her own anguish
mirrored in his dead-dull black eyes. Tori stirred
dizzily, she felt herself being carried. She looked up
into Granger's troubled face. Slowly, the realization
washed over her that their plan had failed ... failed
miserably! Then her thoughts sank into merciful blackness.

Chapter Twenty-Four

The interior of the Owl's Eye Inn was lit with a dim yellow glow from greasy, soot-blackened hurricane lamps, their tallow candles smoking off an acrid odor. Granger sat in a corner of the taproom nursing a mug of mulled wine, inconspicuous among the shuffle of men and a few doxies vying for the men's favors and trade. Every time the tarnished bell above the door sounded he quickly glanced up, his eyes searching for the one person he hoped to find this night.

A few days after the fiasco of trying to rescue Scarblade from Newgate, Ned and Richard had brought word to Granger that Charles was known to have been carousing drunkenly and boasting that he had been one of Scarblade's men. Ned also informed Granger that Charles's natural meanness and brutal behavior had not won him any friends among the riffraff that inhabited the neighborhood. Granger had come to the Owl's Eye to see just how far Charles's bragging had gone and how damaging his boasts were to Scarblade.

At the sound of the bell, Granger looked up to see a tall thin man enter, his face still swollen and bruised from a fairly recent beating. Granger sat quietly listening for any hints of the man's identity.

A group of men who had been drinking at the bar saw the tall man and pointedly took up their tankards and moved to a table across from Granger. They muttered beneath their breaths and looked accusingly at the man they had made room for at the bar.

One's words fell on Granger's ears. " 'E's a mean coot, 'e is, an' badly used, Oi'll gran' ye, but 'tiz no excuse fer wha' 'e done ta tha' poor whore!"

"Whazzit 'e's done?" the second asked.

"As Oi 'ears it, when poor Sally put 'im off 'er 'e took offense an' beat th' poor lass ta death. Thems th' know it wuz 'im fer sure won' do nothin' abou' it becuz we don' loike th' authorities interferin' in our business. Bu' 'twuz 'im, all righ'."

Charles, aware of the hostile glances of the men in the taproom, swore profusely, yelling into the room that if any there among them felt man enough to take him on he was ready for all comers. No one made a move toward him and yet Charles was not satisfied. "Why are ye all lookin' at me tha' way? Tha' little whore is out o' th' way o' trouble now, th' thievin' little tart. Refusin' me th' way she did. A man 'as 'is rights, 'e 'as!" Charles then turned his attention to the tankard the innkeep had set before him, giving the men a view of his back.

Granger shuddered to think that this man had tried to force himself on Tori. Granger wouldn't like to tangle with the man himself, and was more than glad that Scarblade had left the mark of his fists upon the man's ugly face.

Charles again turned to face the center of the tap room. "An' th' gold! All tha' gold an' me wi' na a tuppence ta me pockets."

He was speaking of the tax robbery, Granger was sure of it. And now Scarblade was to lose his life for it and the colony would still suffer. What a shame that Lord Fowler-Greene prevented Captain Elias from sailing to North Carolina with the booty. Scarblade would hang for naught.

Sounds of a scuffle brought Granger from his thoughts. Charles had thrown his tankard at the innkeeper, accusing the man of serving him spoiled ale. The looks of hatred the others laid on the man were enough to make a sane man crawl, but still none of them moved to put an arm on Charles and toss him out. Granger was reminded of the words he had heard a few moments ago, and though he knew they feared Charles and hated him, he also knew they wouldn't call the patrols, for many of them also had a price on their heads and none of them would want the law poking around.

Charles drunkenly mumbled, his words becoming clearer and louder. "Me own brother wuz murdered, do ye 'ear?" He leered a malevolent toothless grin to the room. "An' the dirty bastard'll 'ang fer it, Oi made sure o' tha', Oi did."

Failing to attract attention from this statement, he became more heated in his response. "An' any among ye who thinks tha' th' barstard wuz Scarblade wha' wuz th' brains behind those robberies, let me tell ye a few truths. Oi, Charles Smythe, wuz th' brains an' me brother John me righ' 'and man. An' if anyone deserves th' fame fer bein' Scarblade, 'tiz me!"

A glimmer of an idea was born in Granger's mind as he listened to the despicable man boast. Perhaps . . . he thought to himself, the Newgate jailors have the wrong man after all. Picking himself up and draining his tankard, Granger walked on unsteady feet to the bar. Placing himself next to Charles, he pretended to be the worse for wear due to the wine. When next Charles turned to bemoan the fates that had taken his brother, Granger paid him his sympathies.

Charles, hearing the first friendly voice directed at him in weeks, quickly offered to buy Granger a refill of mulled wine and proceeded to bend his ear with stories of injustices which had been inflicted upon him. Granger kept a sorrowful expression on his face and punctuated Charles's statements in all the correct places with a "tsk-tsk . . ."

Throughout the course of this one-sided conversation, Granger managed enough praise to bolster the man's spirits and led him on to making crowing boasts about himself.

"So, as anyone can see, Oi wuz th' leader o' tha' pack, Oi wuz. It wuz me who gave th' orders an' saw ta it tha' they wuz follered out."

Granger took the lead and said, "If you were the leader then who's that miserable soul who's pacing off a cell in Newgate?"

Charles, sensing he had the reluctant attention of all within earshot, raised his voice to a roar, "Tha's th' rot wha' killed me brother! Bu! 'e wuz jus' a flunky, Oi'm Scarblade, Oi am! Oi'm th' one wi' th' 'ead on me shoulders, no' tha' pig-lovin' dog! Oi'm Scarblade!"

Unable to contend with Charles's boasts a moment

longer, the crowd in the taproom began to sneer and mock. "Scarblade indeed!" One voice was heard above the others! "An' Oi'll be supposin' th' it's you wha' 'as captured th' 'earts o' all th' laidies that ye robbed. Scarblade, indeed!—why a poor workin' girl loike Sally wouldn' bed ye fer thrice th' price!"

Enraged, Charles turned in a fury upon those who had dared to ridicule him. "Oi'm Scarblade, if'n Oi says so. An' who're ye ta talk ta me tha' way? Ye petty thieves an' pimps"—he pointed a gnarled, filthy finger at one of the men—"an' ye, Stevie Nespoint, Oi suppose ye doubt who Oi am, too? There's no doubtin' who ye are, an' wouldn' th' watch patrol luv ta know tha' who they're lookin' fer in a little matter o' purse snatchin' is sittin' righ' 'ere! An' ye," he roared, pointing his finger at another, "what abou' tha' little matter o' settin' fire ta th' roomin' 'ouse so's ye wouldn' 'ave to pay yer rent wha' wuz due? No record, no rent, right? There's bounty fer mos' o' ye, an' those tha' ain' bein' sought wuz at one toime er another. 'Ow would ye loike me ta put th' bulldogs on ye, th' lot o' ye? Tha' would teach ye no' ta mock th' man tha' calls 'imself Scarblade!"

The silence that followed his outrage was stifling, brewing, ominous. Granger knew that Charles was too drunk to know the harm he had done himself.

"Oi'll have another ale," he growled at the inn-keeper.

"There'll be no further service for ye here, Sir Scarblade," the innkeeper said jeeringly, removing the tankard that Charles had been drinking from and throwing it into the garbage that was stacked at one end of the bar.

Charles lunged across the bar, grabbing for the inn-keeper's neck. The keeper, a heavy, robust man, moved adroitly and avoided contact. "Throw him out!" he boomed at three men who had seated themselves near the door.

Kicking and struggling, Charles was lifted off his feet and removed from the taproom. Sounds of a scuffle came through the open door, and Granger pressed through the throng of people in time to see Charles beaten and thrown into the road beneath the hooves of a horse tethered at the rail.

The startled, nervous animal reared up on its hind legs, bringing down its sharp hooves on Charles. Again and again the horse tried frantically to escape the body which lay beneath him. Charles, uttering a last blood-chilling scream, took the full force of the blows about his head and shoulders. Someone unleashed the terrified animal, and it raced headlong down the street.

Tori sat inside the open trap, the only means of conveyance she had been able to hire on this mid December day, the day they would hang Scarblade on Tyburn Hill. It had been three days since she had seen Granger or Josh and indeed she hadn't sought them out. Tori had removed herself from their company and retired to the boardinghouse, in fact the very room that had been Marcus's. Seeking to find some small measure of comfort from being in the same room that she and Marcus had shared on that one night of love, a night she would remember always, she had been overjoyed to find it had not been let to anyone else.

The trap made its way over the rutted, muddy roads to Tyburn Hill. Disinterestedly, Tori brushed at the muddy spots which had splashed up onto her green woolsey skirt. Again she found herself grateful to Dolly, who had thought to send on to her the trunks of clothing and personal belongings that her parents had conveyed to the Fowler-Greene house before their departure for America. Tori received them gladly, not being able to bear wearing the green silk gown she had worn to the opera with Marcus to witness his final debasement on the gallows.

The driver did not think it at all strange that this lovely, well-dressed young lady should direct him to Tyburn Hill. He laughed to himself: If taproom gossip was correct, most of society's matrons would be there to shed a tear for the passing of a most gallant and attractive highwayman.

Tori arrived late, and because the rows of carriages flanking the gallows themselves were already full, the driver of her hack grudgingly contented himself with a place well to the rear of the field.

A young boy selling hot-cross buns ran up to the trap in hopes of a sale. The driver bought one and jerked his thumb toward Tori. "Get away from me customer," he scolded the boy; "can't yer see this mus' be her first 'anging? She's as white and pinched lookin' as me auld mum's apron."

Disgust and nausea surged in Tori as she gaped at the spectacle before her. Children hawked leaflets purporting to contain the last words of the condemned man. Hags sold "relics"—cloth and locks of hair—from past hangings.

Peasant and gentry alike thronged about. Bawds vied for marks and pickpockets had a field day. Youths pitched pennies, old men sold potions and remedies, housewives enticed people to buy their wares of ribbons, laces, smoked meats, fish, and hot breads. Justice, if Scarblade's hanging could be called just, would be meted out in the tawdry, tinselly surroundings of a circus.

Lifting her eyes to the far-off gallows, Tori stared hypnotized by the swaying length of knotted rope which the slightest wind tossed to and fro.

As she watched, several men came from beneath the wooden structure and mounted the stairs. Vainly, her eyes strained across the distance in an effort to see Marcus. One of the men was dressed in black, and he, she supposed, was the executioner. She could not see Marcus, and suddenly she realized she did not want to see him! It was better to remember him the way he was, not this way: stripped of all dignity, denied human compassion, to die without solemnity, the sacrifice at a pagan orgy!

In a voice that quivered with emotion, she ordered the hackney to take her back to the boardinghouse.

"Aaow, miss, it jest be gettin' good! Oi wouldn't want ta miss the 'angin! Hang on fer a minute, it wouldn't be long."

"Now, I tell you!" she screamed in panic, "take me out of here now!" Noting the hackney's continued insolence, Tori commanded him more firmly, her voice holding the practiced note of nobility instructing a servant. The driver's ears perked up, but still he hesitated.

Hysteria mounted within her, choking off all reason. Fiercely, Tori pounded him with clenched fists, pummeling his head and shoulders, forcing him from his seat. With a mighty shove she sent the man flying from his perch to the trodden mud below. Grasping up the reins which were looped over the seat and taking up the whip, she forced the startled horse to veer to the left, taking her out and away from the ghoulish scene at the gallows. Tori had the trap turned about and the whip was held in suspension above the animal's flanks when she heard it!

The crowd had become hushed with anticipation and it came to her ears as plainly as though she were within three feet of it. The clank, the clap, the split, the gasp of the crowd, the sudden thudding yawn of the gallow's trap door, penetrated her being like a shot from a pistol. Her spine stiffened, her head snapped back, and she thought she should be dead. She wished she were dead! But she wasn't. Frantically, mercilessly, she lashed out at the poor beast's flanks, compelling him to make swift her escape from Tyburn Hill!

The pounding became louder, someone was calling her name. "Tori, Tori, open the door! I know you're in there. Tori, open the door!"

Slowly, painfully, she pulled herself away from the webs of a tearful, exhausted sleep. "Go away, I don't want to see anyone," she called back in a toneless voice she did not recognize as her own.

"Tori, I must see you; let me in, it's Granger," he insisted, still pounding.

Reluctantly, woodenly, she climbed from the bed and unlocked the door. Granger burst in, deep concern for her in his eyes. "He's free! Your Marcus is free!"

At first she couldn't comprehend the meaning of his words. Then their significance dawned upon her. Relief engulfed her, making her dizzy and light-headed. Clarity of thought returning, Tori pounced on her cousin with disbelief. "But I was there, on Tyburn Hill! I saw the executioner. Granger, I heard the gallows' trap door! What are you saying?"

"No, no, Tori, Marcus is alive. They hung someone else today, a man who murdered his mistress or something like that. The courts hastened the man's hanging by a week; they couldn't take a chance on disappointing the mob! Marcus is alive and free, I tell you!"

Realizing the shock she suffered, Granger gently led Tori back to the bed and sat down beside her, slowly telling her the sequence of events which led to Marcus's release.

When Granger reported to Lord Fowler-Greene the circumstances surrounding Charles Smythe's death, the lord pounced on this information and put it to his use.

Convincing Captain Elias to go against Marcus's orders and part with the tax money, Lord Fowler-Greene brought the gold directly to the King, boldly declaring that Marcus himself was instrumental in securing the pilfered taxes. Scarblade was dead, having met his destiny beneath the hooves of a crazed horse, and Marcus Chancelor, the man from America who came to plead with the Crown to lift the embargoes and blockades on his colony, had himself, before his unjust apprehension, located the stolen tax monies and delivered them into Lord Fowler-Greene's hands.

The lord explained that he had not gone directly to the authorities with this information because he wanted to bear out the truth of Marcus Chancelor's innocence.

So it was true, remarkable but true. Tori's mind struggled to comprehend Granger's statements. "Where is he?" she asked her cousin.

"He's at Captain Elias's ship! I almost forgot to tell you the best part. The King lifted the embargoes and blockades and bestowed on Marcus a hefty reward which he says will get his colony through the next harvest quite nicely."

Tori's eyes widened. "You saw him, you spoke to him?"

"Yes, of course." The portent of his words as he watched her face stopped him in midsentence. It was all there for him to see, the pained, wounded expression in her eyes, the slight trembling of her lips.

Granger knew his cousin well, and could read her thoughts like a taproom sign. They said, *If he's alive and free, why didn't he come to me? It's true then, he's done with me. . . ."*

Trying to ease her, Granger said gently. "He had arrangements to make, Tori, the reward, the legal documents lifting the embargo and blockade. He hasn't had an opportunity . . ."

Before his eyes Tori's expression changed to one of hard, cold uncaring; her yellow-green eyes became icy and glittering.

"I'm sure I don't know what you're talking about, Granger. I'm afraid your little tale has tired me. If you would please leave now—" She gave a little yawn to communicate polite boredom.

Bewildered by her attitude, Granger allowed himself to be ushered out the door. He heard the *snick* of the lock and knew that any and all explanations he could make for Marcus would be useless. He had often said Tori had a mind like an iron trap, and she was giving evidence of this once again.

Once more alone in the room, Tori flung herself on the high poster bed and buried her face in the pillow. A myriad of emotions filled her mind. Putting aside her joy at Marcus's release, only one thought rose to the surface, and she choked on the inescapable truth: he did not want her! He had quit himself of her and was glad of it. His rejection of her had been real and she was the fool for trying to read some considerate motive into it. She had offered herself to him and he had tried her and found her lacking.

Shame burned her face as she pushed it deeper into the soft pillow, imagining it still carried the scent of him.

Early the next morning, Tori was dressed in her brightest, gayest traveling suit; her baggage was packed and waiting for the footman to bring it down to the coach she ordered.

Her intentions were to throw herself upon Lord Fowler-Greene's mercies, to entreat him to advance her enough money to book passage on a ship to her parents' new home in America.

There was nothing left for her here in England, and truth to be told, she was glad to leave.

Making the last of her things ready, she heard a light tapping sounding at the door. Supposing it was the footman, she bid him enter.

"Tori." The sound of her name dissipated the stillness of the room, seeping into her consciousness and carrying with it the betrayal of longing and want.

Tori spun around to face him, her eyes bright and luminous with unshed tears. He looked dashing, slightly pale from his stay in Newgate, but, nevertheless, the most handsome man she had ever seen. The cut of his coat accentuated the breadth of his shoulders and the narrowness of his hips. His snowy-white cravat set off the darkness of his skin and the ebony of his eyes.

"You!" she hissed. "What do you want here? How did you know where to find me? Go away, Marcus, there's nothing for you here."

"Granger told me—" he began before she cut in on him.

"So, Granger, was it? And what did he tell you? That I was dying for the sight of you? That you had slighted his dear cousin and he begged you for amends? Get out, Marcus . . ."

In two long strides he was upon her, grasping her firmly by the arms and shaking her soundly. "Your cousin Granger warned me about you. He said you had a mouth that didn't stop! Not that I didn't know that myself, you little vixen! Now shut up, and for once in your life listen to me. I didn't come to you immediately after my release yesterday because . . . because . . . Tori," he asked, "do you know how long it takes to shed oneself of the vermin that's picked up in a hellhole like Newgate? And then Lord Fowler-Greene had to fill me in on the story behind my release. Then, finally, came the King. Not even you, my hotheaded little darling, outranks the King!"

His grip on her arms became painful as he shook her again and growled at her through clenched teeth.

"When the King commands an audience poor commoners like me obey! Then I had to see to the loading of the stores which are a gift to Chancelor's Valley from the Crown. We sail today in an hour's time, so it had to be seen to immediately."

He released her with a backward thrust, sending her reeling across the room, stumbling against and falling upon the bed. "All the while we were loading, Granger told me of the scheme you and Josh and he cooked up to spring me out of Newgate! I thought that filthy ape was raping you, Tori. I had no idea it was all part of some crazy scheme to free me."

His face darkened as he thought of that day of doom that had cost Josh his life. She read the pain on his features, and the pain became hers. She, too, missed Josh and would grieve for him. But the sad memory must not stop her; this time he had gone too far. Who did he think he was, what did he think of her? Some child who must be rewarded for her good intentions?

"So!" she shrieked; "Granger has told you of our combined efforts to help you, and now you feel you must be properly grateful! Oh, I knew it, I knew it!"

"Grateful? For what? For almost being a helpless witness to that filthy dog of a jailor raping you? My God! I wanted to kill that pig for touching you! If I could have gotten my hands on him I *would* be swinging from the gallows." He approached her, stalking her, and she shrank from him.

"God, Tori, they told me if I didn't stop raving they were going to confine me to Bedlam! And you think I'm grateful? For your driving me near out of my mind?"

That disastrous day in the dungeons of Newgate flooded back to her. The stench of the dungeons—Josh's death—the roar . . . that blood-chilling, wounded animal roar. That had been Marcus yelling his helplessness to defend her.

"You're my woman, Tori," he said, his voice husky. "I should have known it long ago. Your beauty and courage intrigued me from the first time we met. And now, I realize you have the spirit and compassion that

I've been searching for. Tori, my bewitching vixen, I'll love you always with every fiber of my body and soul."

Cautiously, Tori lifted her eyes to meet his. Stunned by the impact of his words and the meaning in his eyes, she remained still.

Silently, Marcus swooped down upon her and lifted her into his arms. His face was close to hers, his breath caressed her cheek, and when he spoke his tone was soft: "I need you. I want you." Kissing her, he lay Tori back on the bed and with a devilish grin whispered, "We still have an hour till the ship sails."